Emma Heatherington

Rewrite the Stars

HarperCollins*Publishers*

HarperCollins*Publishers* Ltd
1 London Bridge Street
London SE1 9GF

www.harpercollins.co.uk

First published by HarperCollins*Publishers* 2019
1

A catalogue record for this book
is available from the British Library

ISBN: 978-0-00-835563-0

Set in Birka by Palimpsest Book Production Limited,
Falkirk, Stirlingshire

Printed and bound in Great Britain by
CPI Group (UK) Ltd, Croydon CR0 4YY

For my wonderful children who are
the bravest and the best

Author's Note

A key theme of *Rewrite the Stars* is Charlotte's love of music and her desire to fulfil her passion of song-writing. I'm a huge music fan and my very first writing efforts were in the shape of some very cheesy pop songs written on my synthesizer when I was about 12. What do you mean you've never heard of my big hits 'Mystery Man' and 'The Boy Next Door'??!!!!!

When I was writing this book, the idea came up that there could be an actual song featured that readers could listen to afterwards – I'm being careful not to give anything away in the form of spoilers, but thanks to Claire Fenby, Emily Yolland and Iona Teixeira Stevens for the enthusiastic chat about this when Jade and I were over at HarperCollins in London. The seed was sown and as much as I love writing lyrics myself, I thought the book deserved something a bit more polished!

So, I began scouting around for existing songs that would suit the story, but then something even better happened . . . an amazing song was written *especially* for the book by one of my favourite songwriters, Gareth Dunlop, whose compositions have featured in films including Nicholas Sparks' *The Best of Me* and *Safe Haven*, as well as (drumroll) . . . ABC's hit series *Nashville*! I am still pinching myself. The book has its very own song!

I'm absolutely thrilled to bits that Gareth took the time to write and record the song 'You' which features in such a poignant scene in *Rewrite the Stars*. It really is a beautiful, mesmerising and moving song, and even better than I could ever have dreamed of.

A huge thanks to Dianna Maher of Moraine Music Group, Nashville for helping to make this happen – Dianna, you might notice a very subtle thank you in the form of a character being named after you in the story! Most of all, thanks to Gareth for suggesting a brand-new song instead of using something already out there, for following my brief and for coming up with something so wonderful. I'm so honoured to have your beautiful lyrics, melody and voice attached to my work.

And on that note, I urge you all to go and find the song 'You' by Gareth Dunlop via his website (www.garethdunlop.com), then close your eyes, think of your special someone, kick back and give your heart a treat!

Emma x

Be yourself; everyone else is already taken.

Oscar Wilde

i

Dublin, December 2010

I was twenty-two years and nine months old when I first fell in love with Tom Farley.

Elbow-deep in a sink full of suds in our student kitchen, I watched him come in through the back door with my brother Matthew, steal my heart on his way past with his old-school, movie-star-type swagger and I knew my life was never going to be the same again.

My mother used to joke about how I was born cynical, and I was definitely way too sceptical to believe in love at first sight, but this person's very presence hit me like a bolt of lightning.

He turned my head like no other man had done before, and like none would ever do again.

Tom Farley, with his mega-watt smile, tousled brown hair, dark stubble on a chiselled jawline, the cheekiest dimples you ever did see and bold, devilish eyes of turquoise green, made me weak at the knees. Maybe the attraction was in knowing he was musical, like me. Maybe it was his rugged, ruffled, rough-round-the-edges good looks, or maybe love at first sight did exist and I was now living proof and the latest victim of the old cliché.

Whatever it was, I found myself instantly hooked.

'What on *earth* are you wearing?' my brother Matthew snorted, clearly showing off in front of his new friend. Matthew didn't have much room to talk when it came to fashion. He was sporting a pair of lilac spray-on jeans with a hideous see-through lemon linen shirt that clashed with his cranberry-coloured hair. Between the two of us, we certainly looked like the circus had come to town.

I glared out the window onto a red brick wall that divided our terraced house from an identical row behind us, turned down James Blunt who was aptly singing his number one hit 'You're Beautiful' and desperately thought of something smart to say in return, but my head was too busy spinning with unadulterated lust.

I was speechless.

My glow-in-the-dark Disney-themed pyjamas with Doctor Marten boots at three in the afternoon *was* all a bit of an eyesore, but I was a student, on my day off, and how the hell was I to know that the man of my ultimate dreams would pass me by in a whiff of leather and tobacco when I was dressed like a clown?

Yes, Tom Farley, with his air of beauty and superstardom, had just rocked my world and I couldn't wait to see what happened next, so I ignored my fashion crisis, took a deep breath and dried my hands quickly to go and take a closer look at him.

'Stick the kettle on, will you Charlie?' said Matthew when I reached the tiny sitting room where it looked like they were about to set up office. He called me Charlie, which meant he was *really* showing off now. No one ever called me Charlie. No one was ever *allowed* to call me Charlie.

I gulped and tried to compose myself in front of this absolute hunk of burning love who was now looking at me just as eagerly as I was at him. Late twenties, I guessed, no wedding ring which was a good start and, despite his bourbon rock-star looks, he had an air of shyness mixed with an inner confidence that made him all the more attractive. I could feel his eyes burn through me, so I looked around the room instead of directly at him to try to keep my cool.

'Well, I would stick the kettle on, but I was just about to go—'

'Where?'

Nowhere was the answer. I was about to go nowhere but there was no way I was going to be treated as the tea lady in this whole operation without a proper introduction.

A heap of vinyl with names I'd never heard of was stacked in the middle of the brown carpet, the room stank of stale, spilt beer and weed, while a cactus plant we'd named Jarvis Cocker (because it had prickles) looked as gloomy as the winter weather outside, but Tom Farley brightened up everything in my dull-as-dishwater world. Who was he? Why was he here? My brother was in the process of forming some sort of new age rock band, so I gathered they were here to talk business.

'I'm OK for tea, thank you . . . Aren't you going to introduce us, Matt?' asked the dreamboat on the sofa and my mouth dropped open when I heard his voice for the first time.

He had the most delicious, gravelly, deep American-Irish accent, which sounded so deeply mysterious in comparison to my own plain old Irish twang. This man, this absolutely gorgeous being, was becoming more appealing by the second.

'Oh, sorry, this is Tom Farley, our drummer in Déjà Vu,' said Matthew, finally remembering his manners. 'He's probably the best drummer in Dublin.'

Probably the best-*looking* drummer in Dublin, I'd have added to that sentence, not that I knew many drummers in Dublin or anywhere else for that matter.

Tom held up his hands in a display of modesty.

'Tom, this is my sister, Charlotte. The bossy baby of the house I was telling you about,' said Matthew.

I nodded a hello, not knowing whether to thump my brother for calling me bossy, even though it was *him* telling *me* to 'stick the kettle on', or to hug him for bringing this piece of heaven into my life. Then I stuttered out a proper hello and giggled in a girly way that made me want to thump *myself*.

'Nice boots,' said Tom the drummer, looking me up and down. 'Snap.'

He pulled up his faded blue jeans ever so slightly to show off identical cherry-coloured Doc Martens and my heart sang. It was destiny. It had to be. He ran his fingers through his tousled hair. I may have swooned out loud. I clenched my own empty fingers, wishing they could touch his hair, too.

'We're holding a meeting here shortly,' said Matthew, clearing his throat. 'You know, about the new band?'

'Ah, that's right,' I said as if I'd forgotten. As if I *could* forget. Matthew had talked about nothing else except 'the new band' for months now and had been scouring every avenue for the right talent to join him. 'Is there anything I can do to help, apart from make tea?'

Matthew looked at me wide-eyed.

'Er, *no.*'

I knew this was code for 'Piss away off, sister, or just get the drinks in', but I wasn't taking the hint.

'You know, I always wanted to play the drums, ever since I saw the gorilla in the chocolate ad banging out the beats to that Phil Collins song,' I sighed, leaning on the doorframe. I even pouted a little. Boy, I hadn't flirted like this since forever.

Tom laughed, in an endearing way.

'And Larry Mullen Junior from U2, of course,' I added, trying to redeem myself. 'He's a really good, um, drummer too.'

Matthew was gritting his teeth. 'I didn't know you wanted to play the drums, Charlotte,' he replied swiftly. He seriously looked like he was going to throw something at me now.

'I do,' I lied, knowing I was really pushing the boundaries at this stage. 'Do you teach drumming, Tom?'

Tom was still staring back at me, smiling, his chest moving up and down, and I knew for sure now, as much as my brother was about to kill me for my blatant flirting, that Tom liked me as much as I liked him. He slid out of his heavy jacket and I gulped at the sight of his tanned, toned arms under a khaki green T-shirt, his gaze never leaving mine with a smile that made my stomach do a backflip.

'I could certainly try to, er, teach you,' he said, and his voice cracked a little when he spoke. 'So, you're the budding songwriter then? Matthew was telling me that you—'

I was just preparing my response when we were both ever so rudely interrupted.

'I was telling you she writes *country* songs about men in Stetsons who drink too much beer and break too many hearts,' said Matthew, clearly put out by the chemistry in the air. 'She's not a *real*—'

'No, I'm not a *real* songwriter,' I said, finishing my brother's sentence for him. I was evidently embarrassing him with my very presence, so he was doing exactly the same in return as Tom shifted in his seat, watching us battle it out in front of him. We would row about this later.

'Well, I'd love to hear your songs one day,' said Tom, much to my delight and surprise. He leaned forward, resting his drummer-boy arms on his knees. The top of his T-shirt gaped open ever so slightly, allowing me to glimpse a light sprinkling of very manly chest hair, just enough to make me want to reach out and touch him. I may have swooned out loud. Again.

'You really wouldn't want to hear them,' said Matthew. He sniggered a bit. I so wanted to swing for him, briefly recalling a time we took lumps out of each other as we fought over who was the funniest character in *Friends* or when we wrestled over the last mango in the supermarket, much to our mother's humiliation.

'I really would,' said Tom. 'I think we all need to be educated on how to drink more beer and break more hearts. Maybe you could teach me something too, er, Charlie?'

He quickly sat up and drummed on his knees a bit, reflecting my irregular, pumping heartbeat, and all of a sudden I felt a bit sweaty in my Disney pyjamas that had seen better days. I tucked a strand of hair behind my ears, wishing I was looking more presentable, but I was smitten, and so it seemed, despite my somewhat unique appearance, was Tom Farley.

And he called me Charlie.

We stood there in momentary silence, breathing in and

out, not having to say a word as the universe weaved its magic around us.

'Why don't you go get your guitar, *Charlotte*?' Matthew suggested seconds later, with a cheeky grin on his face while emphasising my proper title. It was obviously OK for him to shorten my name, but not for anyone else, especially if it was meant in an endearing way. 'Go on. Give us one of your country songs. No time like the present, is there?'

I took a long, deep breath through my nose then pursed my lips to consider the challenge. He was really trying to get rid of me now.

'But I thought you were having a meeting?' I said. 'You know, about the band?'

'We can wait,' said Matthew. He had just scored a goal and he knew it. 'You have time for a song, don't you, Tom?'

Tom beamed that glowing smile at me again.

'Of course I do,' said Tom, not knowing if he was giving the right answer. 'The others are running late so if you don't mind, Charlie, I'd love to hear some of your work.'

My brother's grin echoed his now, only Matthew's was much wider and full of sarcasm as opposed to Tom's smile of anticipation. He was really going for gold in the embarrassment stakes.

I weighed up my options for as long as I could get away with. I couldn't do it. No way was I going to let myself down in front of my brother's hot new band member by singing my cheesy lyrics of how I'd loved and lost (or thought I had) in my wonder years. I'd only written a handful of stuff and most of it was for my ears only. But then out of the blue something struck me. Something told me that I'd an opportunity to either make a fool out of myself or, on the other hand, to really impress this delight in front of me. Something told me to go for it that day, that in fact I'd nothing to lose, and I think that 'something' was the energy between me and Tom Farley. I had a feeling, despite my brother's indifference, that Tom was going to like my humble efforts, even if my writing was in a genre that turned my brother's stomach.

'OK, I'll do it,' I said, surprising even myself. 'I'll sing you a song.'

'*What?*' Matthew burst out laughing and looked at Tom, but he wasn't laughing at all. He was beaming in my direction, convincing me more that the sudden confidence within me was indeed coming from him. He was giving me strength to take a chance on this, to bare my soul and risk it that he might just *like* my music.

'You go for it, girl,' said Tom. His full lips looked so inviting. I could see his Adam's apple move as he swallowed hard in my direction. 'That's just what I love to see – some good old pride and determination. I'm all ears and ready when you are.'

I stood up straight, and instead of scarpering off like a scared mouse as my brother hoped I would, I put my hand on my hip, took a deep breath and decided to go ahead and call Matthew's bluff.

'No problem at all,' I said to them both. '*You* can get the drinks in, Matthew, while I go and get sorted. Give me a few minutes and I'll be right back with a country song that will break both your little hearts.'

Tom Farley winked at me again and nodded his head in approval.

It was official. I was prime time in love.

ii

Twenty minutes later, now wearing my favourite retro flared pale blue jeans, a crisp, clean grey vest top and with my long, bleached curly hair hanging down round my shoulders, I strummed the last chord on my guitar.

The song I'd carefully chosen to sing for him was called 'By Myself' (a song I'd written about the very first break-up I'd experienced but he didn't need to know that) and I'd picked it out from my humble collection knowing the deep rhythm and sultry lyrics would be just enough to get his attention.

As the final pluck of the guitar strings echoed around us in the little room, I waited for his reaction. I looked up slowly, half closed my eyes and, when I opened them, I realized my hands were shaking.

'I can't believe I remembered the words,' I said, a string of apologies going through my head for making his ears bleed, but I was worrying in vain because when I looked in his direction, he didn't look disappointed or bored at all. He was, in fact, wide-eyed in awe, shaking his head, looking

11

at my face, then at my hands, then at my mouth, and back to my eyes.

'Wow,' he said eventually, wiping his mouth with the back of his hand, and then he applauded slowly. 'I mean *wow*! I'm literally drooling here! That, young lady, was bloody awesome!'

We laughed in relief – at exactly the same time. And then we stopped laughing in disbelief – at exactly the same time. Matthew was not laughing.

'Matthew Taylor, what the hell!' said Tom. 'Your little sister has absolute, magic in her words and melodies! Seriously!'

I smirked at Matthew, feeling his pain and discomfort at the tangible harmony and the intense meeting of minds that had beautifully backfired on him.

'Well, I'm – I'm glad you think so,' stuttered Matthew. 'But you should try living with her. She's—'

'She's incredible,' Tom said, and I fleetingly felt sorry for Matthew who was so removed from this moment between us. 'Matt, you told me she could sing but you didn't tell me we'd the next Stevie Nicks on our hands! She even looks like her, too. And as for those lyrics! Did you write that, Charlie? Really?'

He called me Charlie again.

'Yes, I wrote it. All of me, all *by myself*,' I said to him, quoting my very own lyrics. I sat up straight and put down my guitar then flicked back my hair. It's wonderful how a quick wash, a lick of mascara, a spray of perfume and a change of clothing can help up your game, plus I was feeding off his hunger and energy. 'Oh, and Stevie Nicks? I'll take that. Thank you, Tom.'

I should say that I absolutely *loved* that he called me Charlie and that I *loved* saying his name too. Tom. It was manly enough to make me flutter inside and if I was Stevie Nicks to him, to me he was a scruffy, unkempt young Bradley Cooper. Those eyes could stop the world.

Later I would look up the name Tom online to see what it meant and find out that it translated as 'twin', which wasn't as romantic as I hoped it might be, but then I decided that he was my soul twin. Yes, I liked that. We were kindred spirits, meant to be.

'I'd really like to hear more of your work,' Tom said, still shaking his head in awe. 'Please tell me there's more where that came from?'

I gasped at his approval. No one had ever said that to me before. No one had ever really listened to my songs, not even my mother who, despite being quite cool in so many ways, was totally convinced that for me music was a hobby for behind closed doors and not something I would ever pursue in the real world. With a super-talented big brother like Matthew and a perfectly turned-out sister like Emily, I was never quite sure what to do to get my parents' attention, and any efforts I made didn't always turn out in my favour, you might say.

'You sure you want to hear more?' I asked Tom.

I was shaking inside but doing my best to look cool and confident on the outside.

'For *sure* I'm sure!' he said, standing up from the sofa. 'Look, you need to get those songs out there, big time, Charlie.'

I could feel my brother wince every time he called me Charlie now. At home and to everyone I knew, I was Charlotte Jane Taylor, named after the Brontë sister of the same name and as a nod to my mother's favourite novel of all time, *Jane Eyre*. My older sister was Emily Maria and Matthew James, the first born, often joked that he just about escaped being named Heathcliff as my dad got to choose his name.

'I mean, why are you even busting your ass with university?' Tom asked me. 'You're gifted, girl. You don't need a degree! Your qualifications are all in there already.'

He pointed at his temple to emphasize how I already had all the accolades I needed in my creative brain.

'But I'm going to be a teacher,' I told him. 'So, as much as I love what you're saying, in the real world I kind of *need* a degree.'

Tom hunkered down in front of me and looked me right in the eye. His hands were on either side of me, on the arms of the chair. I could feel his breath on my skin. I could smell his woody, aromatic cologne. I thought I might explode.

'No, no, no!' he said, looking up at me. '*You*, Charlie

Taylor, aren't going to be a teacher. *You* are going to be a huge star.'

My heart rose into my mouth. He had a presence, a charm, and the electricity between us was filling me up and making me feel weak at the same time. He was so close to me now his arms were almost touching my legs.

And you're going to be my muse, I wanted to say in return, wishing he would just stay there right in front of me forever.

He stood up, pushed his hair from his face and, when he sat down again on the couch, I silently thanked my brother for bringing Tom Farley into my life. He was everything. The way he looked at me and the way he just made me feel was nothing like I've ever felt before. I was dizzy with lust and sheer admiration. I was brimming with confidence, more than I'd ever been in my whole twenty-two years on this planet.

'Go on, give us one more,' said Tom, resting back on the sofa now. He put one leg across the other to show he was in no hurry whatsoever.

Matthew was almost green with envy.

'It's almost three thirty, Tom,' he said, really peeved now. 'We could make a start before the others arrive? I really want to go over some poster ideas for our new dates and we've a press pack to pull together.'

Matthew looked at his watch, but Tom was still looking at me.

'I think we should wait on the others instead of having

to repeat yourself, Matt,' he said, grinning my way. 'Plus, I want to see if Charlie is a one-hit wonder, or if there's more to come from such a genius mind. Go on, give us one more song, Charlie.'

And so, I sang another one, and then another, neither of us noticing that Matthew had by now left the room, leaving us to it as we got lost in the music. I was singing for him. I was actually *singing* my very own songs for this beautiful stranger who was making me feel like I was the most important person in his world right now.

'Hang on,' Tom said while I was just about to finish a chorus. 'Gimme that again.'

He grabbed my brother's guitar from the corner of the room and strummed along with me, then harmonized when he caught on to the chorus. All the time when we sang together, our eyes were locked and I felt like my heart might burst.

'Keep singing that part,' he said to me at one point. 'I wanna try something here.'

And so I did what he said and it made perfect sense. We were making music together. It was the most thrilling rush ever and this was shaping up to be the best day of my life.

'You've blown my mind, Charlie,' Tom said to me after the third song. He sat the guitar to the side and shook his head. 'I could seriously listen to you, and look at you, all day. You've got it, Charlie. You've just got it!'

He was in genuine disbelief. I tried to absorb all this unexpected praise from him.

'And you know what? The most beautiful thing is you have no freakin' idea just how good you are!'

I tried to catch my breath in the intensity of it all as we stood there in the middle of this tiny, smelly, hormone-filled student sitting room, our breath patterns moving to the same rhythm. As Monday to Friday university accommodation to my brother, me and our friend Kirsty, the room had hosted many booze-filled parties and late nights over the past four years, but never had I experienced electricity in the air as I did right then with him.

'*You* can sing too and play guitar as well as drums,' I managed to stutter. 'You're a mighty fine talent in yourself, so I can't take all the credit for what just happened.'

I tried to divert the compliment back to him, but he wasn't having it.

'No, no, Charlie Taylor. I can play, yes, but *you* have star quality. You're on a totally different level and I don't say that lightly. You're amazing.'

My bottom lip quivered, and I pushed my hair behind my ears.

'You really think so?'

'I really know so,' he said, holding my gaze. I didn't know whether to laugh or cry at all this attention from someone so gorgeous and talented who seemed to be so much in awe of me.

17

Matthew had always been known as the creative one in our family. He was the colourful one who wanted to sing in a band as well as study to be an architect, so he was the one we all looked up to, cheering him on along the way. I was going to be a teacher and any musical notions I had were brushed under the carpet when we were growing up. It just wasn't how my family saw me. Matthew was the cool, talented one, Emily was the middle child, the quiet, sensible one who obeyed all the rules, and I was the quirky, hippy dippy baby, the rebellious clever kid, and the one with brains to burn whose way with words would be best suited to a classroom where others would benefit from my wisdom. I just dressed a little funny and sometimes found myself in hot water, but that could all be fixed. Or so my parents hoped.

'I've never properly sung these songs for anyone before,' I confessed to Tom. It was dropping dark now outside, so I walked past him and pulled the curtains closed.

He gently took my hand on the way back.

'You have magic, I mean it,' he whispered. 'Please believe me, Charlie. You can't ignore what happened just now.'

We stood there, frozen in the moment. I could barely catch my breath.

'I think I'm going to get you into trouble,' I told him.

His eyes widened. 'I think so too,' he said.

'With the band, I mean!' I retorted quickly. 'I mean, I hope I don't get you into trouble with the band. Sounds like the others are here now.'

Our hands parted and he rubbed his forehead, which told me he'd been thinking of a totally different kind of trouble.

'Yeah, yeah, the band. That's what you meant,' he said, then looked at the ceiling and blew out a long breath.

That accent of his was a killer and could get me into trouble any day, I thought. I closed my eyes for a second. I wanted him to reach out and touch me again, to tell me that he didn't care if he got into trouble. He said I had magic. He said I was amazing. He said so many things I'd never been told before and I wanted to pause this moment so that we didn't have to just leave it at this.

I wanted more of Tom Farley and when I opened my eyes I could see from the pain in his face that he wanted more of me, too.

'I suppose I *should* make a move,' he said, but his eyes told me he didn't want to go. I didn't want him to go either.

Now that we'd stopped singing, I could hear the rest of the band members chatting in the kitchen. Matthew was going to kill me. Not only had I taken up so much of Tom's time and attention, but I'd also taken over the living room with our unplanned mini concert which was totally stealing his thunder.

Tom whispered to me.

'Look, Charlie, between you and me,' he said. 'I know some people who aren't a million miles away right now who would die to have just an ounce of the talent you have.

You can't just hide these songs away or ignore this gift you have. You must send your songs out to some record companies. Believe me, you'd be signed up in seconds.'

Record companies? I'd never even thought of doing such a thing, yet I felt a wave of imagination flood my mind. I laughed out loud at the idea.

'You mean, do this for a living?' I asked him. 'Write songs? As a *job*?'

I laughed again, but he nodded as if it was just as simple as that.

'As a *career*,' he emphasized. 'Long term. Go to London, Charlie! Go to New York City or somewhere else in the States like Texas or Nashville. They'd eat you up out there, I just know it. Music and lyrics are in your blood, I'm telling you. I have total faith in you. Your songs are totally mesmerizing. *You* are mesmerizing.'

The room spun a bit and I felt a hot flush overcome me as I imagined little old me in a big city, far away from Ireland and all that I'd known all my life. In my mind, for just a second, I saw myself sitting at a big window seat in a new city, looking out on a mix of sunshine and flashes of colour and sounds I'd never seen or heard before. The very thought made me both dizzy and excited. A rush filled me from head to toe as I imagined someone singing my songs, *my* actual words to a packed auditorium with a drummer like Tom Farley thumping out the beat and—

'OK, meeting time!' announced Matthew, bursting my

bubble entirely with his bellowing voice as he returned into the living room. 'And someone called Lexi is here?'

His voice drew my eyes in the direction of the door where I saw the most beautiful, exotic creature – small, pale, oriental and gothic – and Tom's eyes diverted briefly from mine for the first time since he'd got here.

My afternoon of heaven was just about to turn into an evening of hell as reality punched me right in the heart.

'Honey!' said Lexi in a raspy, posh Dublin accent. 'Sorry I'm late, babe, but I couldn't find this house for ages! You should have told me it was the one with the letter box hanging off . . . Students!'

She made a face that on anyone else would have looked very unattractive, but she still managed to look like a super-model compared to me, who looked like I was chewing a wasp at the shock of her arrival. My mouth dropped open as she breezed right past me, then wrapped her arms around Tom and kissed him full on the mouth in front of us, giving me just enough time to quickly pick up my guitar and make my swift exit before my brother, complete with smug face, could say 'I told you so.'

'Charlie!' Tom called after me, pushing his girlfriend off his face as gently as he could.

I tried not to look at them again and, when I did, regretted it instantly as I saw her whisper into his ear, almost eating it at the same time. She threw her black, shiny bobbed hair back, showing off a tattoo of Asian text on her long, slender neck, and I touched my own neck which felt boring and bare in comparison.

'My name's Charlotte,' I said to him, hearing my voice quiver. 'Not Charlie!' He caught my eye and I felt my lip wobble, then stomped upstairs with my guitar in my hand, my stupid lyrics in my head, my pride trailing on the floor and tears bursting from my eyes.

'Write a song about it, sister!' I heard Matthew shout to me when they all finally left after what seemed like hours later. 'And don't worry, Charlotte. Everyone who meets Tom Farley falls in love with him. In fact, I might even love him a little bit myself.'

'Oh, give it a rest, Matthew!' I shouted, kicking my bedroom door closed.

If he was trying to make me feel better, it wasn't working. I'd fallen for Tom, hook, line and sinker, not knowing he'd a girlfriend all along. How could I be so stupid and assuming? How could two people have such magic, like he said, yet one of them just walk away and be in the arms of another? I couldn't understand it. I was young and naïve and didn't know life could present you with someone so perfect one minute, and then shove you off in a different direction the next.

I tried to shake away his memory, but I couldn't and, although I didn't see Tom Farley except from a safe distance when he was behind a drum kit at his gigs, he never really did leave my mind from that day on.

Morning, noon and night I dreamed of him and even though it's a bit clichéd and predictable, I *did* put him in a song, just as my brother advised me to. Well, I put him in about twenty songs if I'm being perfectly honest.

I was twenty-two years and nine months old when I first fell in love with Tom Farley, and I was exactly the same age when he first broke my heart.

Life, for all of us, was never going to be the same again.

Chapter One

Dublin, December 2015

Today is my last day of term at St Patrick's National School, meaning it's officially the season to be jolly, and jolly I am.

I've tinsel round my neck, a Santa hat on my head and I'm celebrating at a local watering hole with some of my favourite people in the world. Life is good.

'I'll be right back,' I say to the gorgeous guy at the bar who is buying me a drink.

My sister Emily is very uncharacteristically dancing on a wobbly table held up only by her brand-new husband Kevin, my roommate Kirsty is snogging a random stranger in a booth and the Black Eyed Peas tell me that tonight's going to be a really good night. So, with all looking pretty in my humble little world and just enough time to do so before the bar closes, I steal away out the back of the pub for a sneaky cigarette. I don't normally smoke, but slipping off like this all by myself to do something I know I shouldn't is as rebellious as my life gets these days.

Pip's Bar, on a side street near the house that Kirsty and I share in north Dublin, is the type of place you normally wouldn't drink out of the glass, only the bottle. But with a blanket of snow thick on the ground and the option to skate home and avoid taxis, it's becoming more and more fun as the beer goes down.

'Wooo hoo!' I sing out loud, dancing as I reach for the cigarette in my purse, ignoring a leering look from some dodgy old guy playing a poker machine by the back door.

Being a teacher is fun and fulfilling but on nights like this when school's out for Christmas, there's nothing I love more than to cut loose and just be Charlotte Taylor who loves to sing at the top of her voice, instead of 'Miss Taylor' who sometimes has to *shout* at the top of her voice when my seven-year-old pupils get rowdy.

'Toilets are dat way, me lady,' says the man at the poker machine in a thick Dublin accent and I hold up my cigarette to show him that tonight I'm a nicotine addict who doesn't care that it's minus seventeen or so outside. I push the heavy grey 'Emergency' back door open and then shiver in the chill that greets me, asking myself if leaving the heat and the prospect of a snog with gorgeous Jimmy or John or whoever his name was, who I just left holding a beer for me, is really worth it.

The door slams closed behind me and I realize that I'm

locked out but I'm in no mood to panic. Mr Poker Player will hopefully come to my rescue if I bang loud enough once I'm done.

I can still hear the music from inside, I'm more than a little bit tipsy and I've decided that this Christmas is going to be the best one ever, so I keep dancing like there's no one watching. And there *is* no one watching.

It's almost midnight in a little yard out the back of Pip's where no one my age ever goes unless they've no choice, which is the case for us tonight. I search my pockets for a lighter.

'Ah man, now you've just locked us both out! Do you know how long I've been waiting out here for someone to open that damn door?'

'Sweet Jesus, you scared me!' I gasp in reply to my companion who I now realize is sitting in the shadows.

'Sorry, but we're going to have to wait now until the next smoker comes out if we want to go inside.'

I get my breath back and turn towards the husky American accent that comes from my right. My unlit cigarette waves around and points to the heavens, my feet are still dancing a little bit too ambitiously. I'm in slippery electric blue cowboy boots, which I now know are certainly not the best footwear when there's snow on the ground, but I should be more concerned that I'm stuck in a back yard with a stranger who seems more than a little pissed off at me right now.

27

'You really shouldn't jump out on people like that!' I reply, straining to get a better look at him, and trying to match his tetchy mood. 'I could have fallen over and broken my ankle and that would *not* have been—'

'Charlie?'

My heart stops. He just called me Charlie. No one ever calls me Charlie except my brother when he's showing off or . . .

'*Tom?* Tom *Farley?*'

I must be imagining things. This *cannot* be real. I take a step back and put my hand to my chest, saying a prayer that this isn't some prank or messed-up dream like so many I'd had down the years since I last heard his voice.

I walk closer, towards the silhouette, and I lose my breath when I see his face.

That voice – how could I not have recognized it after playing it over in my mind for so long? Those eyes that I've imagined staring back at me just once more, those lips, that hair, those arms I'd longed to hold me.

It *is* him. It can't be. I don't understand.

'*Tom Farley?*' I say again.

He nods. 'How the hell did this happen?' he asks me, just as flabbergasted as I am.

I can't *believe* this is happening. I can't be that drunk, can I?

I'm locked out of a bar in the back end of nowhere, on a freezing cold night in December, and the one person I find in the same position is the one person I've been basing my whole imaginary future for five whole years upon, even though deep down I thought I'd never see him again.

'This is *unbelievable*,' he says, flashing me a very, *very* sweet smile and obviously just as taken aback as I am. 'Charlie Taylor!! Man, I thought the next time I saw you would be on some big stage with your name up in lights, not out the back of some poky bar like this place.'

He shakes his head, just the same way as he did so long ago. He looks at me, just the same way, with the same wonder and hunger as he did back then too.

'I don't get it,' I mumble. 'What on earth are you doing here? Where on earth have you even been all these years? I can't even—'

'You need a light?'

Stop the whole world and let me off. Stop the clocks and silence the pianos and all that. It really *is* Tom Farley, in the yard of Pip's Bar, in the asshole of nowhere, and there's no one out here with him – only me. How?

I look at the cigarette and realize that yes, I do indeed need a light, but I'm too stunned to even speak. I've stopped dancing, but on the inside I'm still doing a routine to 'Boom Boom Pow' which the DJ inside has followed up with in a Black Eyed Peas' double spin.

I feel like I might faint. I don't know whether to laugh or cry as a whole movie script of emotion attacks my insides. My mouth is saying words, but my brain isn't thinking them through. It's like every part of me is separated, desperately trying to slot together again and make sense of all this.

'I don't even smoke so please don't tell Matthew.'

I'm tongue-tied and I've no idea why I said that, as if I'm fourteen years old or something and will get into trouble with my parents or my big brother if I'm caught. I also think I'm about to have a heart attack and it's nothing to do with cigarette consumption.

'You sure look like you're about to smoke.'

'What I mean is, I don't *normally* smoke, only sometimes when I'm drinking, and after tomorrow I'm never touching them again,' I ramble.

It's actually *him*.

'I don't think I will be telling Matthew, no fear of that.'

'In fact, I'm never drinking again after tonight either,' I rant on. 'Those are going to be my two big New Year resolutions come January. I actually can't believe it's you. It *is* you, right?'

'It's me, yes,' he laughs. 'Still me. Still the same Tom.'

Still the same drop-dead *gorgeous* Tom. Still the love of my life, Tom. Still the one that got away who I've fantasized about meeting again one day, Tom. All I know about him is what I've found out from my brother since, which isn't a lot really. The only thing I've managed to gather is that they're no longer friends after the band they formed had a messy break-up.

I lean into the glow of his cupped hands, glad of the

quick blast of heat, and chug on the butt, puffing the ash until it turns bright orange on grey, then I flick my hair back for effect as I exhale a long stream of smoke. Tom, in turn, smells like a heavy mix of spearmint chewing gum, tobacco and leather, just like he did on that first day we met.

'You still smell nice,' I tell him. 'Musky.'

'You still talk a lot,' he replies with his dazzling smile. 'Chatty.'

I would argue but I have been told this before, many, many times.

'So, do you still sing as much as you talk, then?' he asks. 'Please don't tell me you ignored my advice, became a teacher and your songs are gathering dust under your bed.'

My songs about *you* are gathering dust under my bed, I long to admit to him. My breathing is slowing down now, yet I still can't believe this moment is real.

'I still love to write and sing,' I say with a smile, straightening up and fixing my coat up around my chin. 'But yes, my main collection nowadays does come in the form of "The Farmer Wants a Wife" and other such playground hits.'

'A teacher then,' he says. He's disappointed. 'I mean, don't get me wrong, it's a super career, but I always thought you were destined for even greater things.'

I'm shaking. I'm totally sobered up now. I look around me to make sure there's really no one else around and clench my nails into my hands tightly to make me feel like it's real life. I want to scream in delight. I want to jump with joy, but most of all I feel like I could cry with the knowledge that this is indeed, very real.

'Yes, I teach little people their ABCs and I love it,' I tell him eventually, trying to keep it sane. 'I've just quit for the Christmas break so I'm out on the lash, but I never, ever thought that I'd bump into you.'

He laughs and flicks his cigarette like he doesn't know what to say next. He is equally as flummoxed as me. We stare at each other, examining the moment, trying to absorb that so much time has passed, yet here we are still sharing the same breath-taking moment that has hit us right in the heart all over again. Well, at least that's how I feel, anyhow.

'And you? Are you still drumming?' I manage to ask him. I've no idea how I'm even holding a conversation right now.

'Not much since your brother kicked me out of his band four years ago,' he laughs nervously in response. Then he whispers, 'How is Matt anyway? Is he OK?'

There's a big pause and swift change of mood. Oh, if only he was OK. How I wish that my brother was OK.

'Matthew's doing as well as he can,' I say, looking at the ground. I could divulge so many more gory details of how absolutely not OK he has been, but blood is thicker than water and I would never let my only brother down. 'He doesn't really talk about those days any more, Tom. He doesn't talk about any of the band.'

'I thought as much,' says Tom, kicking imaginary stones on the slushy ground.

'I did ask about you all for a long time,' I confess, 'but eventually I copped on that it was more or less a closed subject. I've a feeling he doesn't like to talk about you guys very much any more. Sorry.'

Tom bites his lip and looks away.

'It really all did turn out so terribly wrong,' he says, his face scrunching into a puzzle as he looks up to the snow-filled sky, giving me an opportunity to drink him in. He still looks like he could be a real rock star in his biker jacket, his dogtooth black and white scarf and his faded blue jeans. He still smells like I want to pull him closer to me. He still sounds like the man who speaks right to my soul and the one who I never could get off my mind, no matter where in the world I've been after meeting him for just a few hours some five years ago.

'So where have you been?' I ask him, pain leaching into my voice. For so many years I've longed for him, pined for him. I travelled the world to try and shake him off, eventually laying his ghost to rest easy in my mind, but he never really ever left my heart. I know that now more than ever.

'I've been . . .' he laughs and scratches his head. 'I've been everywhere trying to recreate what Matt and I tried to do all those years ago, ironically. I've been trying to make it big in music but every time a door opened for me, another one shut in my face. Maybe you were right to ignore me and my big dreams of music, but I'm happy for you, Charlie. You look happy. You look just as gorgeous as you did that first time I saw you with your guitar, your beautiful songs, your silly pyjamas and DM boots that matched mine.'

He remembers it all. My God, he actually remembers it all, but if only he knew how much it was killing me to see him again. He hasn't changed a bit and yet he looks so different at the same time. His eyes are a little more tired but still dreamy enough to wash me away. His lips still catch my breath as I watch them move as he speaks. His hair is shorter now but still magnetic enough to make me want to reach out and touch it, and his arms still look like they were meant to hold only me. I've so many questions I want to ask him. Did he ever think of me like I did of him? Did he feel what I felt that day in my humble living room five years ago or was it all in my loved-up imagination?

'What on earth are you doing here, Tom?' I ask him. It's the bravest question I can ask him out loud. 'Like, seriously, how did you even find this place?'

He laughs at my bewilderment at finding him here.

'No one our age ever goes to Pip's Bar,' I emphasize, 'especially not in the run-up to Christmas when there's so much fun to be had closer to town. This is really, really strange to bump into you here of all places.'

My cigarette isn't as appealing as I thought and I want to stub it out already, but that would be very uncool.

'True. I suppose it's hardly Vegas, is it?' he laughs.

He looks back at me with dreamy, sparkling eyes that crinkle at the sides. They don't dance and flirt at me as much as they did before, but there still is something that makes my head spin a little more than the buzz of the beers I've been on. There's still chemistry between us. I knew I wasn't imagining it all those years ago.

He takes a deep breath.

'It's a long story why I'm here,' he tells me, blowing a long line of smoke out in my direction. 'Maybe I was looking for someone.'

I should have known.

'Maybe I was looking for you?' he says.

My eyes widen. I take a step backwards. I can't tell if he's joking or serious but I'm too afraid to ask.

'I never thought I'd be so lucky, but lo and behold, here I am, talking to you, you're talking to me, and we're freezing our asses off at the same time on possibly the coldest night of the year,' he says. 'Plus, you've locked us out. It could be serendipity after all?'

His voice is deeper now, like it's been well-lived-in, making him sound a lot older than he looks, which I reckon must be a few years over thirty since I'm now the grand age of twenty-seven.

'I love that,' I tell him.

'What? Being locked out in the cold?'

'Very funny,' I say with a nervous giggle. 'I mean, I love serendipity.'

'Me too.'

'You know, fate . . . going with your gut instinct . . . believing that things are meant to be. In fact, you've just reminded me of my third resolution for next year, which is a pretty good one.'

'And that is?' he asks me.

I stand in just a little bit closer to him for effect, urging myself not to make it so obvious I'm still mad about him and have been for all this time. I so want to touch him, just his jacket would be enough. The attraction I have for him is intensifying more than I ever knew could happen and I've all sorts of emotions clogging up my head.

'My resolution is to take more chances in life,' I explain, my eyes widening at the thought, even though if my mother heard me, she'd go mental. In her eyes I've always been one to live life close to the edge. 'I'm going to put things in the hands of chance and fate, you know. Take more risks in life. Go with the flow. Be true to myself and not suppress the real me to please others.'

He glances towards the door, and then looks behind him. There's a gate at the back of the small yard we're standing in but, apart from that, it's just us, some bins, some steel barrels and a very snowy sky.

'Would you like to go somewhere else to talk more?' he asks, looking around him, as if for inspiration. 'Like you said, it's hardly our type of place, is it? Plus, we mightn't get back inside again since the door is well shut.'

Oh my good Lord . . . did I just hear him correctly? He wants us to go somewhere to talk? Just the two of us? This must be a dream.

I can't think of anyone else I'd like to talk to right now but then my heart sinks. I can't really just abandon Emily, Kevin and Kirsty inside even if I do want to run away with him more than anything in the whole world. Could I? And what if I don't go? Will it be something I'll regret the rest of my life? Will I never see him again?

'We could walk around to the front and knock the door to get back in?' I suggest as a compromise. 'I really should go back in to my friends. They'll be wondering where I am.'

He looks deflated now. He licks his lips lightly in defeat.

'No problem, Charlie. Respect to that. I'll walk you round to the door.'

I so want to change my mind. What the hell am I thinking? Maybe I'm becoming sensible at long last.

'Thank you,' I say to him, but I don't make a move to go. Maybe I'm not so sensible after all.

He is looking at my lips now, then my chest, then my hair. He is looking at me like he did that day in our student living room in our matching boots when the air was filled with awe and song and music. I feel the blood fizz through my veins, warming me up.

I can almost read his mind through the hunger in his eyes, and my stomach has now joined in on the 'Boom

Boom Pow' dance. In fact, everything is a little bit dizzy on the inside when I'm standing so close to him.

I gulp. I don't want him to go. I don't want to miss this 'one in a million' chance again.

'I'd like to get to know you better this time, Charlie,' he says. 'If tonight won't work, could we meet up some time soon? No pressure, but just see what happens? See if it really is serendipity that we met again tonight?'

The dancing inside me comes to an almighty stop. My heart is thumping. I look up at him. He's *very* sexy, especially up this close. He's Tom Farley. I've spent so much time for the past few years fantasizing about this very moment and putting him in my songs.

I breathe.

He breathes too.

The snow is really pelting down now and seeping into where we're standing under the half shelter.

I think of Emily, Kevin and Kirsty again inside. Kirsty is probably still talking to that group of strangers at the bar, and the nice-looking guy who bought me a drink just before I came outside might be still waiting for me at our table. Emily might be wondering where I am, but Kirsty will already be planning on a hot night with one of the doctors, not giving a shit that they've all only just met. So, if she can do it, why shouldn't I have some fun too?

It is my third resolution after all, even if it's not New Year for another couple of weeks. My mind swings like a pendulum – what should I do? Should I go? *Should* I go?

'I think we could get into trouble, Tom Farley,' I tell him. 'A lot of trouble.'

'I think you said that to me before,' he whispers.

That's it. I'm going.

'Let's get out of here then.'

He offers me his arm and I take a deep breath, laughing in nervous disbelief as we walk away, slipping and sliding on the white snow, giggling like two love-struck teenagers who are hiding from their parents. Or, in this case, my big brother who might not be so impressed that I've taken a chance with his ex-band-member.

'I have to warn you though, you might have to listen to more of my country songs,' I tease him as we plod through the cold winter night. 'I've quite a few now for you to catch up on.'

He stops and looks at me. He turns me towards him.

'I've wanted to do that for years,' he says, and something tells me he's serious. His thumb wipes a snowflake from my cheek. 'I still know the melody to that one you sang for me, believe it or not.'

'No, you don't,' I laugh in response but then he hums it, filling in the gaps with words he remembers, and I gasp at his recollection.

All of me, all by myself, longing for you, nobody else.

'I can't tell you how much you impressed me that day,'

he tells me, and we walk through the empty streets, the sounds from the bar fading into the distance and the cold biting our smiling faces.

'I can't believe you remembered my song,' I say to him. 'Wow.'

He takes my hand and the touch of his skin rushes through my veins, making my head spin a little. I can't decide if I'm more terrified or excited with the decision I just made, but I've got a feeling, or so I keep telling myself, that this really *is* going to be a good, good night in a way that I would never have expected. That, or else I'm going to be in a whole lot of trouble for something I know nothing about.

Chapter Two

The box-sized bedroom I wake up in the next morning is so tiny that I can reach out and touch the wall from anywhere in the single bed. Navy curtains hang loosely on a long narrow window as condensation drips down on the inside, and a radiator below is lined with multi-coloured socks and white boxers that sit in a zig-zag row. I can smell burnt toast and hear muffled voices downstairs.

Where the hell am I?

I peep under the covers, afraid of what I might see, but I know by the heat in my body that I must be fully clothed. I'm wearing a Ramones T-shirt that is definitely not mine, a pair of old-school tracksuit bottoms and a pair of mismatched fluffy men's bed socks, which explains why I'm so cosy and toasty. I check the time on my phone. It's just gone ten in the morning. Gosh, I slept like a baby.

'Knock, knock. Can I come in?'

Tom pops his head round the door, enters the room and sits on the edge of the single bed as I run my hands through my hair, trying to recollect coming in here in the first place last night. Everything about this room, everything about him, is so new yet so familiar.

'Tom?' I say.

'Still me, Charlie,' he replies. 'You sleep OK? Were you warm enough?'

I go to speak but I can't. He keeps calling me Charlie even though I've warned him it could get him a slap on the wrists if he ever meets my parents again.

'Where the hell are we?' I ask. He laughs a little, and then leans over beside me. I can smell his aftershave. It's very . . . oh God, he looks even better in daylight.

'You told me last night you'd wake up and ask me that,' he says, resting his hand on top of mine. I want to move it, but I can't. 'Don't look so scared, babe. We had fun, but nothing more happened. Well, lots of good stuff happened actually, now that I think of it.'

I take a moment and have a good long look at him, feeling myself relax a little now as the night before unfolds in my hazy hungover memory.

'I remember,' I whisper and close my eyes, recalling now his muscular strong arms and the musky smell of his soft skin, almost feeling again now the way he touched me so tenderly.

'I practically carried you to bed here in my deluxe spare room,' he says and we both burst out laughing. 'I carried you right over the threshold and even gave you some clothes to sleep in. So much for a hot-blooded night of making up for lost time. You were *very* tired.'

I can't help but giggle at the thought of it all.

'So much for it all being meant to be,' I say, covering my mouth with my hand. 'Sorry to disappoint you but once a convent girl, always a convent girl.'

He lifts a pillow and pretends to fight me, and we wrestle until we fall into a kiss that brings me right back to the night before. I inhale every part of the moment, delighted for once in my life that I was too pissed to turn this into a shitty one-night stand, especially not with someone I've dreamed about for so long. All things considered, I'm very, very proud of myself. Sober me may not have been so resilient, but I'll never admit that to him, of course. Plus, he's an excellent kisser – his lips are warm, soft, gentle but firm in all the right places at all the right times.

'Well I guess some things are worth waiting for,' says Tom, fixing my hair round my shoulders when his lips part from mine. '*You* have been worth waiting for. I still can't believe you're here with me now.'

'Me neither,' I whisper. We didn't end up under the covers together, but we had a very good night. A very, *very* good night.

'Brunch?' I say, remembering now how we had made plans.

He nods. 'We're a bit snowed in for now though and could be for a while,' he says, his green eyes twinkling again just like they did last night. He reaches across and peeps out the curtains to prove it.

'It's coming down heavy,' I say to him. 'So, what do we do now?'

'Well, it's not every day you bump into the girl of your dreams in a dead-end pub in the backstreets of Dublin five years later, so why don't we start the day off slowly with a really fancy instant coffee, some toast and just enjoy each other's company?'

I smile in agreement, recalling how he played guitar last night while I danced in my bare feet drinking wine in the poky living room and singing into empty beer bottles. I sent my sister Emily and friend Kirsty a text at the time to say I was OK and told them I'd met Tom *actual* Farley and had gone to a 'party'. I begged them not to tell Matthew but neither of them replied, meaning they were probably too busy having fun themselves to care. Now I've got missed calls, which means Emily is probably panicking. I'd better call her, but not just yet . . .

'So you don't want to ever perform your own songs, then, just write them?' Tom asks me as we lie there on the bed, still chatting over an hour later, too warm now with the duvet draped around our legs. Two empty cups and a plate full of crumbs sit beside us on the floor. I don't think I've ever enjoyed tea and toast as much in my whole life. We're a bit squashed but it's cosy and I wouldn't want to be anywhere else right now.

'I like the writing part better,' I say to him, resting my arm over his hip. 'Maybe I'm too shy and like to hide behind all the words and music, even though to some that might be hard to believe. You see, someone once planted a crazy dream in my head that I could actually be a proper song-writer one day.'

He is still standing by his claim and spent most of last night telling me so.

'It's not a crazy dream,' he whispers to me. 'I totally believe in you. I really think you should ditch the teaching and go on the road with your songs.'

He has no idea how much he is tempting me to do just that, but I know he is telling the truth when he says he believes in me. I knew it the first day we met that no one will ever 'get me' the way Tom Farley does. It's like he can look into my soul and push me to live my life in the way that I should.

'So what are your plans now, Tom? Please tell me *you're* still going to follow your own dreams to make it big in music?'

He stares up at the wall behind me as if for inspiration. I stare at his face.

'Ah, I dunno, Charlie. I'm a fly-by-the-seat-of-my-pants guy when it comes to it,' he says, then turns towards me again, leaning on his elbow on top of his half of the pillow. 'I used to think I was going to be a real-life rock star, and I'd some really good opportunities that got me close, but I bailed out. I messed it up, so now I like to just go with the flow and see where it takes me. Right now, I'm bluffing around in some real estate but it's not for me at all.'

'Real estate?' I say, laughing at the contrast of it all. 'I can't imagine you in a shirt and tie showing people round fancy houses.'

He sits up straight and puts on his best poker face, then laughs in return.

'You know, it pays the bills for now, so I count myself lucky, I suppose.'

So, he messed it up. I've a feeling my brother could tell me exactly how if he wanted to, but he never did.

'Tell me more about you, Charlie girl.'

He pushes my hair back and his eyes dart around my face. He has such a handsome face.

I shake my head. 'You really aren't going to drop that name, are you?'

He looks so blasé. 'Why should I? It suits you. Charlotte is too posh.'

I raise an eyebrow. 'And you think I'm not posh?'

'Are you posh?' he laughs.

'No way,' I say to him. 'But posh girls can be fun too, you know.'

He puts his arm around my waist and pulls me closer into the heat of his body. 'I've a feeling we're going to have a lot of fun, Charlie,' he says with a wink, pulling the duvet up over us again. 'So, go on. Tell me more about what you've been up to since I first fell for you and life got in the way.'

I take a deep breath. He fell for *me*? Although I'd always hoped he had, I never thought I'd hear it directly from him.

'Well, I'm a big twenty-seven years old now,' I say, getting the formalities out of the way. 'I've been a brunette and a redhead since I saw you last and even a shade of purple but I got rid of that quickly. And then back to blonde.'

Now *he* raises an eyebrow. 'I'd never have guessed, my little chameleon.'

I suppose that's one way of describing my eclectic taste in fashion. My father would describe it in a totally different way, telling me some days I'm like a walking charity shop or a love child between Russell Brand and Mrs Merton.

'As well as teaching in a lovely primary school where the kids are ace, I've been working the very odd shift when I can get it in Music City, a singer-songwriter-type cabaret club for about a year now, so I do sing stuff other than nursery rhymes when I get the chance,' I tell him.

'You've done really well for yourself so far,' he says. 'Is it a permanent post at the school?'

I nod and can't help but smile with pride.

'It's just been confirmed. They want to keep me,' I tell him, and he holds up a hand for a high five. Everyone knows it's almost impossible to find a full-time permanent teaching post in Dublin, so it is something I'm very, very proud of. 'But before I became Miss Taylor, teacher of dreams,

I'd some adventures in Australia which was fun. My sister met her husband there – while I met a lot of real-life snakes, you could say. I think that's about it.'

He looks impressed that I've travelled a bit, but what he doesn't know is that he, or at least the idea of him, came with me every step of the way.

'And Matthew?' he asks, unable to look me in the eye when he mentions my brother's name. 'What's he up to these days?'

My stomach flips. I suppose we should just get this part over and done with.

'He's living back at home with my parents,' I tell him, feeling my brow break into a frown at the thought of what has become of Matthew. 'They're looking after him as well as they can, but it's been hard on everyone. It's been so hard on us all watching him lose interest in everything he worked so hard for.'

Tom lets out a deep sigh that sounds a lot like regret.

'I'm so sorry to hear that,' he says.

It's not Tom's fault. It's no one's fault that this darkness has got such a grasp of my once so flamboyant big brother who was always bursting with life and energy, convinced that the sky was the limit when it came to chasing his dreams.

'He's got a job in the little corner shop, which takes his mind off his troubles a little,' I continue. 'Not exactly the architect or big star he dreamed of becoming, but it gives him a purpose and that's what we all need, isn't it? We need something to get out of bed for in the morning.'

I draw imaginary circles on his arm as I speak.

'Are your parents still living further up north?' Tom's face reflects mine as he looks back at me with such a sense of pity. I remember hearing how he visited my home once with Matthew, and of how my mother had rolled out the red carpet as if it was The Beatles coming to visit.

Their band, Déjà Vu, had been offered a record deal at the time with a small label in Belfast and had popped by to see our folks en route to a meeting, which to Mam and Dad was like winning the lottery.

'Yes, they're still up in the little village we grew up in, which suits him, away from the city and all his reasons for giving up on everything,' I tell Tom. Whatever happened between you guys, it shook him. I don't think he ever got over it.'

Tom wears a deep frown and pinches his eyes.

'How much do you know, Charlie?' he asks me. 'What did Tom tell you about why we all broke up?

They'd been going so well. Marketing plans were being discussed, recording studios lined up, even a fairly decent local tour all backed up by a label who believed in them and were just about to sign them up, but suddenly it was all over. It all went pear-shaped so quickly.

I lean up on one elbow now, mirroring him and take his hand from his face, holding it for reassurance.

'He told us nothing more than the band broke up and it broke his heart,' I say to Tom. 'He wouldn't say why, but I'm sure it wasn't anyone's fault in particular, was it?'

I say I'm sure, but then what would I know? Tom, on the other hand, doesn't look so sure.

'He just told me that bands break up, people break up. It happens,' I continue. 'He never wanted to tell me anything more than that, so I respected that. He'd put so much time and energy into the band and the break-up just rocked his whole world.'

Tom looks like he wants to say so much more but I put my finger on his lips.

'Listen, Tom. My brother, as much as I adore him,' I say, 'can be very stubborn when he doesn't get his own way, so you don't need to tell me any more if you don't want to. In fact, can we please talk about anything other than Matthew, just for now? We've had such a wonderful time. Let's not ruin it.'

Tom looks relieved. We've had so much fun since we met up last night, laughing, singing and catching up. I really don't want to dampen the mood.

'OK,' he sighs. 'But I really hope that he finds his way again, Charlie, I really do. He's one hell of a singer and a seriously good guy. He deserves so much more than how we all left things. He really did have big plans but it all just—'

'Come on now, your turn,' I interrupt him deliberately.

There are tears in his eyes, which frighten me a little, but I don't want to face up to this or question why just now. 'You have to tell me more about you, something that doesn't have anything to do with Matthew and Déjà Vu. How did a talented, gorgeous American boy like you end up in Ireland? I'm intrigued.'

He welcomes such a straightforward question, a timely diversion from the heavy cloud of memories that just triggered such emotion. Matthew's depression has rocked our family, shaking us to the very core, and I'm not ready to confront Tom any more on the subject, not yet anyhow.

'My mum is Irish, from Dublin originally,' he says, tracing his finger along my cheek. 'My dad is American but his people are English, hence the name Farley, so I'm a bit of a mixture.'

He takes a deep breath.

'I grew up in Ohio, we moved here when I was seventeen and soon after that my dad disappeared with my mum's cousin, so she went back Stateside and I just stayed here.' He glances away and takes a deep breath. 'The last I heard from my dad, he'd married the other woman and moved to London, so I've been drifting ever since, I guess.'

'Ouch.'

'Exactly,' he says, looking away for a bit. 'Shit happens, though, doesn't it? As Matthew says, people break up, things change. We have to learn to move on and keep going, don't we?'

The sadness in his eyes is back.

'The band was probably the best thing that ever happened to me.'

The band. Matthew. We're never going to get past this one, are we?

'You could form your own band? Make a go of it again?'

I'm excited at my suggestion but Tom just laughs.

'Nah,' he says, shaking his head. 'I tried but it will never be the same. That ship has sailed, and I've tried but failed, I'm afraid. I've also been in and out of jobs, everything from driving cabs in Belfast to selling my soul as a singing stripper for hen parties.'

'No!'

He throws his head back in laughter now.

'I thought you'd like that one,' he says. 'I'm joking! But I've nothing as fancy on my CV as having a degree and being as focused as you are.'

He keeps laughing at the look of shock on my face. I'm trying to be cool at the thought of him stripping for horny young women, even if it was a joke.

'I get by playing the odd pub gig in a covers band,' he says. 'I have a day job and I share a flat here with a Russian guy called Peter who just left to drive to work in the snow, saying it was no big deal even though the whole country is virtually in shutdown. Pete's really cool.'

My heartbeat has settled after the stripper revelation, and I want to know so much more, but most of all I want to hug this lonely boy who has been so lost for far too long. I imagine him as a teenager, abandoned by both his parents who couldn't put him above their own needs.

'You hungry?' I ask him when I think I just heard his tummy rumble.

'I'm starving,' he says in relief, his eyes brightening at the thought of food. 'That toast was good but I'm a growing boy, plus we still have our date today so don't stand me up, Charlie Taylor.'

'As if I would,' I say, looking forward to it more than anything. 'But I'll need to go home first and get changed, which means braving the snow.'

He shakes his head, climbs off the bed and goes to a chest of drawers, which is the only other thing in the room apart from a battered guitar. He hands me a pair of pale blue jeans and a black Guns N' Roses sweatshirt.

'Cinderella, you shall go to the ball,' he says with a heart-melting smile. 'We won't be going too far so don't worry about being too glamorous. There's a great wee pub that does bar food just a few miles away. It's got sea views, an open fire and there's always someone in the corner playing a tune so this will be just perfect.'

I lift the sweater.

'The Ramones and Guns N' Roses all in one day!' I say to him in mock horror. 'Whatever happened to me being a country girl at heart?'

He walks towards me and takes both of my hands.

'Come on, let your hair down, country girl,' he says, kissing me on the forehead. 'It's a brand-new day and life is for living, plus I think it will look pretty cool with your blue cowboy boots.'

I look at the offering and my heart skips a beat. My brother has the same sweatshirt. Stay present, be happy, I tell myself. Matthew would want me to be happy.

I've a feeling he would also have a lynch mob out for me now if he knew who I was with.

'By the way, just so you know, I never, ever do this type of thing, *ever*,' I say to Tom as I pull the sweatshirt over my head to try it on for size. The jeans fit well enough with the help of a belt tied really tight and, although this all feels a lot out of my comfort zone, it does make me feel a bit sexy knowing Tom wears these on his beautiful body.

'You told me last night you'd say that,' he says to me, handing me a towel now. 'Shower is to the left.'

I take a deep breath and make my way out of the bedroom, feeling his eyes on me every step of the way.

It's a snowy winter's day in December, it's the Christmas holidays, so I may as well have some fun with my rock star from Ohio who I've dreamed of for so long. I've waited forever for this moment and no one, not even my brother, is going to ruin it for me.

Chapter Three

We're in the cosiest little pub by an angry winter sea, wrapped up like onions with an open fire by our feet, and I'm looking across the table at Tom Farley who still can't take his eyes off me. And I can't take mine off him.

I'm not sure what heaven is like, but I'm pretty sure this feeling is as good as it gets.

A smell of turf and damp clothes fills the air around us as an old man plays a slow air on a fiddle in the corner, followed by an almost unrecognizable rendition of 'A Fairytale of New York'. It has us all singing along at the tops of our voices, giving the famous Pogues song the Christmas national anthem status it deserves.

I've a bellyful of oysters and Guinness, a heart that's about to burst with joy and I don't ever remember feeling so relaxed and at home in my whole life.

'I think I'm in love with this place,' I whisper to Tom. His sweater is soft on my skin and I'm so at ease, glad to be comfortable in these new but oh so welcoming surroundings. 'I think I've fallen in love with Howth and all it means being here.'

I think I could very quickly fall deeply in love with him, too, and I'm sure he knows it.

'It's one of my favourite places, too,' says Tom. His gravelly voice and rugged good looks make him the icing on the cake in this setting. 'Do you have a favourite place, Charlie? I'd love to go there with you if you do.'

I swoon inside at the idea of us making plans like this together. He wants to do things, see places with me.

'I'd love to go to Paris one day,' I tell him. 'It's been on my bucket list since I was very little. I must be a romantic at heart, even though I've always believed I was a cynic. Something, or someone, must have changed my mind.'

He knows well that I'm referring to him. I never believed in the power of love until I met him.

'We'll go to Paris one day, then,' he says, his eyes lighting up at the idea of it. 'You and me, candlelit dinners overlooking the Seine, evening walks taking in the sights . . . Of course you're romantic, Charlie! You're a writer. Romance is bursting from you.'

I take what he says as a compliment. I suppose I couldn't write country songs with heart-breaking themes if I wasn't romantic.

'I'd love to see Paris with you one day, Tom,' I say to him. 'But I'd also be happy to stay here forever.'

'You'd be very welcome to stay here forever,' he says,

putting a strong arm around me, telling me the feeling is mutual. 'We could live by the sea and watch the world go by, test-run our self-penned songs on the punters at our leisure before strolling home with the wind in our hair. Not the worst type of life if you ask me.'

My heart swells at the thought of it.

'Imagine being able to make a living out of your own creations, being exactly the person you know you want to be instead of being a slave to mortgages and bills in some silly rat race in the city.'

I allow myself to dream of a life here in pretty Howth with its island views, writing songs and playing music, being who I am and not who I seem to have become.

'That's how I thought my life would be,' sighs Tom. 'Don't you ever just wish you could make a living from your talent, your passion and your dreams instead of always going against the grain of who you really are, Charlie?'

He looks like a man with so many regrets as his mind drifts away again from the beautiful moment we have been sharing for the past couple of hours.

'You're too talented to be stuck in a job you hate,' I tell him, sitting up straight. 'You used to steal the show on stage with the band, even from behind the drum kit. Plus I've heard you singing so I know you'd make a great front man if you wanted to.'

He smiles lightly but I know he doesn't believe me.

'I'm thirty-two years old,' he says to me. 'Maybe it's about time I stopped dreaming of being the next Bob Dylan and earned some money for a change.'

'Maybe it's time you stopped trying to be someone you're not by working in an office,' I say, knowing I'm talking to myself as well as him.

'I'm a free spirit, Charlie,' he says as if reading my mind. 'So are you. We should both be earning a living doing what we love instead of where we both are now. But sometimes life gets in the way and we need to do what we need to do. Does that make sense?'

I nod slowly. Of course it makes sense.

I think of my job at the primary school and how much I love it, yet since Tom told me how talented I am five years ago, I've always feared I might be a square peg in a round hole, ticking boxes, robotically following systems I don't even believe in just to keep a roof over my head and to have a career that gives me a steady income.

I think of Matthew, a truly tortured artist now working in a corner shop in the middle of nowhere and living with our parents as he battles with his mental health issues which have suffocated him when all his dreams folded. He couldn't make his passion work, so why would it be any different for me?

Then there's my friend Kirsty who wants nothing more than to be someone's wife with two-point-four children, and my sister Emily who travelled to Australia with me and met the love of her life on the way. Always content with the simple things in life, Emily has forever been my role model and the one I look up to with her carefree attitude and happy-go-lucky ways.

I don't know how I became who I am now on the outside, but on the inside I'm bursting to be different, to take risks, to follow my heart and soul instead of my head. Inside, I'm longing to be the real me and so far in my life the only one to recognize that is this man in front of me. He sees in me something that I have only ever seen myself. He believes in me so much that it's almost catching my breath.

'Do you mind if I call my sister really quickly?' I say to Tom, needing a moment from this realization and perhaps some familiarity before I really am tempted to run away with him and pack in all that I've worked for. 'It's not that we need to know each other's every move, but I did abandon them all last night so it might be good to see how they got on.'

Tom gladly gives the go-ahead then goes to the bar to get some drinks in, giving me time to check in with Emily. She misses the call then rings me straight back and I'm excited to tell her all about my very quaint surroundings here in this brand-new place where life seems so free and easy.

'Happy school holidays, Miss Taylor!' she sings down the phone when I pick up. 'Are you still with that absolute ride Farley? Our Matthew will murder you, you do realize that? I get a feeling he *hates* him and everyone else who was in that band.'

I can hear Kevin, my brother-in-law, mutter in the background something along the lines of Matthew being all right if nothing falls on him.

'I'm with him, yes, in a little pub in Howth,' I tell her. 'I think I've fallen in love with Howth, not to mention the company. Oh Emily, he is just the best. I'm feckin' mad about him.'

Not that I need to tell her that as she's listened to me go on about all the 'what if' scenarios and fantasizing I've done about Tom Farley over the years.

'I swear,' she says to me. 'I can't believe this, Charlotte, he's a dream! He's *your* dream! Did you tell him about the songs you wrote about him? Oh my God, it's like a movie! Did you tell him how mad in the head you've been about him for five years now?'

For the first time ever, I want to gag my big sister as she states the obvious as if she's on speed.

'And did you ask him what happened with our Matthew and the band?' she continues. 'I'd *so* love to know the real story there. Like, why on earth would Matthew leave Dublin and go back to the sticks over a silly row? It must have been really bad for it all to get so messed up. Ask him, I dare you! You better ask him, Charlotte!'

I don't want to ask him. In fact, I feel panicky at the very thought of knowing the truth in case it ruins everything. I know it must have been bad – we all know it must have been bad – but I don't think I want to know any more than that. What if it was Tom's fault? What if it was so bad that it meant we could never be together?

I glance across at Tom who is thankfully engrossed in conversation with the barman and can't see the worry in my face.

'He's everything I hoped he would be,' I whisper to Emily, feeling tears of fear prick my eyes at the thought of this all going wrong. 'I really hope that Matthew can forgive him for whatever it was and see how good we are together.'

My sister gasps in a high-pitched tone.

'Sorry, I'm just really happy for you,' she says, getting emotional now, too. 'I can't believe you just bumped into him like that. Like, five long years later, too. Kevin, did you know that she has waited five years to find this man? Even the hunks Down Under couldn't change her mind and believe me, I tried to distract her from him. But look, she was right. It's fate!'

I wait as my sister and her husband update each other on what Kevin knows and doesn't know about my five years of pining for Tom.

'So, anyhow, I just thought I'd check in so that you knew I was alive,' I say quickly, trying to divert the subject, 'and to apologize again for abandoning ship last night. I hope Kirsty isn't too mad.'

I say that with the ultimate tongue in cheek as we both know that Kirsty, as long as she has a man stuck to her face, couldn't care less if any of us disappeared to Outer Mongolia.

'She's worried sick about you.'

'I'm sure she is,' I laugh.

Tom comes back to our seat and I feel slightly nervous. Not nervous to be with him in the slightest, but nervous that my sister will let me down by declaring my forever love to him not knowing he is beside me again and he might overhear her.

'Last I heard from Kirsty, she was planning her wedding. Yes, another one,' says Emily, while Kevin continues to commentate in the background. 'I mean seriously, I don't know how she does it. I'm still de-stressing from my wedding a year later, never mind contemplating another. She's like, what do you call her? What's the name of the actress with all the husbands?'

Tom can definitely hear her now. We glance at each other. He catches my eye and smiles.

'What's the name of the famous actress who was married eight times?' I ask him, not wanting him to feel left out.

'Liz Taylor,' he whispers.

'Liz Taylor, yes! Kirsty would make Liz Taylor look like a spinster at this rate,' I joke to my sister. 'Look, I'd better go but you two enjoy the rest of your day and I'll see you soon.'

But Emily doesn't seem to want to go. She's totally caught up in all things to do with me and Tom, it seems, and wants to hear more.

'Is he there right now? Beside you?' Emily says just as I'm about to hang up. 'You know, our mother fancied him more than any of us when he was in the band with Matthew. She totally had the hots for him and said if only she was twenty-five years younger!'

I take that as my cue to go and we swiftly say our good-byes, then I lean back on the booth and drop my phone beside me.

I can't believe she said that my mother fancied Tom but, let's face it, he probably has women of all ages swooning after him all the time. He's the type of man that older women float towards in a giddy mix of maternal instinct and phys-ical attraction.

'So, your friend, is it Kirsty? She's been married more than once or was that just a joke?' he asks, out of the blue, and I'm a bit taken aback at his interest in the brief mention of Kirsty's exotic love life.

'Yes, Kirsty is a real romantic who would consider marrying Mickey Mouse if he asked her to, why?' I ask, taking a gulp of my drink.

'Just asking,' he says to me. 'Funny old thing, marriage. I'm just curious.'

OK, then, since he's just curious . . .

'Well, her first marriage was when she was twenty-four to a Turkish lad called Demir who she met on holiday,' I tell him. 'They'd known each other two weeks when he proposed.'

'Sweet.'

I smile at his sincerity.

'That's one word for it, I suppose,' I explain, 'but as soon as he got his visa just over a year later, she was history.'

His face changes. 'Ah, not so sweet then. Poor Kirsty.'

That's what we said at the time, but we needn't have worried.

'Second of all was James, a forty-seven-year-old divorcé she met online who only wanted someone to look after his children so he could work around the clock,' I say, and Tom's eyes widen. 'So this time *she* jumped ship after two years, realizing that being Fräulein Maria was not her destiny, after all. She's twenty-nine now and still hasn't given up on her happily ever after.'

Tom sits back and raises an eyebrow. I can't tell if he's impressed or just intrigued that someone in this day and age could be so gullible.

'I guess we all make foolish mistakes when we're young and think we're in love,' he says, a tinge of regret in his voice. He looks like his mind has drifted again for a second. 'Do you fall in love easily, Charlie?'

'What?'

'You heard me.' He squeezes my hand and my heart flutters.

I hold his gaze as I wonder how to reply. If only he knew how I'd longed for him after only minutes in his company five years ago. How I'd spent hours of my life pouring my thoughts into love song after love song and how every single man I've met since him failed to give me the intense feeling in the pit of my stomach like he did. I'd thought that maybe I'd imagined him to be something he wasn't, that I'd dreamed him up in my head, yet here we are having the most relaxed, perfect time together and it tells me that I was right all along.

'I don't think I've ever been in love before,' I say to him, wanting to hold back from spilling my whole heart out to him so soon. 'I'm a bit of a cynic, maybe. My mother always said I should lower my expectations instead of dreaming of Mr Perfect For Me.'

He laughs now with a tiny hint of embarrassment at the mention of my mother.

'So, you've never been in love,' he says. 'Ah, come on.'

If only he knew.

'Same question back to you,' I say to him, feeling brave but unsure if I want to know the ins and outs of his love life. I already know that it's been, let's say, very busy.

He takes a sip of his frothy pint of Guinness and then leans forward and clasps his hands.

'I've certainly *thought* I was in love before,' he says, not afraid to look me in the eye as he does so. 'Many, many times I thought, wow, this must be it, but then it would wear off and I'd wonder if that's how it should be. I've been searching and hoping for something deeper, you know? Something real that lasts and that doesn't give up when the novelty and lust drug wears off, but to be honest, I'm still wondering if I really know what it's all about at all. What even is love?'

We both take a deep breath and sit in silent contemplation. I feel tears prick my eyes when I think of the words I put into songs about him, yet I didn't even know him at all back then. Is that love? Or how I dreamed of this moment when we'd be reunited and it's just as perfect as I'd imagined it. Is that love?

'What I do know?' he says, breaking our silence and looking my way, 'is that when I first met you, Charlie, I think I felt something that I hadn't before.'

He pauses. I try not to gasp.

'And I also know that I haven't felt the same with anyone ever since, no matter how I tried to convince myself otherwise,' he continues. 'That probably sounds ridiculous but it's true, Charlie. I find your talent, your presence, everything about you just so mesmerizing, which is why what your brother thinks of me just can't get in the way any more. Not this time. Not ever.'

I inhale this moment. Could this really be happening? Is it true what they say, that when you know, you just know? What is it about the two of us that makes this all feel so unique and real? When I see him, I want to touch him, to hold his hand, to take every part of him in. When I speak, it's like he hangs on every single word and answers in exactly the way I want him to – actually no, he answers even better than that.

I swallow hard. 'Thank you,' is all I can say. 'I'm really honoured you think I'm so talented. I've always feared my songs might be a bit twee and simple.'

He looks at me in disbelief. 'You should be shining brightly, Charlie Taylor,' he says, leaning closer, touching my face. 'You absolutely impressed me and have rarely left my mind ever since that day, no matter where I've been or who I've been with.'

I want to ask him why he didn't come and find me back then if his feelings were so strong. What stopped him from looking me up and saving us both from all this misery for so long? Even if it hadn't worked out, why didn't he try and make it happen in the first place? And so I take a deep breath and ask him just that.

'I think you broke my heart that day,' I confess to him in an outburst I've been trying so hard to hold back on. 'My heart went to pieces when I saw you with your girlfriend, not to mention all the different girls I saw you with after that.'

He bites his lip, then runs his fingers through his hair.

'I think that when you're ready you should ask your brother why I never made that move,' he says to me, and for the first time since last night I see a different look in his eyes. A little bit bitter, maybe.

'Matthew?'

Oh no, not this again.

'Or I can just tell you now some of what happened, and

you can make your own mind up if you want to see me again?'

We sit together, in a slightly uncomfortable silence, each acknowledging the dip in the mood and the onset of reality. I can almost hear my heartbeat. I don't know if I want to hear this or not.

'Just tell me,' I say, closing my eyes as I concentrate on breathing. I've a feeling my whole world is about to be pulled from beneath me, just when it was all going so well. 'No matter what it is, I'm sure it can't be that bad.'

He swallows, holds my hand a little tighter, and I can see that this is just as difficult for him as it is for me, but it's like an elephant in the room now and we have to get it out of the way.

'The girls I was with back then, they never meant a thing and Matthew knew it,' Tom explains to me. 'It used to irritate him that I got all this stupid attention. Not that he was jealous or anything, but more that he wanted me to focus on the band itself, or him at least, rather than the women who followed us. Then, one night after a gig, I got the courage to ask him for your number. I made some excuse about wanting to hear more of your songs and he flipped, like, totally flipped, and told me that he never wanted to see me near you again. Called me a womanizer and a . . . well, you can imagine the rest.'

I shake my head and smile a little, but Tom isn't smiling

at all. This is a big thing for him to tell me and even talking about it is really opening up old wounds.

'I can imagine.'

'I totally got that he was your big brother and of course he was worried, but no matter how much I tried to explain to him that to me you were different, he wouldn't have it,' says Tom. 'He was the big boss at the time, it was his band and I had to do what he said if I wanted to keep my place. We were really going places and he made me choose – go after you like I wanted to or stay in the band. At least he said that was why he was mad.'

I bite my lip as it all falls into place. Maybe this isn't as bad as it seems. Unless there's more?

'But there's no band now, right?' I say to him. 'There is no band so none of that matters any more, does it? We can be together now if we want to. It's nothing to do with Matthew any more.'

I think of my brother and all the times he seemed to stand in my way when in his head he was standing up for me. He was always so super protective and I hated him for it, but maybe he had a point. He saw Tom as a Casanova who would break my heart. He was looking out for me as any big brother would, but that time is over now. We are where we are now. We can live in the present.

'No, there is no band now, and I'd a big part to play in that too,' says Tom, dropping his head and looking away.

'That's when the story ends, and it wasn't a happy ending, as you know.'

Oh. So I haven't heard it all yet. There *is* more . . .

'Why did you guys break up?' I ask him. 'Please don't say it was over me?'

Tom wets his lips with his tongue and exhales long and slow. My stomach hits my mouth.

'We were having silly rows up until then,' he continues quickly. 'There were cracks. Me and Matthew were clashing left, right and centre. He wanted to be the star of the show, I wanted to have more say in what direction we were going in. It was a clash of ego, of power, a real-life case of too many chiefs, and I told him he was jealous, but I always had a feeling it was more than that.'

I dab my nose with a tissue as I try and absorb my part in all of this.

'Jealous? You mean, jealous of you?'

He bites his lip. 'Yes, I guess in a way he was jealous of me,' he says, his eyes heavy now and sad. 'But not *just* jealous of me. He was jealous . . . he was jealous of what me and you could be if we got together.'

It all starts to make sense now, even if it seems so petty and ridiculous on Matthew's part. He used to make every excuse he could think of to put me off Tom Farley. He used to love to tell me that he'd a woman at every gig, a different one every night, and because he knew I fancied Tom he'd remind me that I'd always just be the same to him. I'd offer to help out at gigs, but Matthew would have anyone but me come along and hang out with them. He would never let me get close.

'I felt there was something deeper going on with him, something I couldn't control, and I just couldn't work around his negative energy any longer so I stormed out and we all became history after that,' says Tom. 'It cost me my whole musical future, but it also lost me a very good friend and any chance of seeing you again. Maybe that was a big mistake. Maybe it was a selfish, childish move that backfired as it broke up the band and it broke . . . well, it broke Matthew too, I suppose, didn't it? I never imagined he would take it so badly.'

I can't think straight. I put my hand to my forehead. Do my parents know this? Did Matthew tell them he was jealous of the idea of me and Tom getting together? I still don't understand why. My family have been to hell and back with Matthew for four years now, but do they know I had a part to play in this too, even if I'd no idea?

The music in the bar is irritating now instead of entertaining and the punters are suddenly too loud. I'm uncomfortable instead of cosy. I'm sick instead of happy and content.

I can't speak right now. All I can think of is my brother and his mental health problems that have driven him to some very dark places, of the recluse he has become, of his rejection, of his avoidance of any mention to do with the band he set up with such love and attention. He refused to tell me what happened, but I'd never have guessed any of this.

'And you're sure that's all it was?' I choked. I've a feeling there was more. There had to be. 'It seems pretty trivial to build up a band for a year then throw it away over you asking for my phone number.'

Tom's chest rises and falls, and he looks away, his face etched with pain.

'I dunno, Charlie,' he sighs. 'I tried to talk to Matt. I really tried to dig deep with him, you know? He was acting so strangely around me, and I couldn't get it out of him if there was something else. Are you sure he never told you anything?'

I shake my head. Matthew's darkness moved a black cloud over our whole family as we battled to help him, but he refused to talk. He just closed up and said he'd had enough of life. We've been on a time bomb of nerves with him ever since, watching his every move. Tom's return could be enough to tip him over the edge again.

My phone rings, giving us both a welcome distraction until we see who it is.

'Oh God, you'll never believe it but it's Matthew calling me,' I whisper, wishing I could just run away from all this mess between these two men who I've so much feeling for. Could he have found out where I am today?

'You should answer it,' says Tom, rubbing his temples. 'Would it help if I spoke to him?'

I look at the floor. The smell of Guinness is turning my stomach now and the fire is too hot. I can't answer. I can't answer Tom and I can't answer my phone. Matthew leaves me a voicemail message, but I don't need to listen to it. I know how his moods have been lately. If he's heard I'm with Tom, he'll just spit out a rage at me and I can't cope with what he has to say right now.

Plus, I'm angry at him. I'm so angry that he couldn't see past his own ego back then, his own big brother macho attitude or his own jealousy that I might have just an inch more talent than he wanted me to have or might stamp on his toes. How dare he make that decision for me when it was none of his business?

I'm angry at Tom now, too. I can't believe he didn't stand up to Matthew more and push through with the band when it was all he ever wanted in life and when they were showing so much potential. How petty of them to throw it all away over some jealous row – unless there was more to it than I'm being told?

'Aren't you going to call him back?' Tom asks me and I shake my head.

I feel a bit sick. I don't want to talk to Matthew right now.

'I think I need some fresh air,' I tell him, lifting my coat.

'Me too.'

He follows me outside and we stand in the slushy snow watching waves crash on a grey foamy sea in the near distance. I shiver, clutching my bag that holds my dress and other bits and pieces from last night, while Tom paces around me, smoking a cigarette and waiting for a reaction. But I can't give him one right now.

'None of this has to ruin us, does it?' pleads Tom. 'We can't let it happen again, no way. I have feelings for you, Charlie. We can't keep letting other people get in our way. Do you have feelings for me, too? Tell me.'

He puts his cold hand on my face and rests it there, looking deep into my soul. A hot tear trickles down onto his fingers from my eye but he doesn't move his hand away.

'I do,' I say to him. 'More than you'll ever know.'

He slips his arms around my waist now and pulls me close to him, the warmth of his body soothing me instantly. I close my eyes, lean on his chest and feel the rush that fills me up from head to toe. I have to be with him. I just have to.

'Last night at the bar,' he says to me, like he's breathing his last words to me. 'Charlie, I didn't just turn up there unexpectedly, you know that.'

I'm confused now. I look up at his face.

'I was hoping you'd be there,' he says. 'I had absolutely no idea if I was on some wild goose chase, but I went to Pip's Bar because I was looking for *you*. I had this mad hope you might be there, just because it's the area of town you used to live in, and then I gave up and went out the back for a cigarette but . . . well then, there you were. It was like it was meant to be. Mad, really, when you think of it.'

I gulp, stunned a little that it worked out as it did. My friends and I hadn't planned to go there last night. It was only because of the weather that we did. He couldn't have known. He took a gamble. He's telling the truth.

I look up to the black, snow-filled night sky and the moon that reflects down over Dublin Bay. We didn't just meet last night by accident. Sometimes things are meant to happen. Some things are meant to be.

'You should be a detective,' I laugh, and he kisses me on the forehead, not lightly like he has done before, but a long, lingering kiss that makes me hold him even tighter. I give myself to him, leaning in and absorbing every ounce of the man I've wanted to hold me and touch me for so long.

'I wish we could stay here forever,' he whispers to me, and I feel exactly the same. I love this place more than anywhere I've ever been. This moment, this kiss, this knowing that for once in my life the planets aligned and brought us here together again.

I think I love Tom Farley, but then I always knew I did.

'Look, just let me talk to Matthew once and for all,' I whisper and when he looks at me, I can see the pain and worry in his eyes. 'I'll explain to him that he can't get between us, no matter what happened before, and we'll see where this all goes. I can't take a chance on losing you again, Tom, and I know you feel the same.'

'You sure?'

I nod at him. 'I've never been so sure,' I tell him. 'We've waited five years for this. I don't want to lose you again. Never. It's happened once and it will never happen again.'

Chapter Four

Matthew James Taylor, my one and only brother, was my hero every day of my life when I was a little girl. He was the big brother of dreams, the one who all my friends adored and wished they could be around, no matter what stage of life I was at.

As a child I'd hear him sing in his bedroom, everything from Elvis Presley to Oasis, and I'd watch him in awe when he took the lead in school concerts, drama groups and anything that allowed him to take centre stage. Other boys were mad into following football and chasing women, but Matthew had one dream and one dream only and that was to sing.

At first my father tried to push him into sports of all sorts, thinking he wasn't manly enough if he didn't play rugby or cheer on the reds or blues or whoever was the popular soccer team of the day. But Matthew was always to be found in his bedroom with a guitar strumming along to the Top Ten hits, or in the music room that used to be our garage but was soon filled with second-hand keyboards, drums and everything under the sun that Matthew could gather to build his own idea of a 'man shed'.

In many ways he was an isolated boy growing up, because in rural Ireland it was only cool to have alternative interests as long as you could still score points and goals when it came to Gaelic games and show some rough and tumble.

But Matthew wasn't that type at all. He was quiet and gentle and the only time he'd raise his voice was when he was hitting the high notes of a Guns N' Roses song.

'He's a deep boy,' my mother used to say, as if in apology. 'He thinks too much. Maybe his passion for music will be his saviour one day.'

And so, it became his thing.

I, on the other hand, could have stood on my head and done a jig to try and impress, but even if I could I'd never be seen to be talented like Matthew was. Emily often joked she was the invisible middle child, while at least I got some attention being the youngest, but Matthew was always the one to watch – the one who was destined to be different – and everyone came to adore him for it.

Now, to see him put down his tools as such, to have abandoned his university degree in architecture (which was a back-up plan he never thought he'd need anyhow), and to be working in the village corner shop back at home as he battled with the demons in his head was a bitter pill to swallow.

I follow the stone walls into Loughisland, a drive I could

do with my eyes closed, and my heart swells when I see the familiar faces making their way up and down the little street where I will always call home.

It's a quiet-looking place to the naked eye, but behind the scenes it's a bustling little village, where the tiny primary school is the heart of the community and where everyone lives and breathes for football matches on a Sunday after Mass. I loved growing up here – a world away from Dublin and the city life that caught my stride since I left here almost ten years ago.

I park the car on the side of the street and walk towards Sullivan's corner shop, which even in December has a huge ice cream cone outside advertising its famous 99s that everyone who passes through will stop for. The shop is attached to a pub of the same name where you'll also find the local undertaker, should you ever need to plan a funeral when you're doing your grocery shopping. Well, you never know, do you?

Across the street is the chapel with its adjoining cemetery, and I notice some very entrepreneurial thinker has opened a new florist's alongside, meaning that every event or occasion, be it a christening, a wedding or a funeral, is well catered for. A tall, somewhat overpowering evergreen tree is decorated with bulbs of green, red and blue and a string of clear lights hang to tell us that it's the season to be jolly.

I was christened in that very chapel on a sunny Saturday in April many years ago. I made my First Holy Communion there in a white dress handed down from Emily when I was seven, and it was the first place I heard a choir singing 'Ave Maria', which made me fall in love with live music when I was barely tall enough to see over the pews. We sang carols every year beneath a tree in the exact same place, which would then be replaced when spring came with pots of daffodils and snowdrops, then bursts of colour in summer that always made us proud of the locals who made such an effort to make the place so pretty.

The snow has thawed a little now, but a bitter winter breeze catches my breath, forcing me to tighten my scarf and quicken my step towards the shop front of Sullivan's. I get there and stop, despite the sharp weather, to watch Matthew through the window serving a friendly local. A wave of sadness overcomes me from deep inside.

This is my hero, my big brother. How did he ever come to this?

His eyes light up when he sees me through the window before a familiar-sounding chime above the door marks my entrance. The shop smells of my childhood – of warmth, boiled sweets, newspapers and ice cream in wafers – and I rush across to give him a hug which he receives shyly. He is thinner than he used to be and his hair, which once upon a time sported every colour of the rainbow, is pale brown, lank and light. He is thirty-two years old now but he looks at least ten years older in his navy apron, worn-out jeans and with his tired, drained face.

'You got my message then?' he asks, his eyes wide in anticipation. 'I probably wasn't making much sense, but I hope you understood my rambling?'

His eyes crinkle as he smiles, which tells me he may have some good news. It's far from what I was expecting. I didn't listen to the voicemail he left me last night, but I can't bring myself to tell him so. I just couldn't do it. I was too afraid he may have found out about me and Tom and I wanted to speak to him in person, hence my unannounced visit.

'Oh, did you leave me a voicemail?' I bluff. 'Sorry, I'm so bad at picking up messages.'

'Some things never change,' he says, wiping his hands on his apron. 'I just said I wanted to meet up with you in the next day or two, so looks like we're on the same wavelength, after all. I've something to tell you.'

I know by his face that it's good news, which is a huge relief. Something to tell me? What on earth could it be?

'I did see a missed call,' I confess, feeling guilty now, 'but decided on a visit home instead. I miss my big brother.'

Never one for big affection, he rolls his eyes and goes back in behind the overcrowded counter as another customer approaches. It's the type of shop that used to feature in every Irish town or village but has died out over the years, replaced instead by heartless chain-stores that don't reflect the soul of a community like this one does. Here, you can buy everything from a loaf of bread to your morning paper, but you'll also find hardware, a pub and you can choose a coffin out the back if you need one.

'I've a few things to tell you, one biggie and the other is a really cool idea for Mam and Dad, if you and Emily are up for it,' he says as he punches numbers into an old-fashioned till, without acknowledging any further that I've no idea what he's talking about. 'I think it would be something different and would give Mam a lift this Christmas.'

'Of course,' I say with as much enthusiasm as I can muster. 'We can talk more when you've finished your shift.'

I'm a little bit worried but only because this all seems too good to be true. Matthew wanted me to come here to share some big news, and to plan a Christmas surprise for our parents. It's like the old Matthew is back, the one who used to be so bright and full of ideas and excitement.

He glances through the hatch behind him that looks into the bar where, as always, there is horse racing flashing on a TV high up in the background.

'I can finish up here now,' he tells me. 'Look, do you want to pop next door and I'll buy you a drink? Mrs Sullivan can mind this place too when I need a break. We have that sort of arrangement.'

'Cool,' I say to him. 'I'll let you get finished up.'

I make my way out onto the blustery street again, my head lost in wonder and steeped in time as it always is when I come back here.

Mrs Sullivan knows the score, I think to myself, realizing

that Matthew's 'job' at the shop is more for his benefit than theirs, of course. It's a baby step back into society for him and a subtle level of responsibility that gives him a reason to keep going.

Four years of this have passed, though. We'd all hoped he'd have got better a whole lot sooner, but depression knows no boundaries and the black dog inside him doesn't seem to want to move on just yet. Well, not until now perhaps, as he shows this light glimmer of excitement for the first time in a long, long while.

Mrs Sullivan, or Angela Martin as I know her as she was only a few years older than me at school, is the third Mrs Sullivan to run this place for as far back as I remember. She greets me shyly, a bit nervous as most people are around us city types who left Loughisland for wider shores, but she soon relaxes when we start chatting like I've never been away at all.

'He's doing so well,' she tells me, wiping her hands on a brown and white tea towel. Nothing in here has changed a bit. The old chocolate-coloured stools at the bar are the same with their black metal legs that I used to have to climb up to reach my seat when Daddy and I would slip in here on a Saturday afternoon for a sneaky bet on the horses. I'd be fed Tayto Cheese & Onion crisps and bribed with a glass of Fanta while he chugged down a quick pint of the black stuff and prayed that his luck would come in.

'I think working here can only be good for him,' I say to

Angela. 'We're worried sick for him, to be honest, but thanks to you and your family for giving him this chance.'

'You know he wants to start a folk club?' she says, as if she's telling me she's won the lottery. 'Now, that's a good sign! He's showing an interest in music again at long last. Your mother is *thrilled*!'

We keep our voices down as the open hatch that adjoins the bar to the shop means noise can travel, but we don't get to chat any further as just then Matthew makes his way in and joins me.

'Have you ordered?' he asks. 'Have what you like, it's my treat.'

He seems so chirpy and excited, which now all makes sense. The folk club here in the village, the job in the shop and whatever this Christmas surprise for Mam is. I dread the thought of bursting his bubble when I get round to mentioning Tom, but maybe, who knows, it could be good timing if he's other more positive things on his mind.

'I'll have a gin and tonic,' I say to Angela. 'What are you having, Matthew?'

'The usual,' he says to Angela. 'And don't be expecting any fancy berries or glasses like goldfish bowls in here, Charlotte. A gin and tonic is a gin and tonic in Loughisland, not a bowl of mixed fruit.'

He laughs at his own joke and Angela pretends to be offended.

'The original and the best,' I say to them both and soon

we are clinking our glasses together in true Christmas spirit. 'So, what is it you want to tell me? It's good news, I take it?'

Matthew sits up straight on the stool. 'I thought, well it just came to me yesterday before I rang you . . .'

His appearance may be changing each time I see him but somewhere in there is still my big brother, still the one we all looked up to.

'I was thinking,' he continues. 'Wouldn't it be a great idea if we were to take Mam and Dad on a summer holiday next year, just the five of us? Well, Kevin too, I suppose, as he's family now,' says Matthew. 'It's their thirty-fifth wedding anniversary this year and I think after all the crap we've been through over the past while, it might be something to look forward to? As a family?'

I almost choke on my drink in delight. 'I love it!' I tell him.

'You really think so?'

He's showing so much hope for the first time in ages. He's making plans. He's excited about something once and for all. I lean across and hug him.

'That's the best idea ever!' I say to him, and I really mean it. 'Let's get onto Emily and Kevin and we'll surprise Mam and Dad with all the detail on Christmas Day. Is that what you're thinking?'

'Exactly,' he agrees. 'You know, Charlotte, I remember when I was just a nipper how Mam used to stand at the kitchen sink and say that if she ever came into money, she'd love to take us all to see the pyramids in Egypt. Now I know it will take a lot of money, but if we booked it for, say, August, it would give us all eight months to save the fare and some spending money. Does that sound OK?'

He has thought it all through and it's breaking my heart in two.

'That sounds absolutely spot on, Matthew! Oh, look at you! You're looking so much brighter,' I tell him. 'How are you feeling? Are you coping any better these days? You definitely look like you are.'

He stares at his pint for a second and then breaks into a smile.

'Well, the truth is I'm feeling stronger, yes. I've met someone, Charlotte,' he reveals to me, circling his finger on the top of the glass, and his face instantly brightens. 'Would you believe that I've managed to find another music type, just like me, who was visiting relatives here in the back of beyond? We started as friends, and it's still early days, but it's given me a whole new lease of life. We're thinking of starting up a folk club here in the pub once a month. Don't laugh, I know I'm a rocker at heart, but I'm excited. At long last I'm excited about something.'

I lift my drink and clink my glass against his with tears in my eyes.

'Well, blow me down, big brother!' I say to him. 'That's the best news in the world! Does she sing or what? Tell me more about her. This is just fantastic! Do Mam and Dad know yet?'

He looks away shyly. I've often imagined Matthew's wedding day, him making a heartfelt speech, maybe singing to his bride at some part of the ceremony and my father speaking of his son and new wife, saying how much he is looking forward to welcoming her into the family. If this is really happening for him at last, I'm over the moon.

'I told them last night,' he whispers. 'I wanted to tell you first, but in person, so I just had to tell them over dinner last night.'

I'm taken aback at that. 'You wanted to tell me first? Why?'

'I suppose you've always been the one I've felt closest to,' he says. 'The one I trusted the most. I know I may have pissed you off sometimes by looking out for you a little too much, but you've always been special to me, Charlotte.'

Ah . . . I feel my opportunity arise.

'Sometimes a little bit too much,' I say with a light laugh. I remember I've the car outside and decide to leave it there and walk the mile or so to our parents' house so I can have another drink. That's the effect Loughisland has on me. 'Can I get another G and T please, Angela?'

Angela looks flustered as a new couple enter the bar and I can see the shop has a few customers too. Matthew really should be working and I'm relieved when he offers to get the drinks while she attends the adjoining shop. When he sits back down, I fear the moment to tell him about Tom may have passed.

'So, before I get into all the gory detail about my love life, what about you, little sis?' he asks me when we get back to our conversation. 'I know you're busy being teacher of the year but is there anyone special in your life right now?'

Yes! It's all happening so organically so I decide to grasp the opportunity. I can quiz him further on his mysterious new lover in a while, but this is my big moment to tell him about Tom.

I take a deep breath. I've practised this the whole way from Dublin to Loughisland and now it's time for the big reveal.

'I've met someone too, yes,' I tell him softly. 'And, just like you, it's early days, but I'm feeling it, you know? I think when you know, you know.'

He brightens instantly. 'That's so true, sis. So, who is he? A work colleague, I bet! I always thought you'd end up surprising us all by falling for Mr Sensible who teaches Year Fives and wears corduroy trousers and—'

Oh no, no, no. I am so not going down this road for a second.

'You mean you *hoped* I would,' I interrupt him, unable to disguise the jag in my voice. 'Oh Matthew, I've no interest in Mr Sensible with corduroy whatever, you must know that? I could never go there, in fact I'd run in the opposite direction from anyone remotely beige. Please cut me some slack for goodness' sake.'

He looks offended now but I'm not sorry. I didn't question or judge his type of woman when he just told me he'd found a kindred spirit so why should I let him do the same to me?

'What I mean is, I hope you've met someone who matches your intelligence,' he quickly covers up. 'Someone good enough for you, who will be good to you, someone who isn't like—'

'Someone who isn't like Tom Farley, you mean?' I interrupt him and he actually jumps.

'What?'

'Is that what you're getting at?' I ask him, still nipped by the very idea of me falling for Mr Sensible. 'You'd love me to be with anyone on this earth as long as it isn't a womanizing rock wannabe like Tom Farley who maybe *is* my type after all?!'

'Where is this coming from?' he asks me, as if someone has just punched him in the stomach. 'Why are you talking about him?'

This is not going as I'd rehearsed it at all, but I can't hold back. I'm losing it. I've lost my way, and everything goes into some strange sort of slow motion as the name Tom Farley seems to catch the back of my brother's throat.

His mouth twists a little and he grabs his beer and takes

a long, thirst-filled drink then slams it down just a bit too hard for my liking. Here we go . . .

'What on earth do you have against him?' I ask him, wanting to know once and for all the truth behind the stupid row that changed their whole future. That changed *my* future perhaps, too.

'Why the hell are you bringing *him* up all of a sudden?' Matthew asks me. He looks ashen now as opposed to the bright happy chappy I just witnessed. 'We weren't even *talking* about Tom Farley! You *know* I've a history with him that I can't discuss. My doctor told me never to indulge in conversation with him or about him. Do you know why?'

'No?' I say, afraid now of what is to come.

'You really have no idea?' he says to me, looking at me now as if I'm telling lies. I shake my head.

'I don't, Matthew,' I tell him. 'I mean, I know that he asked for my number and you turned on him and—'

Matthew's voice is shaking when he responds. I really seem to have hit a nerve more than I ever could have expected to.

'Are you *trying* to upset me?' he asks, his face crumpling now. 'Is that what you came here for? Are you bringing him up just to test me or tease me? Why are you talking about Tom Farley, Charlotte? I've left all that behind. I'm trying to move on!'

I realize that I'm shaking now too as he raises his voice. It's not like him. It's so not like him and it's frightening me.

He downs the remainder of his pint, leaving me dizzy with where I'm going now with this conversation, and calls for a vodka and Coke from Angela who looks like she'd rather be anywhere than near us right now. She pours him a drink and sets me up with another gin and tonic and I feel like I'm going to need it.

'Look, I just need to be honest with you. I met him a few days ago, OK?' I say to Matthew.

I can't stop now. I have to finish what I came here to tell him.

'I just bumped into him on a night out really unexpectedly and we spent some time together catching up. He is so, so sorry for whatever happened between the two of you, and the whole breaking up of the band that meant so much to you all, but we've all moved on like you said, Matthew. Can't you forgive him? It's not good for you to hold onto so much anger.'

Matthew drums his fingers on the bar. He shakes his head really slowly.

'It's you and him again, isn't it?' he says to me, closing his eyes in disbelief. 'I don't believe this! That's what you came here to tell me, isn't it? *Isn't it?*'

I'm afraid to go any further now. I want to change my mind and tell him no, of course it isn't, but then I remember Tom and his kindness, his way of knowing me, of how he makes me feel, of how we were pushed apart when we were meant to be together, of the second chance we have and of how I drove all this way to make sure that nothing and no one would ever come between us again.

'We want to give it a try,' I whisper to Matthew. 'Is it really that bad for you if we do?'

I reach out to touch him, but he pushes my hand away.

'Charlotte, please!' he says defiantly, and then downs his vodka and Coke in two gulps.

'Are you denying me being with the one person I want to be with over a stupid band?' I ask him. 'Are you really going to hold onto this forever? Why don't you want me to be with him?'

He inhales and I fear what is coming next. There is more to this story, I just know it.

'He will only ever be trouble, Charlotte! You're making a big mistake, believe me, but hey, maybe I'm wrong? Maybe you two *will* live happily ever after,' he spits at me and gets up from the stool. 'But I very much doubt it.'

He walks away, leaving me puce-faced in front of Angela who is finding it hard not to look in our direction.

And at that he is gone.

My head is spinning with what just happened. I just don't understand. What on earth could spark such a reaction? Why is he so angry at Tom, so bitter and mad that he can't even stand the mention of his name? I look at Angela in utter confusion and embarrassment that she witnessed such an uproar, but she looks away until I say a quick goodbye to her, deciding to go after him and demand some answers.

This time she does meet my eye, but her look is now one of pity, like I'm the last to know on this sorry occasion. I jump from the bar stool to follow my brother out onto the street where I'm met with a furious blizzard of fresh snow.

'Matthew! Matthew, where are you going? Wait for me, please!'

I'm blinded by the wind, the snow and the haze of alcohol that's pumping through my veins and blurring my already confused state of mind.

'Matthew!'

I reach into my pocket to find my car keys, knowing that even out here in the middle of nowhere it's too risky to drive. My head is racing, my heart is thumping, and I know there's no way I could get behind the wheel to follow him, wherever he has disappeared to. I've had almost three drinks in a very short space of time and my emotions are running high. I can't drive, I just can't.

But I don't know what else to do. The snow is thick and heavy now, and then I see him. I can just about see Matthew getting into his car across the street.

'Matthew, no!' I shout into the roaring wind. 'You can't drive in this weather! You've had too much to drink! Matthew, please don't!'

But he can't hear me of course, so I try to cross the street to get to him and a car slams on the brakes, the driver shouts obscenities at me and I take a step back onto the safety of the pavement, cursing myself for being so careless in my despair. I can't see him any more. He's in the car. Oh no, he's in the car!

'Matthew, please!' I call out into nowhere. 'Don't do this, I'm begging you! It's too dangerous!'

I hear the windscreen wipers scream and I too scream out in frustration. The engine roars and I roar too, but it's too late. He is gone.

Chapter Five

I'm standing in a sticky, roasting hot, hospital corridor back in Dublin city, waiting on a doctor to update us on Matthew's condition. It's one of the coldest nights of the year when most people are at home, snuggled up in front of the fire and getting into the Christmas spirit with some old-fashioned movies and a cup of something seasonal.

I haven't felt the cold all evening though, not even as we trudged through the snow in the hospital car park, or when we stopped at the scene of the accident in horror to see Matthew's car on its roof, showing up only under the flashing blue glare of a police siren at the side of a country road. We're all in shock, too numb to feel anything just now.

My mother sits on a bench beside where I stand in the hospital corridor, her pale fingers entwined with pearl-coloured rosary beads, my father's arm around her frail shoulders. Nurses in soft white plimsolls go about their business up and down the wards, very much business as usual and doing a job they should be canonized for, while hearts break around them and everyone is watching them

95

in anticipation, waiting, pleading on a smile and some good news.

'It's just not like him,' Mam keeps whispering when she's not blessing herself or humming prayers as we wait. 'Our Matthew would never get into the car with a drink on him. He's not well sometimes, but he's more sense than that. What on earth got into him? Paddy, you'll have to have a good stern word with him when he gets home.'

My father, a tall, unassuming man who only ever ventures into the city when he really has to, lets out a deep sigh, catches my eye and the fear in his face melts my heart.

When he gets home.

If he gets home is what we're both thinking, but we can't say that to Mam who is holding onto those holy beads like she's grasping onto Matthew's life.

If I hadn't spontaneously gone to Pip's Bar that night, I wouldn't have met Tom Farley.

If I hadn't left with him, if I'd gone back inside to my friends, I needn't ever have mentioned his name again.

If I hadn't come home to tell Matthew when I did, this would never have happened.

So many decisions, made by me, that led to this horror right now. And yet, no matter what is going on or how much I can dish the blame on myself, I still want to see Tom again so badly. I've never felt so alone and I need his strength and how he makes me feel so safe and strong like no one else can.

Emily and Kevin have gone for a cuppa in the canteen a few floors down, Mam and Dad are literally propping each other up and I'm standing here on my own up against a hard wall. I'm so confused in my thoughts and wanting the one person whose name drove Matthew into such a state in his head that he jumped into his car and had a head-on collision just two miles out of the village. Where on earth he thought he was going, we might never know.

I check my phone, my thumbs lingering on the touch-screen over the phone, longing to tell Tom what happened but afraid to at the same time in case he blames himself. There's more to this, I know that by now, but I've no idea as to what that could be.

'You must be Emily?'

I look to my right to see a handsome stranger extending a strong hand out to me. He's wearing a three-quarter-length navy woollen coat, his auburn hair is flicked to the side and his face is grey with worry.

'Martin?' he says as if I should already have guessed. I must have the appearance of a startled rabbit because he drops his hand after I give him a very limp handshake.

'I'm Charlotte, not Emily,' I explain. 'I'm sorry, have we met before, Martin?'

He looks down at my mother and father to say hello but they're too busy praying to even notice he's here.

'Charlotte, of course,' he says. 'Matthew has told me all

97

about you. You're the very talented teacher, yes? God, this is a nightmare, isn't it?'

We glance at the theatre door where doctors are operating on Matthew as if the door can give us answers but it's just a waiting game for now.

All we know is that Matthew's car spun off the road following a head-on collision with a people carrier – a mother and her children who were on their way home from seeing Santa. His head injuries are severe, theirs aren't life-threatening, thank goodness, but Matthew is going to take the guilt of this to his grave should he survive it at all.

The dark place he'd been in for four years is set to get a whole lot darker, and just when he was showing some signs of hope again. Just when he had found a nice girl, just when he was making plans for next summer with his family, along I come and mention the one name that he couldn't cope with hearing. And now he's lying on an operating table fighting for his life.

I burst out crying and Martin, whoever the hell he is, puts his arm around me and pats my back like I'm a baby.

'It's my fault,' I sniffle, conscious that I'm set to ruin his very expensive woollen coat. 'I don't know why but he stormed off on me without giving me any explanation. Why didn't I just get on with things instead of going home to cause trouble? I'm always causing trouble, it seems. It's all my stupid fault.'

Martin continues to hush me. I may have no idea who

he is but I'm glad of the comfort. For a moment I pretend he is Tom who would hold me even tighter and make me feel so safe if he were here now. Why is life so bloody complicated and unfair?

I hear Emily and Kevin whisper in hushed voices as they make their way back towards us, so I pull away from Martin to greet them. They've only been gone less than half an hour but it feels like forever, and I'm so glad to see my big sister who links her husband as they walk towards us.

'This is Martin,' I say to them both. 'Martin, this is my sister Emily and her husband, Kevin. Martin is—'

I stop, realizing of course that I've no idea who Martin is, only that he has a nice coat, gives good hugs and smells like a fresh Christmas in a mix of oranges and cloves.

'I'm a friend of Matthew's,' says Martin, extending a hand in a firm shake that almost takes my sister's arm out of her socket. She's white as a ghost with worry and has barely spoken since she got here. None of us have spoken much, come to think of it, apart from hurried whispers of the type normally saved for wakes or in the pews of the church. 'Angela from the bar rang me to tell me what happened and I came straight here.'

'You're a good friend,' says Emily, clasping Martin's hand with both of hers. 'Thanks for coming along to support us.'

Martin looks at us in confusion. He's probably just as distraught as we are.

'Matthew and I were due to meet in Sullivan's later tonight

to talk about the folk club we're starting up together,' he sniffles, 'yet here we are instead in hospital. God, I hope he's going to pull through from this. I can't understand it. He would never drive the car after a drink. Never.'

They were going to start up a folk club together? Matthew's friend? I'm fully aware my mouth is gaping open now as I stare at Martin and try and put the pieces of the puzzle that has just formed in my head together. Martin is Matthew's new friend, they were going to start a folk club together. Matthew told me he'd met someone special . . .

'Martin, are you . . . are you Matthew's new partner?' I ask, wanting to kick myself for being so presumptuous and blind to what's been going on in my brother's life. Emily looks like she's going to faint as Martin nods, glancing at us both, wondering why we are so behind the times.

'Yes,' he says, embarrassed now. 'I thought he may have told you by now?'

I don't know what to say. I feel like I've been holding my breath for hours as the penny drops, making a lot of things about Matthew make sense, but also making me a lot more confused. He said earlier he had big news, that he wanted to tell me first, after having told Mam and Dad, and I could kick myself now for stealing his thunder when he was just about to tell me something he's been holding in all his life.

'Charlotte, did you know about this?' Emily asks me, her face twisted in sheer confusion. 'I mean, it's no big deal to me, it's just a bit of a—'

'I'd no idea,' I whisper, 'but it does make sense now. He asked me to come and see him. He was going to tell me this evening.'

Matthew was just about to tell me in the bar, but then he stopped and asked me about my love life, and I took the opportunity because I was on a one-track mission to tell him about Tom. I hadn't for a second thought he wanted to see me for something as huge as this.

'I'm sorry,' I say to Martin, rubbing my forehead. 'We aren't home as much as we should be, but I think Matthew was going to tell me all about you, just before . . . just before this happened.'

Martin takes a deep breath and opens the buttons of his fine woollen coat, then takes it off, wrapping it over his left arm. My mother notices him at last and gets up, then falls into him, hugging him tightly while my father stands beside her staring at the ground. He then glances at Martin and nods in his direction.

'We didn't think this would be coming to our door, did we, Martin?' Dad says, his chin tilted up in a way that tells me he is fighting back tears. 'Only last night we were having dinner with the two of you and loving how happy Matthew was at last, and now . . . one day later. One day later.'

My father breaks down and both me and Emily race to his side, wrapping our arms around his waist like we used to when we were little girls.

So my brother's special person is not a woman like I'd automatically assumed, but a man, and he was going to tell me today. Just as Matthew had paired me up in his mind with Mr Sensible who teaches Year Fives which drove me insane, I too had made my own assumptions about his love life without pausing to notice who my brother really wants to be with. So why the big reaction over Tom Farley? Was it because . . .? Oh my God.

I might even love him a little bit myself.

The words he said so lightly on that very first day I met Tom come back to me.

I slowly let go of my father and stumble down the corridor, grasping my phone in my pocket. I push through two swinging doors, briefly noticing a strange double-take from a doctor on his way past me, and I charge out through a glass-paned connection until I find a soft seat by a potted plant. I collapse down on it and hit Tom's number.

'Charlie, thank God,' he says after the first ring. 'Please tell me you're OK? I was going to call you but didn't want to in case I interrupted you and Matthew. So did you tell him? What did he say?'

I close my eyes tight, wanting the glare of prissy celebrities on the fronts of the magazines that share my space on the hospital sofa to piss away off.

'Tom, you said you thought there was more on Matthew's mind than some petty jealousy between you and him, or me and him or me and you or whatever—'

I don't sound like myself. I am breathy and panicky. I need to slow down. There is a pause. A very long pause.

'I had my suspicions, but I could never say to him, Charlie. Did he tell you? Did he tell you what it was?'

I'm so unbearably hot right now. A glare of winter sun scorches through the floor-to-ceiling windows beside me and I try and catch my breath to keep calm.

'Tom, did you ever think that Matthew might be gay?' I ask him. 'Do you think that all the fuss and over-the-top reaction over you and your popularity with women was because *he* wanted to be with you?'

Tom doesn't pause this time. He just comes straight out with it without giving it a second thought and his voice is one of relief.

'Yes,' he says. 'I did think that, but he would never admit it to me, Charlie.'

'Oh my God!'

'I couldn't ask him,' says Tom. 'I was so afraid in case I'd got it wrong! I've wondered about this for years, torturing myself, but all I did was watch him break up everything that meant so much to him. Did I do the wrong thing by not asking? I should have asked him.'

I shake my head as if Tom is here to see me now. I want to scream at my brother for being so unnecessarily secretive for all these years, yet I want to cry for him at the confusion he must have been feeling. He's thirty-two years old! Why on earth has he been hiding this for so long, living a lie and not telling me or Emily or Mam or Dad how he really was? We would only have loved him more, but this? This is an awful mess now.

'I think he was going to tell me earlier today in the village pub,' I explain to Tom as it all clicks into place. 'He was in such high spirits. He told me he'd met someone and he'd lots of good stuff coming up, but then when I mentioned your name he freaked a bit, then stormed out into the car and had a really bad accident. He's in hospital, Tom.'

'Ah, Jesus.'

'He's critically ill and we're waiting to hear from the doctors just how bad things are. I just can't believe this is all happening.'

I hear Tom gasp and allow him a moment for this to sink in. Matthew let his feelings for Tom ruin a record deal with the band they'd all worked so hard for, his own mental health suffered immensely and the whole thing kept me and Tom apart when we both were thinking the same thing all along. We wanted to be together. We wanted to give it a try. But Matthew wanted him too. I wasn't the only one who fell in love with Tom Farley all those years ago.

'What a mess,' Tom whispers. 'Imagine the pain of hiding who you really are all your life, living a lie and pretending to be someone you're not, Charlie. I feel so sorry for him but he's going to pull through this, isn't he? Matthew's a strong spirit, he won't let this beat him. He's going to be OK, I just know it.'

I think of my mother clutching her rosary beads in that busy corridor, believing they hold some sort of magic that will make Matthew survive this, and maybe they do? I'd turn to anything now if it meant my brother was going to be up and alive and healthy, living the life he always wanted to. Oh, how could I have been so blind, so naïve not to have known this all along? How did he keep this to himself and, more to the point, why? And the most ironic thing of all is that he left Dublin, a cosmopolitan, diverse city where anything goes, to find himself back in Loughisland where the chances of him meeting someone were very, very slim – and yet he met Martin and was on the road to happiness. All until I mentioned Tom. What the hell?

'I'd better go back to my family to see if there's any more news,' I say to Tom, not wanting to end our conversation but knowing there should be some updates by now. 'God, I wish you were here with me. I could be doing with one of your hugs.'

I realize as I say it that it's very unlikely to happen, and Tom's response isn't as enthusiastic as I'd hoped it would be either.

'I think I'm the last person your family needs around them right now, Charlie,' he says to me. I hear his voice quiver. 'I shouldn't have gone looking for you like I did, stirring up old feelings and trouble. What on earth was I thinking? I'm so, so sorry for all the mess I've caused you all.'

'No, Tom, please don't say that!' I plead with him. 'It's not your fault! And I don't want to give up on us now. Not after yesterday. Please don't say that.'

But in my gut, I know that he's right of course. If Matthew's feelings for Tom awakened his sexuality, drove him into a dark depression that caused him to lose his beloved band and almost his mind, how could he ever watch me and Tom together? It's never going to work, no matter how much we want it to.

'We can't just leave it like this, can we?' I say to him. 'I don't want to leave it like this. You know we've something special, you even said it yourself.'

Tears are streaming down my face now and my throat feels like it's closing in panic. This is all too much to process. Yesterday we were so happy, we knew it was all meant to be, and I had so much hope in going home to tell my brother once and for all he couldn't control other people's feelings . . . but this? This is more than any of us could ever have imagined.

Life can take a turn for the better in the flick of a switch like it did when I found a second chance with Tom, but then just like my dad said, in one day it can all change for the worst. It's cruel and unkind, but maybe a blessing in disguise that tomorrow is blind and we don't have any idea what's coming our way.

Tom Farley is a thorn in Matthew's side for all his tomorrows and also his yesterdays – a reminder of an old him, a wake-up call that came to him in an unrequited love, that it seems he just isn't quite over yet, no matter how long has passed. Out of sight, out of mind, was working for him but if this is what the mention of Tom's name can do to him, imagine what it would be like if he had to see him with me. It feels like everything is slipping away from Tom and me, and it's totally out of our control.

'Do you think we'll ever be able to make this work between us?' I ask him, knowing in the pit of my stomach that we won't.

'I guess we don't have to make any decisions just yet, Charlie,' Tom says to me. 'Let's not panic, and please don't cry or you'll start me off. I'm parked outside a really posh apartment in Dublin where I've to show some Kardashian-type sisters round and try to make a sale, so red, puffy eyes won't get me off on the best foot.'

He's trying to make me laugh but all I can do is imagine him in his suit, shirt and tie, his tousled hair all tidied, and I just want to run to him even more.

'I'm not crying,' I lie, losing my breath into a deep sob. 'I don't know if I can take this all in. This will ruin us. I fear it already has.'

And now I can tell that he is crying too. I know it by his voice, his gorgeous, gravelly voice, the way it cracks when he speaks to me. I've a feeling this is the start of a long goodbye and he knows it is, too.

'Look, I'm always on the end of the phone so talk to me

when you want to, no matter what time of day or night,' he says, clutching at straws like I am. 'We can meet up once we know Matthew is on the mend and see where we are then, OK? We don't have to give up just yet, do we?'

I look up at the ceiling.

'No,' I say, as my heart sears in pain. 'Not yet.'

Not yet. But I know that day will come very soon with so much against us. How can I possibly pile any more pain on Matthew? I would never forgive myself.

I look at the clock on the wall ahead of me. It's after nine in the evening, reminding me we've been here for four hours now. The longest four hours of my entire life.

'Stay strong, Charlie Taylor,' Tom whispers. 'You're made of solid stuff. You're going to be fine and so is Matthew, I just know it. I'm here for you, always, even if it's just someone to vent to when you feel like it. Look, I'd better go. Please know I'm thinking of you constantly, every second, and I mean that. I'm going nowhere. I'll be there for you always, no matter what.'

I grip the phone. I don't want him to hang up. I don't want to go back in there and hear what I'm going to hear from the doctors. I don't want to just vent to Tom when I need to, I want to be with him just like we were yesterday, so close, so at home, making plans and celebrating our second chance of being together.

'Thank you, Tom,' I whisper, unable to hide my sobbing now. 'I'll be in touch, OK?'

'Yes,' he says, trying to be strong. 'We'll chat again really soon. I'm here for you, always, Charlie. I mean that.'

And I so want to believe him, but deep in the back of my broken, muddled, loved-up mind is the knowledge that me and Tom Farley will never be simple. In fact, after today, I fear we might never, ever make it happen at all.

Chapter Six

Dublin, March 2016

There are days, when I sit here in my classroom, staring out at the spring sunshine spilling onto the daffodils and snowdrops in the school garden, that I wonder how on earth nine weeks have passed since I said goodbye to Tom Farley.

We tried so hard to keep it going, but no matter how much we tried to disguise it or deny it, the enormity of Matthew's brush with death was like an elephant in the room and we just couldn't get past it.

'Go away somewhere for a few days, just the two of you,' said Emily, forever our cheerleader. She knew I was crazy about Tom and how long I'd pined for him, but no matter how much I tried, I just couldn't lay my guilt to rest. I needed to be near Matthew, morning, noon and night when I wasn't working, and soon Tom felt like he was only adding more pressure to my already messed-up mind.

'When Matthew gets better, maybe you'll get round to

clearing the air with him once and for all,' he said to me one day when I managed to escape from the hospital. 'You're breaking my heart, Charlie. I can't watch you suffer like this. You have to stop blaming yourself. Stop blaming us.'

But I couldn't, and so when Tom was offered the opportunity to audition for a band in London, I knew I couldn't for one second hold him back.

'Come with me, please,' he begged me when we were lying in bed one Sunday morning in late January. 'We'll rent somewhere small and take every gig that comes our way. Maybe you could ask for a career break from school? I know someone who took six months out to travel and they kept the job open so when they—'

I must admit that my gut instinct was to just pack up and go, to follow my heart and live a life in London with the man I love, doing what we both love, living a life that I know is true to my soul, but the decision was out of my hands.

Another decision to stay or go – this time I wasn't taking any chances.

'Oh Tom, I would love to go with you more than anything, but I can't, not yet,' I told him, watching as I broke his heart once and for all. 'I can't leave, not for a long time. But who knows, maybe I could follow you when things get better here?'

Matthew had by now come out of the critical stage but still had a mountain to climb and it was consuming all of our lives. We'd worked out a rota between the six of us – Mam, Dad, me, Emily, Kevin and Martin – which meant that we could make sure he was never alone, even if at times he didn't know we were there at all. New words and phrases like 'blunt trauma', 'haematoma', and 'axonal damage' flood our everyday vocabulary while we lean on doctors who we now know by first name.

Emily thought I was mad not to take up Tom's offer.

'You're only a few hours away for goodness' sake,' she told me. 'You can't carry this burden around forever, Charlotte. You've punished yourself enough. Go with Tom! Go and try it out and we will all still be here if you ever want to come back. Sometimes you have to make decisions for yourself. You want to go, right?'

I nodded, crying as always when I thought of Tom leaving.

'Then go!' she said. 'Matthew will understand eventually. You can't let what happened to him define the rest of your life. His feelings have done that for long enough already.'

But I couldn't do it. My own guilty conscience was in battle with my breaking heart, and my conscience won.

Tom and I spent our last day together in Howth where we walked the Bog Linn loop with its spectacular views, grabbed some lunch at the artisan market and sat on the grass looking out at the famous Bailey lighthouse. It was a quiet day compared to the joy we felt when we last visited this part of County Dublin, but a gentle acknowledgement to what we both knew could have been had circumstances not piled up against us.

'I'm going to miss you so badly,' he said to me, out of the blue, as we sat with the wind in our hair and the sea at our feet. 'Please say you'll come and visit soon.'

I turned to him and gently touched his beautiful face with the back of my hand.

'I'll be with you as soon as I can, I promise,' I told him.

'I love you, Charlie Taylor,' he said to me, his eyes filling up with tears. 'I don't have to go, you know. You could tell me to stay and I would.'

I shook my head and held him close. 'I love you too, Tom,' I told him. 'But I can't hold you back from this opportunity. Go to London and I'll be with you someday, I promise.'

And so, he left for London, his heart in pieces and mine the same, not knowing if I'd ever find the space in my mind to let go of my guilt and follow my heart and soul to where I knew it belonged – with him.

The days passed into weeks, the weeks into months and, as Matthew slowly got better, we never talked about what happened that day in Loughisland when he stormed out in the snow. We just focused on his daily progress, teaching him to sit up straight, to eat with a knife and fork, to say words that used to roll off his tongue but which he now couldn't find. But there were times when I'd catch him staring at me and I'd wonder what was going on in his tortured mind.

Does he hate me for what happened? Does he blame me? Or will he ever be able to let it go and move on as we all have been trying so hard to do? Now he lies in a different ward in a new hospital where he's learning to pick up the pieces of his splintered life, still unable to walk and neither of us able to discuss the elephant in the room, the man we both were in love with at the same time.

'We've got a name for the band at last,' Tom told me in his weekly phone call where we try and catch up and keep our precious connection. 'You're going to think it's awful, I know it.'

'Hit me,' I said to him, drinking in the sound of his voice and longing for the distance between us to lessen soon.

'The record company want to call us The Band with No Name,' he said, then waited for my inevitable reaction. I just burst out laughing and he did the same.

'What genius came up with that?' I ask him.

'I was telling the label all about you,' he says, his voice glowing with anticipation. 'I said you could maybe send us some new material when you get a chance? I want this to be an opportunity for you too, Charlie. I can't wait till you come here. You'll love it.'

My heart soars when he talks like that and I picture it all in my head. Me and Tom, walking around London, somewhere like Notting Hill or Camden Town, exploring the culture, drinking in the diversity and writing songs that come to us like magic.

But deep down, I don't know if the guilt I feel over Matthew's brush with death will ever let that dream I have come true.

'Miss Taylor, I drew you a picture.'

My daydreaming and reflecting is interrupted as usual by one of my seven-year-old pupils, little Gracie Marshall, who hands me a sheet of paper with a very circular-looking me, complete with my guitar and long, flowing purple gypsy dress. Above me is the most magnificent yellow sun with a smiling face that only a young child can draw.

'Well now, Gracie, that has just brightened up my day, thank you,' I say to her, putting the picture up on the wall beside me with my ever-present stash of Blu Tack. She grins from ear to ear and swings from side to side, so I know she has something else on her mind. I wait with a smile, wanting her to know she can ask me anything.

'What is it, darling? Are you OK?' I ask her.

She looks around, then up at me from under thick, dark eyelashes.

'Will you . . . will you sing us a song, please, Miss Taylor?' she eventually asks me, her brown eyes wide as saucers as she twiddles with her dark hair. 'You haven't sung to us in ages and *ages* and I love it when you sing your songs.'

I take a deep breath knowing this is very true. I don't sing at all these days. I just can't. Every time I lift my guitar and try, either at home or here in school, I feel Tom near me and I want to cry for how sore my heart still is without him.

He wants me to sing again, he told me in his last call. Maybe today, with the joy of spring in the air and an audience of very non-judgemental children, is as good a day as any to give it a go.

'I'll try my best, Gracie,' I say, feeling my lip wobble as she brings me over the guitar from the stand where it's been gathering dust for weeks and weeks now. 'What would you like to hear? Any special requests?'

With the familiar cool feeling of the shiny dark wood in my hands, I twist the nuts to tune up, run my fingers down the bumps of the frets and feel the firm strings under my fingers.

A chorus of voices cheer from their desks and I manage to smile from ear to ear in a way I haven't done in so long. Tears prick my eyes. There's no doubt about it, music is what I'm meant to do in life, I just know it. Tom is right. It's in my soul and it makes people happy to hear my songs just as much as it makes me happy to write and sing them.

'Sing the one about the lucky number,' says one of the Jackson twins from the second row of the small classroom. Even after teaching them for almost seven months, I still sometimes can't tell the difference in the two little red-headed boys, which is made more difficult when they constantly swap seats to confuse me.

'Ah, the lucky number song, of course,' I say to a rapture

of enthusiasm from the other twenty-five faces that stare back at me. 'OK, I'll give it a go.'

I quickly recount the words of the 'lucky number song' in my head, and to my delight and surprise they come flooding back like I've never stopped singing it.

I wrote it over a year ago for the pupils who were in my class and, as I think of life back then, I realize how much things have changed for me and all around me. The words of the song were penned right here at this very desk one evening after marking homework, long before Matthew's accident, and long before I fell in love once more with Tom and then lost him again.

The song, a simple, gentle lullaby, was written to instil a sense of love and joy in such young innocent minds, based around the idea that we all have a lucky number, a sense of hope and a guardian angel. The words never fail to make me cry as I know it will do now, but in the nicest way, stripping the idea of happiness down to the simplest things in life like a hug, a smile or a kind word to another.

I pluck the dreamy opening notes and my heart fills up when I look down onto the rows of tiny faces in front of me, some leaning their faces in their hands, some swaying along and others even mouthing the lyrics as I sing. When it comes to the chorus they all join in and I give up disguising the tears that flow from my eyes.

*Your lucky number, lucky star, will keep you safe when
near or far
Angels watching you and me, guiding light so you can
see
Every step that you will take, even when you make
mistakes
Doesn't matter where you are, lucky number, lucky star*

We all applaud at the end of the song and I put the guitar back on the stand, feeling a new energy that I haven't had for a long time. The sun is shining outside, the children I teach are blessings sent from above, my brother is doing better as each day passes and I know that Tom, although he isn't here with me in person, is in my heart and will always be, even if it's not in the way that I'd always dreamed of.

'Thank you, Gracie,' I say to the little girl who encouraged me just now. 'You've made me smile again, right from the tips of my toes.'

Gracie gives me a toothy grin and gets on with drawing another picture, but alas her artwork has to be interrupted as I announce for the class to take out their arithmetic books. As always, this is met with a series of groans and I marvel at the honesty of children, who keep me on the tips of my toes every single day. Music is my inner passion, my great love, but teaching is what gets me up every day and gives me that sense of purpose that Tom and I spoke of on that day in December. I don't feel as if he has really left me yet. I don't think he ever will.

While I fill my days with the joys of little people, in the evenings I make the short journey out to Malahide to the respite and rehabilitation centre where Matthew has been recently moved for long-term residential care. The hospital promotes a home-from-home environment for patients with acquired brain injuries and Matthew is enjoying the taste of independence, where the focus is on dignity and social activities as well as recovery.

'You look nice,' he says to me, when I make my way into the lemon and grey decorated single room which we have personalized for him with photos, music stations and memories of his life from before the accident in a bid to make it cosy and comfortable for him. A multi-coloured blanket knitted by Mam sits over his feet, and I'm glad to see him out in his chair instead of lying in bed.

'I had my hair done before I came here,' I admit, 'but thanks for noticing. Just a blow dry but it's a pick-me-up I was in need of.'

He looks out the window and then across at me. Every day I see him stronger, every day I wonder why I never knew before the agony he was in, and every day it eats me up inside that a row with me over Tom put him in this position.

'You just missed Mam,' he tells me. 'She's exhausted, you

know, Charlotte. She doesn't have to keep coming here every day and neither do you. I'm a big boy, you know.'

I do know that, but I also know that no matter how many times Matthew tells us, we couldn't go more than a day without calling here with him, so afraid are we of his mind slipping back into that dark place we've been willing him out of for so long.

'I've a new consultant,' he says, as if reading my mind. 'Cool guy, I really like him. His name's Jack and I'd a really great session with him yesterday evening just after you left. Probably the best chat I've had with anyone since this all happened.'

'Oh,' I say, sitting up straight on the armchair beside the bed that lies between us. Each of us cling so badly to any positive signs shown by Matthew so I can't wait to hear more. 'How often will you see him?'

Matthew twiddles with the sleeves of his hoodie in a way that reminds me of myself. We have so many similarities, and always have had. He's the same colouring (despite sharing my love of experimenting with hair products), the same brown eyes and he is slight of frame like I am. In fact, we're so similar that we fell in love with the same person at the same time . . . Even I could never have predicted that one.

'He'll be here any minute so you'll get to meet him,' he says to me. 'And no, before you feel like you've to panic or worry, I don't talk to him about anything that happened before or what led to this. We only discuss what's going on now that I've been honest with everyone, most of all myself.'

I don't know what to say. It's the first time Matthew has even hinted at the history to his accident and it hits me like a punch in the stomach. But I don't have to say anything, thank goodness, as a swift knock on the door marks the doctor's entrance.

'Good evening, Matthew!' says a cheery voice and I turn my head to see Dr Jack Malone, the new consultant, the 'cool guy' he was just referring to.

'Speak of the devil,' says Matthew. 'I suppose your ears were burning, Doctor. I was just telling my sister about you.'

I do a double-take and so does Matthew's new doctor.

'I think we've met before,' he says, when I stand up to shake his hand. 'Charlotte, isn't it?'

I nod, feeling my cheeks flush pink with embarrassment. It's him, the guy from Pip's Bar! It's the lovely man who bought me a drink before I did my disappearing act that night before Christmas. Jack. Yes, that was his name. Jack Malone!

'Hello Jack,' I stutter. 'I mean, Doctor Jack, or Malone. Doctor Malone, sorry.'

He smiles and his blue eyes crinkle at the sides.

'Just Jack is fine,' he whispers.

He pulls over a chair from against the wall opposite the bed and sits down, confident and astute and no way as embarrassed as I'm feeling, it seems. He wears a pristine navy suit, and a crisp white shirt that's wide open at the collar, showing off his tan. I wonder where he goes on holiday to pick up a tan like that? His brown hair is cut shorter than it was when I first saw him and he's cool all right. Plus, he's handsome, even more handsome than I noticed before. He smells good, too, of bergamot and the sophisticated scent of Creed, an expensive aftershave I know from an early Saturday job in a pharmacy when I first came to Dublin. What was I thinking leaving such a beauty? I must have had a few more beers than I remembered. He's a real dish.

'I'm a bit mortified at how I left your company that night in the bar,' I say to him, wishing I hadn't bothered the minute the words leave my mouth. He is flicking through notes, his stance casual and confident, and I realize how it's hardly appropriate to discuss social activities in front of his patients. He rubs his knuckles on his chin as he contemplates his notes in front of him and gives a brief smile my way, then looks back at his notes, which tells me he doesn't want to chat about it any further.

'Anyhow,' I continue, 'I'll go grab a coffee in the canteen and leave you to it. Lovely to see you again, Jack, I mean, Doctor. Doctor Jack.'

I scurry out of the room, knowing that Matthew is now left with a million questions in his head as to how on earth I know this lovely man who has been doing such great work with him. I lean up against the wall outside Matthew's room and want to kick myself for being so unprofessional, then hide in the canteen for almost an hour until I see him come in there too, telling me it's safe to go back now to my brother.

'Charlotte, there you are,' says Dr Jack, just when I thought I'd escaped undercover. 'I didn't mean to chase you off earlier, but Matthew and I have a lot to get through. He's had a rough ride. It must have been a huge shock to you all.'

I rub my forehead, and nod my head in agreement, afraid of saying the wrong thing again.

'He's very lucky,' is as much as I can think of to say. 'We're all very lucky to have him still with us.'

Jack glances at an empty table beside us.

'I've fifteen minutes before my next appointment, then I'm done for the day,' he says to me. 'Could you manage another coffee? I'd love to chat to you more if you've time. About Matthew, of course.'

I take a seat and within minutes he is sitting across from me with two steaming hot coffees between us. The canteen is quiet at this time of the early evening, as the staff prepare for the rush of staff and family members in for dinner. Soon we are knee-deep in an emotional talk about my brother and I find myself opening up to him in ways I never thought I could.

'We had a row over a mutual friend,' I confess to Jack, who looks like he has heard it all in his job. 'Matthew couldn't bear the sound of his name and he stormed off. I tried to stop him, but it was too late. I'll never forgive myself.'

Jack stirs his coffee and adds more milk, listening to me without interruption as I pour my heart out to him, the night in Pip's Bar so irrelevant now. Once again I regret even mentioning it to him.

'Matthew has made it clear to me he doesn't want to discuss that friend,' he says to me, drawing a line under it from the get-go. 'He'd been receiving some counselling before, dealt with it then and was advised to try and move on from what happened, so the work I'm doing with him now is in respect of that. We're focusing very much on where he is now, what he has to look forward to and the acceptance of his new identity.'

'Of course.'

'He's had a lot to deal with in his own head and letting go of the past will hopefully help you all move on – as hard as that may be.'

'I'm trying to,' I say to him, trying not to choke on my emotion. 'I'm really trying to but thank you for bringing me up to date. Matthew is the most important one in all this. If he needs to just move on, then that's what we'll do with him.'

Jack's eyes tell me he knows it's not as easy as that, especially when he can see mine are full of regret and sorrow.

'Maybe you need to talk to someone about the way you're blaming yourself?' he whispers. 'I know Matthew doesn't blame you, Charlotte. You need to go easier on yourself. You have a life to live too, you know.'

'Thank you,' I say to him. 'It means a lot to hear that from someone like you. I can see why Matthew trusts you so deeply.'

He smiles as if he's heard it all before.

'Start living again, Charlotte,' he tells me softly. 'Even painful endings can lead the way to new beginnings.'

His voice is soothing and comforting, his words are exactly what I need to hear, and they resonate with me because he can be objective in all this. Tom could tell me it's not my fault until he's blue in the face, but he's too involved, whereas Jack is a professional, an outsider. In the time it's taken to drink a coffee he's made me feel like I do have hope when it comes to self-forgiveness.

'I'll certainly try,' I tell Dr Jack, feeling much better in myself in such a short space of time. 'Your words of wisdom will certainly help Matthew, just like they've helped me. I better go see how he's doing.'

And so I walk back down the corridor of the small hospital, with a sense of hope in my heart that I haven't felt in a very long time.

Chapter Seven

Dublin, December 2016

'Merry Christmas, boys and girls! Have a lovely break and I'll see you all in the New Year!'

The children chorus back. 'Merry Christmas, Miss Taylor!'

The school bell rings and the stampede for the door begins until I raise my voice and call for home-time etiquette, which means to form an orderly line at the door, in alphabetical order of course.

By my desk, I have two huge bags of presents from my wonderful class, containing everything from photo frames, chocolates, candles and bubble bath to mugs with 'Best Teacher' on them. My heart is full but somewhat empty at the same time, as I think of the joy I felt on this very day twelve months ago and how I could never have predicted what was round the corner. The day we broke up from school, the night of the big snow, the night we went to Pip's Bar, the night I spent with Tom . . .

My phone rings just as I'm getting into the car once everyone has been picked up and wishes of merriment for the festive season have been shared with parents, child-minders, bus drivers and taxi drivers, who all play their part in seeing the children home safe every day of the year. Even Patricia the lollipop lady, who rarely seems to have anything to smile about, has a string of tinsel around her generous waist and looks jolly despite the persistent drizzle of rain that hangs over the school yard.

'Mam,' I say, cradling the phone under my neck as I fasten my seatbelt. 'How's things? I'm just finished so—'

'Well I know you're just finished, that's why I'm ringing,' she sings down the phone. I know immediately it's either good news or bad news. Mam never calls me just for the sake of it or for a cosy catch-up. 'You'll never believe it, but your friend, that nice doctor Jack Malone with the twinkly blue eyes, just called to say that Matthew is going to be able to come home for Christmas after all! We're over the flippin' moon, Charlotte!'

I don't tell her that I'd an idea this would be the case. I knew this already from Jack, but I don't want to burst her bubble. However, Mam has more to tell, an additional announcement that I didn't know about.

'But the best part of it all,' she gasps, 'is that it's not just for Christmas, Charlotte! It's for good! Almost a full year later to the day and my baby boy is coming home at last! This is going to be the best Christmas ever!'

My head falls back onto the headrest and I let tears of relief trickle down the sides of my face, thankful that the car windows are steaming up quickly so that no one can see my reaction. He's coming home for good at last! The release of this moment is immense. The wait is over. Thank God the wait is over and we can all start properly rebuilding our lives, away from hospitals and appointments and the worry that has taken over our everyday conversations.

'Oh Mam!' is all I can say. 'That's such good news. It's just what we've been hoping for and such perfect timing before Christmas. I'm so, so happy for you and Dad and Matthew! For all of us! This has been the longest year ever.'

I get a flashback in my mind of my mother's fragility a year ago in the hospital corridor and all the hours she has poured into doing all she possibly could since then to ease Matthew back into life again. Every prayer, every spiritual cure, weekly novenas, blessings from the parish priest, she did everything she could to pull him into this stage and now the time has finally come. Matthew is coming home for good.

'Your dad is getting the car ready now and we're lifting him tomorrow morning at St Benedict's,' she sings. 'Oh Charlotte, give that nice Doctor Jack a big hug from me tonight when you see him. I'm so happy I could shout it from the rooftops!'

The respite and rehabilitation centre near Malahide, where Dr Jack Malone attends as a consultant neurologist, has been a home from home for Matthew for about nine months now. This weekend will mark the end of such a long, emotional run of events that we never thought we'd see the light at the end of it.

'So will Jack be joining us for Christmas dinner then?' asks Mam, almost as excited at the prospect of having a real doctor in her humble abode as she is about Matthew coming home. 'He's very welcome! I know he doesn't have much time off on Christmas Day but we're only an hour up the road and we'd love to have him.'

I pause and twiddle my hair, unable to help a light smile creeping across my face. Something flutters in my tummy at the sound of his name and as I picture his handsome face. Jack and I have become close, very close, and as Matthew has improved our relationship has grown into something quite special. He's funny, he's drop-dead gorgeous, he's strong both of mind and body and, if it weren't for him, I don't know how I'd have coped with everything this far. He's a good guy and he has really helped us all in so many ways.

'I think he will be joining us, yes,' I say to Mam and she relays the news back to my father, who seems equally impressed. He likes Jack. We all like Jack. He practically saved Matthew's life in so many ways this year, not only with his medical expertise, but with all the extra effort he put in to making his rehabilitation easier, so we've a lot to be grateful for.

'I'd better order in some of those posh home-made

desserts then from the bakery in town. What's it called again, Paddy? The bakery? The fancy one?'

She's talking to my dad now even though I'm still on the phone.

'Anyhow, we'll get some extra wine in too so if you can find out if he drinks red or white that would be really helpful. Oh, this is wonderful, Charlotte! This is all just so wonderful!'

And I suppose the past few months have been a bit wonderful. The summertime brought great hope as Matthew's recovery came on in leaps and bounds; he learned to manoeuvre around in a wheelchair and his speech improved by the day. Tom continued to write to me or call me once a week, and just as we were planning some time together when I broke up from school for the long summer break, his band were offered a tour in America – another opportunity we just couldn't afford for him to turn down.

'We have two days off when we hit Boston at the end of July,' he told me, his voice dipping in despair as nothing was going our way. 'How about you and Kirsty take a road trip and meet us out there? I need to see you, Charlie. I'm still waiting. I'll always wait.'

And although the idea of a week or two in Boston seemed so simple and ideal, nothing could take me away from the commitment I'd made to my family and to see Matthew's recovery through to the end. He was thriving on routine and familiarity, the nurses told us. He needed that stability, love, encouragement and a positive outlook, no matter how we felt behind the scenes, and most of all he needed hope that he was going to get better.

No one can ever imagine the loneliness of sitting by the hospital bed of someone you love until you experience it for yourself – the pressures on the family dynamics, the arguments between us all when things were going wrong or just from fear and frustration. Even though Jack had told me to start living again, there was no way I could just pack up and leave for America.

So I was faced with yet another decision – go to America to see Tom at last, or stick it out for another while to see Matthew's recovery through until the end.

This very subject was to be our very first row.

'I'm starting to think this is never going to happen,' Tom said in despair. 'To be honest, Charlie, I don't think you've any intention of coming to see me, never mind make a move over here. It's all about Matthew. He's your priority, not us. He always has been.'

A knot in my stomach twisted and I felt tears prick my eyes.

'How can you say that, Tom?' I asked him. 'You know I'm going through hell over what happened, no matter how much I'm told to just let it go and move on. I'm not saying *never*, I'm just saying not now. A few more months is all it will take. The doctor said—'

'You have to let go of this stupid guilt!' he told me. 'It's unhealthy and it's gone on far too long. You didn't get behind the wheel of a car that day, Matthew did! He's held you back before and now he's doing it again.'

A few more months, I promised him. But in a few more months, so much changed. The phone calls became less and less frequent. I was spending more and more time with Jack over coffee, then over lunch, and while his words of wisdom were all about Matthew's hope for the future, all Tom and I seemed to do was argue about when Matthew was going to stop holding me back.

'I'm heading out for drinks with some of the guys from the record company,' Tom told me one Sunday evening in late September when I was watching *Strictly Come Dancing* at home alone. The fire was lit and Kirsty had gone out on a date with some guy she'd met at the gym. I'd poured a glass of wine and I fancied a chat with Tom, determined not to go over the same old nonsense like a broken record. His American tour had been and gone, he was back in London again, we still hadn't met up and the gap between us was getting wider and wider.

'Oh, I won't keep you then,' I said, apologizing for inter-rupting his plans. 'I'll chat to you later in the week. Have fun!'

The butterflies in my tummy I normally felt when we had more positive conversations had now turned into creepy, crawly spiders.

'No, no, it's fine,' he said, half-heartedly. 'Chat away. I'm just getting ready. I can put you on loudspeaker as I get dressed.'

I pictured him, choosing his outfit for his night on the town, and I felt the gap between us getting wider and wider than ever, physically and emotionally. I felt my stomach go sick. This was it, I knew it.

'So tell me, how's life in the Fair City this week?' he asked. 'What's going down?'

I could hear him rummaging around, humming along to music while he searched for whatever he needed for his night out.

I, in the meantime, looked around the living room, wondering what excitement there was to inform him of. I longed to be able to run to him, but I knew it was already too late – the moment I had dreaded, the moment I knew would challenge us one day, had come.

'Well, Kirsty's on a date with a sailor,' I said, keeping it light, and he laughed at the very idea of it. Kirsty's love life always did entertain us, no matter what else was going on in the world. 'Only Kirsty could go to the gym and meet her very own Popeye.'

Tom paused for a moment.

'I miss your humour,' he told me from his apartment in London, which looked very white and smart from what I'd seen on video calls. 'God, this is really shit, isn't it, Charlie? We're just going in totally different directions and it's killing me inside.'

I knew what was coming.

'I've met someone, Charlotte,' he said to me suddenly. The fact he called me Charlotte made the gap feel even wider. 'I wasn't looking for someone, but it just happened.'

I wasn't surprised at all, but it still wasn't easy to hear. If truth be told, I'd been enjoying my daily chats with Jack, and although I knew it was nothing more than friendship, it had made me realize that Tom and I were going in very separate ways.

'It's that girl, Claire, isn't it?' I said to him, grasping a soft woollen throw from the back of the sofa and pulling it towards me for comfort. 'The one from the record label who took you all to the States in the summer?'

More silence.

'I'm not mad at you, Tom,' I whispered as my heart cried sore for what we were facing up to at long last. 'I don't expect you to wait for me forever. You've been so patient for so long, but I can't hold you back any longer.'

His voice cracked a little, just like it did that day when we first met, which told me he was nervous.

'She's a really nice girl, Charlie.'

I closed my eyes tight and was so glad he couldn't see me.

'I'm sure I'd really like her.' I forced out a fake laugh as I blinked back tears, feeling like my whole insides had just been ripped in two. 'Look, we don't have to kid ourselves any more.'

'I'm not saying it's anything serious, Charlie,' he said, clutching at straws. 'I mean, it's been six months since we saw each other and I didn't want to even like anyone else, but it's a big lonely place here and—'

I just wanted this conversation to stop already. 'Tom, please!' I begged him. 'You're thirty-three years old, you sing in a band that's going places, you're living your big dream and I live in a different country. Like you say, we're going in different directions. I think the world of you, Tom, but I can't keep this hold on you. You deserve more.'

I still love you and always will was what I really wanted to say, but I wouldn't make him feel any worse for what was going on in his life right now. We'd come to a natural ending, led by circumstances and odds stacked against us.

'You'll always be the one,' he whispered to me and my stomach flipped. 'I mean it, Charlie Taylor. No one will ever come close to you. You know that and I do too.'

I dabbed under my eyes with my pyjama sleeve and focused on the glitz and glamour of the *Strictly* performers on telly. They all looked way too sexy and glamorous for my mood so I turned it over to the *X Factor* where someone was singing an Adele song about how 'we could have had it all'.

Wonderful. I turned the TV off.

'If you tell me not to do this, I won't,' he said, giving me one last chance to salvage the crumbs of our so-called relationship, whatever type of relationship it even was to begin with. I could feel his longing despite the distance. He wanted me to tell him to wait just a little bit longer. He wanted this mention of another love interest to buck up my ideas and move me to take action at long last.

I never wanted to make this final call, but I knew, no matter how much my heart was breaking, that I couldn't switch off from the deep, raw guilt that lay within me. I couldn't rub Matthew's nose in it by bringing Tom into our lives again, no matter how much I wanted to be with him. It was out of my hands, or at least that was what I was trying to convince myself.

'I can't tell you to do that, Tom,' I whispered, gripping my sleeve as hot tears poured down my face. 'I wish you well with everything in life. I wish you all the love in the world, always.'

'No, Charlie,' he pleaded. 'You don't want this. I don't want this. I won't even go out tonight. I'll wait for you, even if it takes forever.'

I pictured Matthew in his wheelchair, his whole life wasted over feelings he couldn't control, an identity that he hadn't been able to face up to for so long, and now a life of suffering over a bad decision he had made because he was so upset at me and Tom.

'I'm sorry, Tom,' I told him. 'I can't hold you back any longer. Goodbye.'

He hung up at that and I spent the entire evening wailing like a banshee over how life was so shit and so unfair. I wanted to jump on a plane and interrupt his evening with the 'lovely Claire from the record company' and just be with him once and for all. But I couldn't do that.

The phone calls stopped. The emails stopped. And in the meantime, Dr Jack who had coaxed my brother into a wheelchair in public for the first time, who read inspirational books aloud to him when off duty, who sat with him when he cried and held up a pillow for him to feebly punch out his frustration, became more and more involved in my daily life.

And now my parents are mad about him and I might quite like him too. And deep in the back of my mind is that Matthew ended up in a wheelchair because of me and Tom Farley but, because of Dr Jack Malone, he is learning to live with it.

In some strange way, being with Jack helps to ease the guilt I've held onto since this whole sorry accident happened, and for the first time in a long while, my parents, it seems, are proud of me. I have a place in the family that extends beyond my title as a teacher, or the quirky baby of the house. I am Charlotte, the caring one who is seeing Dr Jack Malone, the man who will be forever credited with getting my ailing brother back on track at long last. I have a well-respected, reliable man by my side with no turbulent historical connection to my family. Something I could never have had with Tom, so I'm on the right path at last and the guilt I've been feeling is slowly settling, or at least simmering for now.

'Are you sure your parents want me to join them for Christmas dinner?' Jack asks me as we sit across from each other on the train later that evening. We're on our way to meet some of his friends in Dun Laoghaire (pronounced Dun Leary), a vibrant, cultural harbour village on the south side of Dublin city where Sarah and Harry Darling live. I hope they aren't as fancy as their names suggest.

'Of course I'm sure!' I tell him, laughing as I picture how flustered my mother will be when serving him his turkey and ham next weekend. 'You're definitely a hero in our family right now. In fact, I've never seen my parents so excited. The preparations are already underway.'

'That's sweet of them,' he says, rubbing his chin. 'They've been very kind to me, way beyond the call of duty. I was only ever doing my job with your brother.'

I look at him knowingly. He's done so much more than just his job. He's been a guiding light in Matthew's recovery since he came on board shortly after I bumped into him that day in the café. I've developed a deep friendship and admiration for this young doctor who treated us all with such care and attention, managing always to shine some positivity and hope in Matthew's darkest days.

'It's like Doctor Doug Ross is coming to visit,' I tell him, 'so the finest crockery will be pulled out that day. My mam was a big fan of the series *ER*. She thinks you're like a younger George Clooney in your white coat. I think she'd faint if she ever saw you in green scrubs.'

He looks away shyly and I take a moment to admire him from where I'm sitting across from him. Jack is easy on the eye, there's no doubt about that. He's neat, he's tidy, he's well-groomed and impeccably dressed, always. He's sexy in his scrubs, which he wears when on surgical duty at a different hospital, he's hunky in his casual pale blue shirt that he wears now under a tailored black jacket and he's equally handsome in a T-shirt when he's just been to the gym. His short brown hair, charming blue eyes and wholesome smile could light up a room, and anyone who's met us both lately believe we're a match made in heaven. The doctor and the teacher – we look good together, we laugh a lot and he's invested months of his career in saving my brother's life.

So why do I still feel like there's something missing?

Sophie and Harry Darling, Harry and Sophie Darling.
I go over and over the names of Jack's friends in my head, desperately hoping I don't get them wrong when I see them later. I'm hopeless with names and these two sound like they belong in the royal family, but I'm looking forward to meeting people from Jack's world. So far in our 'relationship' it's been all about my family, especially Matthew.

Psychologist Sophie Darling, née Walsh, is a lifelong

friend of Jack's from boarding school and her husband Harry is an ex rugby player, now a dentist, who moved here from Wales when they married two years ago. We're going for drinks in an award-winning wine bar, then to dinner in a top seafood restaurant and tonight we'll stay in Harry and Sophie's spare room in their apartment they share with their two Yorkshire terriers.

I feel incredibly out of my depth for some reason. I'm a working-class girl from the asshole of nowhere. Maybe it's just nerves.

'Do you think we could go for a quick drink somewhere first, you know, before the wine bar?' I ask Jack, as we whizz past the breath-taking moonlit views of Dublin Bay. The very sight of the Irish Sea, even when it's only twinkling black in darkness, makes me think of Howth and Tom. It makes me imagine how he and Claire are getting on now, which makes me feel a bit queasy, which makes me feel a bit guilty for even thinking of him when I'm here with someone else – someone who isn't him . . . someone who is the total opposite of him in so many ways.

'We can slip into a pub along the way, no problem at all if that's what you want?' Jack says, sensing how uneasy I am.

The train is full of commuters on laptops dressed in dull greys and blacks. As well as my anxiety over meeting 'the Darlings', I feel very overdressed with my tea dress, vintage sapphire earrings, extra high heels and funky purple patterned tights. But I reassure myself that I needed to make an effort tonight, plus I should be celebrating.

Matthew is coming home for good. He's actually coming home at long last. OK, so he's in a wheelchair and the whole house has had to be adapted to suit his needs, but it's a fresh start, it's a new beginning and tonight is the start of the rest of my life.

'I just feel like I need some Dutch courage before I meet your friends,' I mutter, a bit mad at myself for feeling in any way out of my depth. 'Sorry, I won't be like this every time, I promise.'

'You have absolutely nothing to worry about, Charlotte, I promise you,' he says. 'They are going to love you just as much as I do.'

I ignore that he casually used the 'L' word, telling myself that he didn't mean it in that way, and look out the window onto the darkness of the bay as we fly past, further down the coast. We sit in a comfortable silence until we reach our destination minutes later, then Jack helps me into my faux-fur jacket and my heels click onto the platform, out into the wintry evening. It's damp and cold but more typical weather for Ireland in comparison to last year's record-breaking minus figures and snowfall.

I need to keep reminding myself that although tonight will forever stick in my mind as the anniversary of the night I got to know Tom Farley in the snow outside Pip's Bar, it's also the same night that I first met Jack Malone, and he is who I'm with right now.

I need to do as Jack once told me and stay focused in the here and now and try and enjoy my evening. I need to stay in the present and let go of my longing for what could have happened in the past.

'Because leaving each other or being apart was never a choice you made of your own free will, neither of you,' she tells me emphatically. 'You didn't want to see him go to London and he didn't want to go without you, Charlotte. Your feelings were never in your own control. You made a decision, not for you, but for others, and sometimes that happens in life. Do you still feel for him? If you do, you need to do the right thing by Jack and let him go, darling.'

Her words, although soft and subtle in tone, hit me like a freight train and I lose my breath for a second.

'I can't do that,' I say, shaking my head again.

I think of how far Jack and I have come, of how no one on earth makes me feel as safe as he does when he wraps his strong arms around me. I think of some of the road trips we have taken together, how we've laughed at the silliest things, how excited he gets when I tell him about the kids at school and how much we lean on each other as we talk about our day when things don't go as planned. I think of him asking me to move in when I was already living out of a drawer here most of the time anyhow, and how excited we were when we shopped for bits and bobs to make this place 'ours' more than 'his'. I think of how I've moved on in my heart and mind so much and how I've healed by being with someone as tender, loving and strong as Jack. I would never throw all that away.

'I love Jack,' I tell my sister. 'We have a great life here in this apartment and I've met some of my dearest friends through him. I couldn't just up and leave.'

I think of Sophie Darling in particular who I've become so close to. We have everything in common, even if our upbringings were poles apart. She's a former professional dancer, a violinist, and oozes creativity. She lost her only sister to a sudden illness when she was a teenager and has never got over it, so she understands exactly the ties I have with my family since Matthew's accident.

I've created a very full life with Jack. We have the full package.

'I can't throw this all away for some whimsical idea of a life with Tom that I don't even know is real any more,' I whisper.

Emily takes two cups from the frosted-glass cupboard, pops a teabag into each and fills them with steaming hot water from the kettle as I stare out through the sash windows again.

'If it wasn't real, you wouldn't react like that over seeing a photo of him in a magazine, would you?' she says. She hands me a cup after squeezing out the teabag and adding a dash of milk. 'And he wouldn't be still texting you when he's drunk or lonely or both.'

I know she has a point.

'Just saying,' she continues, 'but if I thought Kevin reacted in any way over a picture of an ex, I'd be having second thoughts about our relationship. I'd much rather he let me go than go on living a lie.'

I hold the cup with both hands, blow into it then take a soothing drink that warms me and settles my insides.

'Would you like it if it was the other way round with you and Jack?' she asks me to drive her point home. 'Would you like it if seeing an ex hurt Jack as much as it hurts you?'

I go to speak but she does so for me.

'Please don't live a lie, Charlotte, love,' she tells me. 'For goodness' sake, don't ever live a lie. Look what doing just that did to our Matthew. It's not worth it.'

I also know that for Matthew's health and for the sake of his future progress, I don't really have a choice. But am I living a lie?

Jack has picked me up when I was on my knees with worry over Matthew, he has spurred me on when my confidence was on the floor, he knows from how my voice sounds if I'm worried about something or when I need one of his manly hugs. He knows I love spring more than summer, that I prefer dark chocolate to milk, that I take two sugars in my tea at certain times of the month but don't bother with it the rest of the time. Jack knows me inside out. Tom has only seen me at my best, whereas Jack has seen me at my worst and he loves me even more for it.

Would I give up what I have with Jack for a stab-in-the-dark chance of another me? No, I wouldn't. I've turned a corner at long last.

'Happy birthday, gorgeous!'

It's the most beautiful Saturday afternoon in late March, the streets are lined with fluffy pink cherry blossoms and I'm celebrating my twenty-ninth birthday and the beginning of my thirtieth year on this planet with a glass of Prosecco, a picnic lunch of exquisite bites, including black-bean crunch wraps and stuffed focaccia, in Phoenix Park. It has all been prepared and arranged by Sophie, who is sitting with me watching the world go by.

'Is turning thirty as scary as it sounds?' I ask her, feeling the bubbles from the drink in my hand making me merry already. The sun is shining, Sophie's dogs Milo and Jess are running around enjoying the freedom of the open space and I turn my face up to the sky to catch some rays.

'It definitely raises some questions,' says Sophie in her clipped Dublin accent, which is so different to my own more rounded, country twang. 'I know that when I turned thirty, even though Harry and I were just married, was when my mother stepped up her game in wanting me to push out a set of triplets in a puff of smoke, but I still don't feel ready for motherhood. Do you?'

I take a sip of my Prosecco and contemplate the question.

'It has crossed my mind, yes, especially when my days are filled with children and mothers with babies at the school gates,' I admit, 'but to be fair, I can't say that Mam expects anything from me just yet. She understands that Jack and I are still in early days.'

I hasten to add that my mother and Sophie's are like chalk and cheese in every way possible, plus I adore my mother. Sophie hates hers.

'And your sister?' she asks. 'Doesn't she feel the pinch now she's married or is that a really personal question? Gosh, my mother will have a fit if I don't give her a grand-child to show off sometime soon. The pressure!'

I scrunch up my nose, wondering if it's appropriate for me to talk about Emily and Kevin's fertility issues.

'I suppose it's each to their own when it comes to things like that,' I say to her, hoping she will read between the lines. 'Sometimes it doesn't happen just as easily as we'd like it to, unfortunately.'

Sophie leans across and squeezes my arm, telling me I needn't say any more on the subject. She has fast become one of my dearest friends since the night we met at the wine bar in Dun Laoghaire back in December. In fact, any nerves I had about meeting her and Harry were swiftly shoved to the side when she asked to try on my shoes in the middle of the very upper-class seafood restaurant, then paraded to the toilets and back in them to see if they suited her as much as they suited me.

We spent the whole evening in fits of giggles and walked home in our bare feet, even though it had been a rainy night at the height of winter, and when we got back to her apartment we talked until morning about our shared love of music. Sophie had been a concert violinist in her school days and we ended up singing into the early hours, much to Jack and Harry's surprise, who recommended we start up our very own girl band and let them retire early.

'Do you ever think that there is a parallel version of you existing, doing the things you could have done had you made different decisions in life?' she asks me, staring up at the blue sky. 'Like, another you? Is that a weird question? Am I drunk?'

I burst out laughing and turn towards her, totally getting her drift and loving the topic of conversation. 'Oh Sophie, I think about this all the time! I can't believe you think that way too!'

She pushes her sunglasses onto her head, squints at the sun and puts them back on again. Sophie is pixie-like, with her cropped black hair and petite, dancer's frame, and to me she is a darling by name and by nature.

'You're going to laugh your head off at this but at one point I did think I'd end up with Jack, you know, in one of those "if we're not married by the time we're thirty" pacts you hear of in the movies?' she giggles. 'We didn't have an agreement at all, but it was always in the back of my mind.'

I throw my head back and laugh. 'Don't hold back there, Soph!' I joke with her. 'Ah, that's kind of sweet in a way.'

She is laughing now too. 'But instead my future was

formed because I spontaneously went to Wales for a rugby match with my dad, only because I felt sorry for him as his brother had to cancel last minute. I was at a kiosk ordering a hot dog, chatted to Harry who was quite pissed and the rest is history,' she says, in genuine wonder. 'Like, if my uncle hadn't had man flu, I wouldn't have gone to that match, I'd never have met Harry, so what on earth would I be doing right now? Where would I be and who with? It's weird, isn't it?'

It *is* weird when you think of it. I've thought about it so often my head spins, but I've never actually had a conversation with anyone who thinks the same way about it.

I wonder all the time if I'd taken Tom's advice that day when I sang for him back in 2010, if I'd had the courage to send out my work to record companies, would I be living in America now like he suggested? Would I ever have crossed paths with him again, would Matthew ever have had to hear his name again, would the accident have happened, would I have met Jack? One thing in life leads us to another and another and another – how much of it is really under our own control and how much is already mapped out for us, no matter how we try to change it?

Sophie sits up to pour us another drink, both of us lost in our own 'other version' of ourselves, and I feel a little dizzy. I stop her pouring mid-flow and she looks at me with a hint of concern.

'You know, Charlotte, I also often remind myself that just

because things could have worked out differently, doesn't mean they'd have been better,' she says to me, a little bit more serious now. 'That's what I tell myself anyhow. There's no point worrying about "what if" even though it's sometimes fun to wonder from time to time.'

I look at her and smile. She's absolutely right. I briefly imagine how I'd be travelling the world with Tom had we stayed together. I'd be living out of a suitcase, I'd barely see my family, I'd find it hard to do something as simple as have a picnic in the park with a friend like I'm doing right now. It could have been fun, but that's all it is now – something that could have been.

'Yes, sometimes it's fun to wonder,' I agree. She continues to fill my glass to the top despite me stopping her seconds ago.

I love spending time with Sophie, and I love going home every day to Jack.

We clink glasses.

'So, back in the real world, what are your plans for your thirtieth year on this beautiful planet?' Sophie asks me as she lies back again on the grass. One of the many things I love about her is how she always brightens my day by looking ahead, discussing the possibilities of the future and finding something to plan or look forward to.

'Well,' I contemplate, plucking some daisies from beside me. 'I would absolutely love to get a break away from here, you know, and I don't mean that I want to run away from anything. I just would love a change of pace, a change of scenery.'

'Ooh,' says Sophie, liking my style already. 'So what are you thinking? A city break? A week in the sun?'

'Paris,' I say, feeling a gnaw in the pit of my stomach for a city I'd always dreamed of going to. 'I really want to go to Paris.'

I picture it in my head – the most romantic city in the world with its boulevards and gothic architecture filling my soul and feeding my creative senses.

'I'd also love to start writing some songs again,' I confess. 'I'd love to see if I could still do it, but I'll need to search inside myself to find the courage! But I've a feeling it will come back to me one day soon.'

'Yes!' Sophie tells me. 'You need to be true to your soul and Jack would be behind you one hundred per cent. Don't ever hide your talent in a box in your head, Charlotte, or wherever you've been storing your writing since Matthew's accident. Get it out there. The world deserves to hear the wisdom of Charlotte Taylor, and you know it.'

In a way I believe her. I can feel the urge to write niggling at me in a way no one understands unless they write themselves. It's like an itch waiting to be scratched, a part of you that can't be ignored.

'I'd love to someday show that side of me to Jack,' I say to Sophie. 'He honestly has no idea how much I've hidden a whole part of who I am for way too long now.'

It does sadden me to think that Jack doesn't know the depth of my passion for music, and it's by no means his fault, only mine. I've muted it, I suppose, unable to separate my passion for writing songs from my history and long-time thirst for Tom Farley. Jack knows I can play guitar and that I use it to entertain the little people I teach sometimes, but he will never really understand how much it runs through my veins and is bursting to get out. If only I could let it.

'Well, on that point, I think the main thing that struck me when I turned thirty was how important it is to make changes where you need to in your life,' says Sophie from behind her Gucci sunglasses. 'Relationships mean more, being around the right people, finding your own tribe you might call it, I suppose. Does that make sense?'

I put my glass down onto the dainty little wooden holder that Sophie bought for the occasion today and contemplate her words. I have so, so much to be grateful for right now. I'm healthy, as is all my family, even if Matthew is sometimes a grumpy bugger to be around when he's having a bad day for any one of many reasons, from the serious to the simple things. I have a job in a school I adore, I have the most beautiful home in the city in a top location, I've great friends both old and new, plus the man in my life treats me like I'm the most important person in the world. I'm one of the lucky ones. I've plenty to celebrate today, and lots to smile about.

I lift my glass again and raise it to my new close friend, Sophie.

'Here's to my next trip around the sun and all it brings,' I say to her, feeling a tiny glow of excitement at all I have to look forward to in my life. 'I'm glad I met you, Sophie. You're one of my tribe for sure.'

Even though I don't like to admit it, Sophie gets me, more than even Emily or Kirsty does. She knows I've an itch to travel, she knows I've creativity and music bubbling in my veins, she knows I'm a free spirit longing to break free from the ties to my brother but that I am afraid to do so at the same time. It's like she can see the real me behind the façade I sometimes feel I've created and, in many ways, the way we connect reminds me of the only other person I feel that way around. The one I'm so determined to disconnect from. I'm glad I've found a soul mate in Sophie; it reassures me I'm moving on at long last.

After a few hours' shopping for new clothes, a trip to the hairdressers for a revamp of my usual look, which takes me away from the long tousled do I've sported for so long now into a sleek, slightly darker shoulder-length style with a blunt fringe (all booked and paid for by Jack), new Chanel perfume and some make-up treats from Sophie, I'm feeling spoiled and special in a way I haven't done in a long time. So much of my energy over the last year and more has been consumed by fear and hope about Matthew's recovery, but now, I decide, it's time for me to really step up on my own self-care.

In the original plan, now that Matthew is on the up, it would be the perfect time to go and find Tom to see if we can start again where we left off. However, twelve months later, he has his new 'actress girlfriend Joanie' and I have Jack. I can't keep thinking 'what if' any more. This is where life is taking me, and so this is where I'll keep going.

Jack Malone loves me and he isn't afraid to show it, not only in materialistic ways like he did today, but also by being there for me and cheering me on in so many ways in my teaching career when self-doubt creeps in. When I get home that evening, he has more surprises in store for me than I could ever have imagined.

'Hang on a minute! You're taking me *where*?' I say to him, my lip trembling with raw emotion. 'I don't understand! When? How did you know?'

Jack pops open a bottle of champagne, expertly fills two flute glasses and hands me one, then kisses me on the cheek.

'Happy birthday, beautiful,' he says to me. 'Let's just say a little birdie told me this afternoon how it was on your wish list, so I booked it while you were off getting your hair done. We go at Easter when you're off school so you don't have to worry about taking time off. Is that OK? We're going to Paris, Charlotte!'

A shiver runs through me from the tops of my shoulders

to the tips of my fingers and I start to cry, totally over-whelmed that he would do something like this for me.

'I can't believe this! Oh Jack, I love you,' I say to him, meaning every single bit of what I've just told him. 'How on earth did I ever find you?'

He smiles at me and pulls me close to him, kissing me firmly on the lips, then lifts me up onto the kitchen table and shows me just how much he loves me too.

Chapter Nine

Easter Monday, Paris, April 2017

I gasp from the tips of my toes as a burst of colourful fireworks explodes over the banks of the River Seine, each pop making me jump a little more into Jack's arms that snuggle round my waist from behind. Like a wide-eyed child, I gulp in the view through the window of the restaurant, totally mesmerized and pinching myself that I'm actually here in Paris, the most romantic city in the world.

'I just can't believe we're here.' I can see the lights of the Eiffel Tower from where we're enjoying our aperitifs in the upper-floor champagne bar of this haute cuisine restaurant. I can smell the finest of food welcoming us in, and the sound of jazz piano music tinkling in the distance over the chitchat of other loved-up couples is making me feel very excited indeed.

'Is it everything you dreamed of?' Jack asks me. 'I arranged this all just for you. Fireworks are much more expensive than I thought.'

I turn towards him and burst out laughing.

'And for a split second I actually believed you did,' I say to him, my voice ever so slightly slurred as the bubbly champagne swirls through my veins, making me feel tipsy but elated.

'Sounds good, though, doesn't it?' he laughs back. 'I was hoping our friends over there might have heard me and believed that I'm boyfriend of the year.'

He takes my hand and kisses it, his eyes twinkling with giddiness that we're finally here in Paris.

I'm in Paris.

And it's even more impressive than I could ever have imagined.

'Do you love it?' he asks me.

'I do love it very much,' I tell him. I lean on his chest and we sway gently to the music, the sound of distant celebrations ringing in my ears. 'It's even more romantic than I could have ever imagined. Thank you so much, Jack. This is a birthday present I'll never forget.'

And it really has been picture-perfect since we arrived here yesterday evening. After an early night in our Moulin-Rouge-style hotel with its red velvet, almost gothic décor, we spent this morning walking the banks of the River Seine, taking in the galleries and cafés of Saint-Michel and strolling along at our leisure, stopping when we felt like it to admire painters and buskers, sip coffee and taste ice cream along the way.

My mouth dropped open as we sailed down the river this afternoon on a boat trip, and I was wowed as our tour guide pointed out the Louvre on our left and Notre-Dame cathedral which stands near our hotel, majestic and magnificent under a pink April sky.

And now, here we are in a top-class restaurant which normally has a six-week waiting list, but Jack managed to get us one of the best tables by talking nicely to the owners once he realized they had a mutual friend. The mood is light and dreamy, the setting is out of this world and right now I feel like the luckiest girl in the world.

'I can tell you the exact moment that I knew I was in love with you,' Jack announces, out of the blue, after I enjoyed the most superb dinner of chicken with lemongrass and ginger, while Jack chose duck grilled with yakitori sauce. The French-Asian chef even came out to greet us personally at one point, making it all the more special when he wished us *bon appétit*. Nothing, it seems, is too much on this visit to Paris and every moment has been the most delightful experience.

'You can?' I ask him. His words catch my breath as I wait for more.

'Of course I can,' he says to me from across the table. 'Do you remember the day we went fishing and you wore my jacket, which was miles too big for you?'

I nod. 'Yes, I remember,' I reply, rolling my eyes. 'It was lashing wet but you insisted on braving the elements.'

I scrunch up my face, wondering why he found that day so special. We'd been exploring local beaches and stopped at a place he knew well to try out some sea fishing, even though the weather was much more suited to a warm pub with an open fire. I hated it. He loved it. I have no idea where this is going.

'I've never seen anyone so determined in my whole life to try something new,' he says to me, fondly recollecting the moment. 'Even though I knew you were absolutely terrified standing on those slippery rocks, you wouldn't give in and tell me you were totally living out a real nightmare. You did it, and you did it well.'

I smile now at the memory. 'There's no way I was going to turn down a challenge, even if I was freezing cold and soaked to the bone,' I agree with him. 'And you're right. I hated every moment of it but would never admit defeat.'

His eyes are glassy with emotion. 'That's when I knew,' he tells me. 'The look on your face, the way you stood with your dress hitched up and your clunky boots and thick socks finding their place on those rocks. You showed me how much fight you have, how determined you are to do something well, even if you don't like doing it. It reminded me of how determined you were when your brother was so down and needed a push. I knew right then you were special. I knew you were the one for me.'

I've always been seen as strong-willed, that's for sure, but I don't know that anyone has seen a raw fighter in me before. I suppose I have been strong lately. I've made some pretty big decisions in my life, not entirely for my own benefit, but more to help my brother.

Jack has noticed something in me that I hadn't even taken time to notice myself. Maybe I am stronger than I think I am. Maybe I've a bigger reason to be here than I ever thought I had. I'm a caring teacher, I know that, but looking after Matthew gave me something that nothing else has done before. It brought out a side to me I didn't even know existed.

My eyes reflect my surprise that he has noticed this, and also to his reference that to him I am 'the one'. Yes, we're living together, we share friends and have a great connection, but 'the one'? Wow.

'Ah Jack, that's really sweet of you,' I say to him. 'You're a sentimental old thing behind that cool, handsome front, aren't you?'

He knows it's true. The good thing about being with Jack is that I'll always know exactly where I stand with him. He wears his heart on his sleeve, that's for sure, and I never have to wonder. If he feels it, he says it. It's one of his finest qualities, in my opinion.

The waiter invites us to enjoy some after-dinner drinks back in the champagne bar, showing us to a high round table with two stools, perfectly positioned against a full-length window that looks right out onto Paris's most spectacular sights.

'Dinner was exceptional, thank you,' I say to Jack, knowing how much effort he has made to make this trip away so special. 'You know, the past year and more has been such a strange experience since Matthew's accident. I don't know how we'd have got through it all without you.'

Jack shakes his head as he always does if I ever try to give him too much praise when it comes to Matthew's recovery.

'My brother was in a very dark place even before that night,' I explain to Jack. 'I know you've heard about his mental health problems before, but I think it's nice to remind you sometimes just how much you played a part in getting him back on track.'

'Charlotte, Matthew still has a long way to go,' he reminds me. 'Life in a wheelchair is a bitter pill to swallow for such a young man but he has the best support around him. You should be so proud of the strong family unit you have to get him this far.'

'Yes, we've come such a long way,' I agree, sipping my champagne, glad to be a world away from hospitals and the medical jargon of the recent past.

'You've played a leading role, giving up all that time to nourish and encourage him,' he continues. 'His recovery to date has been a huge team effort of medical staff and a dedicated family, but you could easily have left it to the doctors and got on with your own life, wherever it was leading you to back then.'

Wherever it was leading me to back then . . . it was certainly leading me in a very different direction to where I am now. A life by the sea in Howth with Tom perhaps, or a busy life in London and America selling my songs? I try to avoid it but, more so since Sophie mentioned it, I can't help but imagine what my life would have been like had I followed my heart back then instead of what my head felt was best to do. Another version of me might be living a life with Tom, supporting him as his music career soared, writing songs and making a career doing something that comes so easily to me and that gives me such a high. I miss playing music, so I can only imagine how much Matthew misses it too. It's like we both left that part of our lives behind that evening of the accident and closed a door we've never opened since. It's like we're afraid to.

'It's funny where life takes us, isn't it?' says Jack. 'I mean, after that night in Pip's Bar I thought I'd never see you again, then it turns out Matthew would become one of my patients and the rest is history. It's like out of a tragedy came a second chance for us. We've had some fun times, haven't we?'

We *have* had a fun time together, there's no way I could ever deny that. In fact, since Dr Jack Malone came into my life everything seems to keep getting better and that's something I can't ignore. We've laughed so much, we've travelled and explored, I've made the most wonderful friend in Sophie Darling, we now share a beautiful home in a spectacular part of Dublin city, our social diary is always fresh and exciting and, to top it all off, my family, especially Matthew, adore him.

On paper, Dr Jack Malone ticks every box and I know I'm one very lucky girl to have him in my life, so once again I push any memories or notions of 'what if' out of my mind and remind myself how it's good to be present and mindful.

I look out onto the evening Parisian sky and count my blessings to be here with such fine company. Then I close my eyes and savour this special moment, feeling Jack's breath on my neck as he gets up and snuggles into me again, his strong arms round my waist from behind.

'I've something to ask you, Charlotte,' Jack whispers into my ear.

'What's wrong?' I ask, dread swimming in my tummy. 'Is something wrong?'

I've been waiting on the day when he'll realize my dedication to Matthew was motivated by guilt as much as love and he'll ask what happened to make me feel that way. He turns me round to face him.

'Nothing is wrong,' Jack smiles back at me. 'It's the opposite, in fact, because everything is just perfect. Look, I know it's only been six months since we started dating but so much has happened since then, don't you think?'

I nod. Yes, it has, I suppose.

Jack is always reflective and dreamy, sentimental even, but tonight he is more emotional than I've ever seen him.

'I'm so madly in love with you, Charlotte,' he says, 'more than I think you even know. You're caring, gentle and you deserve the best that life has to offer. I hope you'll let me help you to get the very best in life after all you've suffered lately.'

I'm just about to crack a joke but I don't get a chance to as Jack puts his hand in his pocket, takes out a small, black velvet box and opens it to reveal the most exquisite, white gold, solitaire diamond ring that twinkles as it catches the light from the restaurant's chandeliers.

My hands automatically go up to my face and I lose my breath.

'Charlotte Jane Taylor, will you marry me?' he says, shocking me to the very core. I can't speak. I had absolutely no idea this was coming, and it's hard to find the words to respond, even if it's only a simple one-word answer. I'm also aware of the faces of so many other diners who are enjoying their after-dinner drinks in this most romantic setting around us, waiting in anticipation to see what I'm going to say.

I shake my head in disbelief. I try to speak but I almost choke.

I wasn't expecting this. I'm in Paris, not with the man I thought I'd be here with, and I've just been proposed to, but not by the man I'd dreamed of hearing those words from one day. A collage of images flash through my head, a bit like how they say your life flashes in front of you.

Suddenly I'm at the sink in my student house again, Tom Farley walks past me, then we are singing together so intensely, we're out the back of Pip's Bar, we're holding hands in the snow, he takes the snowflake from my face, I'm in Howth wearing his T-shirt, I'm driving back to Loughisland, I'm in the bar with Matthew, I'm in the flurry of snow outside, I'm shouting at Matthew, I'm in the hospital corridor.

I've got to let this go.

'Yes!' I say to Jack, and the entire restaurant bursts into a round of applause, while Jack and I burst into tears. 'Yes, I'll marry you!'

I put my arms around him, and he kisses me with delight and relief. I am relieved, too, and inside I hope that by making this decision, by being Jack's future wife, it will make me realize that this life, this perfectly beautiful life with Jack Malone, is exactly where I'm meant to be right now. I hear Sophie's words of wisdom. *Just because things could have worked out differently, doesn't mean they'd have been better.*

I don't think I'll ever get any better than this.

Chapter Ten

Dublin, April 2017

Marjorie and Jack Malone Sr arrive fashionably late to our door in Merrion Square armed with air kisses, fancy drinks with names I can't pronounce and a hamper of goodies from the very upmarket Brown Thomas department store that probably cost the same as a week's rent on our apartment.

'It's so good to finally meet you, Charlotte, darling!' says Marjorie with a majestic hug in a generous whiff of Dior. 'And on such a wonderful occasion, too! We've sent an announcement to *The Times* and it should be featured any day soon, isn't that right, Dad?'

I suppose calling her husband 'Dad' is easier than saying Jack Jr and Jack Sr when both men are in the same room . . .

'*The Times?*' says my mother, who is keen as mustard for an introduction to her new extended family. 'We'll have to buy it then. Paddy normally reads only the farming sections

173

of the papers so it's hardly worth our while getting them half the time. I'm Mary, Charlotte's mother. I'm so very pleased to meet you, Mrs Malone.'

Mam is really enjoying her second glass of Merlot, having been first to arrive at our engagement party, and I try and signal to her that she has two little black marks at either side of her mouth which do nothing for the new *pink nouveau* lipstick she bought especially for the occasion.

'Nice to see they showed up,' Jack whispers in my ear in reference to his own parents. His only sister, Caroline, is on her way but so far my family are well outnumbering the Malones when it comes to the turn-out at our party. Mam, Dad, Matthew and Martin were first to arrive, with Matthew thrilled to bits that there were no accessibility issues to access our first-floor apartment and delighting in telling everyone so.

'It really shows the difference in city life and rural life,' I hear him say to one of Jack's friends. 'I keep saying to Martin we'll have to move back to Dublin very soon, but I think he's too well settled now in Loughisland, isn't that right, Martin? You're a country boy, now, aren't you?'

They both share a look and a laugh, which makes my heart swell when I think of all the years my brother wasted pretending to be someone he wasn't.

Martin, who has the patience of all the saints not to mention the heart of a lion, has been the best thing that ever happened to Matthew, and we tell him so as much as we can. With his love and support, Matthew is gradually learning to adapt to his brand-new life on so many levels, and a lot of that has to do with Martin who has stood by him every step of the way.

'You're in for a treat tonight,' Martin whispers to me when he gets the chance. 'Matthew would like to sing a song or two later if that's OK with you?'

I put my hand to my chest. 'Really?' I gasp. 'But he hasn't played music in public in years. Wow, that's really special, Martin. Thank you.'

'All I did was a little bit of coaxing here and there,' he says. 'I also didn't want to land it on you without some warning as I know how much it will mean to you to hear him sing again. It's an emotional evening for all of you. We're thrilled to bits for you, Charlotte. Matthew adores you. We all do.'

I get a lump in my throat even thinking about hearing Matthew sing and the memories it will bring back from our childhood and from more recent years as I watched him work so hard with the band. In fact, I'm dreading hearing him again, but so proud of him at the same time as it really does mark another step in the right direction for him.

'That's going to be a very special moment,' I say to Martin, giving him a hug in appreciation. 'Thanks for the heads-up though. I will probably bawl my eyes out, I won't lie, but what's an engagement party without a few sentimental tears from the bride-to-be!'

All in all, in fact, it's shaping up to be a great party. Emily, Kevin and Kirsty, along with her latest squeeze, a 'man child' called Bryan 'with a y' from Cork, are mingling and making everyone feel welcome. Each of the girls are quietly battling it out for a role as chief bridesmaid while Sophie and Harry are already getting into the swing of things, having created a mini dance floor to test-run tunes from the iPod I bought Jack for his birthday.

A cluster of my colleagues from St Patrick's, some of Jack's friends from the hospital, two of my aunts, Bridie and Bernie who I haven't seen in years but who Mam insisted on inviting (no doubt, just so she could brag about her new doctor son-in-law), and my dad of course, who is taking in the view of the park from the window and talking all things Oscar Wilde to anyone who will listen, make up the rest of the party.

'Did you know that Oscar Wilde died in Paris? Now there's a link, seeing you two got engaged there,' he says to me on my way past. 'What a marvellous view you have here, my girl. Imagine looking out at Oscar Wilde every day. That's culture. It sure makes a change from sheep and cows.'

Canapés are being served, the drinks are flowing and, by the time Jack's sister Caroline and her husband Daniel arrive with ten-year-old twins Joseph and Sarah, things are really warming up. Caroline is an angel, a female version of her gorgeous brother, and I welcome her with open arms.

'I'm so bloody over the moon for you both!' she coos, when we break out of our embrace. 'I bet you can't wait to start planning the big day. Come on, tell me everything you have in mind so far!'

We find a quiet corner and get stuck into all things 'wedding' orientated as I explain the type of day Jack and I are planning. A handful of carefully selected guests, an outdoor ceremony perhaps (weather permitting of course, given our unruly climate) and an evening of dancing at a luxury hotel near the spectacular Inchydoney Island in County Cork, one of Ireland's most southern points. I feel nerves in my tummy as other party guests join us to swoon over the diamond on my finger and talk about cakes, flowers and dresses.

'Did you know that Oscar Wilde might never have even said those famous words about being yourself?' I later hear my father say to my mother, who has thankfully changed her wine to water, having realized how much the Merlot was messing with her lipstick.

'Where on earth do you find these facts, Paddy?' Mam replies, rolling her eyes. 'You must have more time on your hands than I think you do.'

'The one about how it's good to be yourself since everyone else is already taken,' Dad tells her. 'Turns out he might never have even said that at all, you know! See, I'm not all just about manure and silage. I do have a brain. Now, put that in your pipe and smoke it!'

I ignore the banter between my parents, instead choosing to think of the famous quote and how much it always resonates with me. Every time I look out onto that statue I question if I'm really being myself, or if I'm putting on a mask and being an easier version of myself – a version that my parents love, my brother loves, that Jack loves, but that I sometimes don't even recognize. It's a strange feeling and one I mostly try to ignore when it creeps up on me. I keep telling myself it won't last forever.

'Ladies and gentlemen,' I hear Martin announce on Jack's instruction, with the polite tap of a glass. He has put so much effort into this and he catches my eye, letting me know that this is the big moment. 'We've a very special treat in store for you now, but mostly for the bride-to-be.'

The noise in the room drops to a hush and I feel all eyes and smiles on me before attention shifts back to Martin and Matthew who sit on the sofa, each with guitars on their laps. Even though I knew this was coming, I'm so not prepared.

'Please put your hands together for Matthew Taylor, former lead singer in the band once tipped to be even bigger than Bono's ego, Dublin's finest, Déjà Vu!' says Martin, as proud as a peacock of my brother's 'semi-famous' status.

A sea of 'wows' filters through our audience, with excited

whispers and stories quickly circulating as to how they remember the band on the local circuit when, according to *Hot Press* magazine, they were destined to be 'the most exciting Irish export since Guinness'. The media had been crawling over them at the time, with Matthew's face almost becoming recognizable on the streets amongst women of a certain age.

'No way! I can't believe your brother was the lead singer of Déjà Vu!' says Caroline into my ear. 'Don't tell my husband, but I'd have eloped with their drummer in a heartbeat, given the chance! He was something else!'

She throws her head back in a rapturous fit of laughter, nudging me for effect, but to me her voice is miles away. All I can do is stare at Matthew as he plays the accustomed opening of a song that brings me right back to where I used to stand on my own, at the back of music venues, longing and yearning to talk to Tom Farley, settling only for a brief glimpse from afar or a quick hello before they were rushed away at the end of the night.

Matthew plays those oh so familiar notes and speaks over the music to introduce the song, just like he used to when the band was on the rise.

'Before I sing, I'd just like to say that about sixteen months ago,' he announces to his audience in our living room, who hang on every word he speaks with bated breath, 'about sixteen months ago I made a very stupid decision to drive my car on one of the most treacherous nights of the year.

Not a wise decision on any account, but an even lesser one when I'd had a few drinks and was in possession of a very tortured mind. I'm not proud of myself and I've paid the price since, as have my family.'

Everyone gathered in our apartment goes totally silent now.

'I haven't played my guitar in public for many years and, after the accident that almost killed me, I vowed I never would again,' he says, looking directly at me, his eyes etched in pain. 'I didn't think I deserved the joy of playing music any more. But as tonight approached, I realized that being true to yourself is always much more important than punishing yourself. It's always better to be yourself.'

I swallow, feeling my eyes sting.

'I want to dedicate this song to my very brave, very supportive and very patient sister Charlotte who sacrificed so much to look after me, even when she knew sometimes I didn't deserve it,' he says softly. 'I'm so happy for you tonight, and I love you more than you'll ever know. This is one of your old favourites. So this song is for you.'

I stare at the floor now, unable to look at my brother any longer as Martin joins him on guitar and they launch into an acoustic version of a song called 'Love and Pain', which I remember Matthew practising for hours on end back in our student digs between band rehearsals.

It was a co-write between himself and Tom and the words

now resonate with me so differently, as I finally understand the true story behind it from both Matthew's point of view, and Tom's of course.

> *I might never touch you, it drives me insane, oh*
>   *nothing hurts more than your sweet love and pain*

I feel a hand squeeze my shoulder and, when I glance up, it's my sister Emily who looks at me knowingly. I take a deep breath, I grasp her hand, then, before the song is finished, I get up from my seat and quietly slip out into the bathroom where I desperately try to compose myself. But I can't stop the tears that flow.

Not tonight, I tell my own reflection in the mirror. Please don't let this ruin tonight. A knock at the door makes me jump.

'Hello,' I call out. 'Just a minute!'

'It's just me,' says Jack. 'You disappeared very quickly there. Are you OK, Charlotte?'

I squeeze my eyes shut and gulp back the emotion, but it sticks in my throat, refusing to go away. He doesn't deserve this. I don't deserve him.

I keep telling myself this will pass, that time will make me forget Tom Farley, but then something simple like a stupid song can bring everything to the surface again and I'm back to square one.

'I'll be right there,' I call out to Jack, feeling like I'm

betraying him with my very thoughts. 'Everything's fine. I'm just freshening up.'

My mind runs overtime as I dab under my eyes, trying my best not to let my tears ruin my mascara. I need to get a hold on this. I'm haunted by Tom's ghost and that's all he is – a ghost, a figment of my overflowing imagination. I don't even know him any more. It's been months since I saw or heard of him. I have got to let this go. I've got to get over him once and for all. I hate him for making me feel this way, I hate myself for feeling this way.

'Do you want me to come in?'

'No! No, I'll be right there,' I say to Jack.

Handsome, kind, beautiful Jack, who loves me more than I can ever imagine. And I love him too. I *do* love him.

I don't want to go out there just yet, but I know I have to, so I paint on my best smiling face for my guests and my future husband, open the bathroom door and he greets me with a kiss.

'You're shaking,' he says. 'Did that song upset you, Charlotte? Martin thought you'd love to hear Matthew sing again, but maybe it was too much?'

Oh, if only they knew.

'I haven't heard his voice in a very long time,' I say, only half explaining but it's as much as I can tell him. 'I just got a bit more emotional than I thought I would, but it was lovely, Jack. I'm so grateful he felt strong enough to sing for me.'

We go back and join the party where Martin has now taken the lead, totally changing the mood by singing 'Amarillo' which has everyone dancing. Before long, Sophie and I are in fits laughing as we lead everyone in an Abba tribute, singing and dancing our hearts out.

I catch Matthew's eye as I sing about being a dancing queen and we both silently acknowledge the bridge we've both crossed this evening. He is back doing what he does best with the man he loves by his side, I am singing again with a friend I adore in an apartment I love and with Jack who I'm planning a future with.

Life is moving on in the right direction and I'm singing from the inside out. Even Marjorie and Jack Sr take to the floor, followed by my own parents who I feel are going to do everything they can to show that anything the Malones can do, they can do better.

'Oscar might come in and join us for a beer,' Dad says to me at a musical interlude, still dancing as he speaks.

'It's the curse of the working class!' I say, impressing him very much with my Oscar knowledge. 'I'm a big fan too, Dad. You brought me up to have good taste!'

He dances on very smugly, hugely pleased with himself, and I shed a tiny tear of happiness, thinking of how far we've all come since we sat in that lonely hospital corridor willing Matthew's life to be saved.

'That I did, my girl!' he says, tilting his chin out again. 'That, I did!'

The evening passes with no more tears, except from Kirsty who after way too much wine called her new beau by her ex's name and he stormed out, oh and my aunt Bridie who was just so proud of me she couldn't stop blubbing (though I do think it was the Chardonnay). By the time the last of the guests leave, I'm delighted to hear nothing but silence and the sound of Jack pottering around in the bathroom as he gets ready for bed.

I remove my heels, marvelling in the feeling of my toes in the warmth of the deep pile living room carpet, and take my phone from the charger to have a quick glimpse at what's been going on tonight in the outside world while we've been celebrating.

Streams of messages filter through from well-wishers and guests who joined us tonight, thanking us for such a wonderful evening, and I smile as I read them, but then my heart jumps when I see an email in my inbox from an address I used to write to all the time.

The subject matter just says '*Congratulations Charlie*' and the sender is Tom Farley.

It catches my breath for just a few seconds, but I don't even open it. I want to, but I can't, so I just press delete.

Chapter Eleven

Wicklow, May 2018

'Jack wants to go to the seafood restaurant as usual, but I'd love to try somewhere different,' I say to Sophie as I drive through the Wicklow Mountains on my way home from school. 'What do you think? There's the new steak house near Bray if you wanted to come out this direction?'

It's our monthly catch-up dinner with our two very closest friends and as always I'm looking forward to hearing all that's going on with Sophie and Harry, especially now that we live a bit further apart geographically and it's not as easy to meet up for coffee or chats during the week.

'Jack's such a creature of habit!' laughs Sophie. 'He would eat in the seafood place every month for the rest of his life if you let him! Does he still insist on washing the cars every single Saturday at nine thirty?'

'Yes!' I tell her, nodding in agreement. 'Even if it's blowing a gale or a hurricane, he'd still be out there with his yellow bucket and sponge in his wellies and waterproofs. Honestly,

I think he's getting worse! He just loves a routine and if he missed the ten o'clock news with a cup of tea in his hand the world would end!'

I hear Sophie's hearty laugh echo through the Bluetooth system in my new gleaming white Land Rover Discovery, which I'm still getting used to as I manoeuvre through the winding roads. The new vehicle was a present from Jack that came straight from the showroom in celebration of my new role at the prestigious Holy Trinity School in Dublin and our new home near the picturesque town of Ardara, in County Wicklow.

'That's married life for you, Char,' says Sophie. 'I swear, Henry never once wore slippers in his life, well not since he owned a pair of Thomas the Tank Engines when he was a nipper. But now that we're all sensible and married, he wears the most hideous velvet navy pair round the house and it makes me want to vom!'

I laugh as I imagine Henry, all six foot four of him, skulking around in his slippers on their fancy porcelain floors, all the time listening to Sophie rant about how much they make her sick! They're a comedy duo for sure, and she's bang on about how settled Jack is now that we're also married.

Our wedding, back in July, was a dream from start to finish, with everything going exactly according to plan. Sophie's string quartet of friends from university re-formed to play me down the aisle to a haunting rendition of 'I'm

Kissing You' by Des'ree, I wore a Valentino-inspired lace vintage dress that felt as exquisite as it looked, Jack was dashing in an emerald green suit and the sun shone for us all day. Even Emily and Kirsty played the role of bridesmaids to perfection and managed not to try and outshine each other too much in the glamour stakes. When Matthew sang our first dance, a medley of our favourite songs, there wasn't a dry eye in the house – or on the patio, I should say, as that's where we were blessed to have the ceremony just as we'd planned it.

I never did hear from Tom again after I deleted his message of congratulations on the night of our engagement party. Even though I yearned to know what he had written in his message, I reminded myself that I'd done the right thing by not opening it when I was already so vulnerable and emotional after hearing Matthew sing.

I had decided I couldn't allow myself to keep looking back in life. My future was with Jack, a life with him in Dublin, my job in teaching and in making sure the wedding everyone was so looking forward to would be one made of dreams, so I put my feelings on autopilot and drove on.

The only unplanned moment of the most perfect day was when Matthew had taken me to one side in the hotel foyer as guests danced to country jives in the adjoining function room, oblivious to the moment we were about to share when we'd finally put the elephant in the room to bed.

The look of fear on his face told me what was coming.

I sat down on one of the plush velvet armchairs and he pulled his wheelchair in as close to me as he possibly could.

'Charlotte . . . I need to apologize . . .'

'Matthew, you don't have to say anything,' I told him, taking his hand which was cold and shaking. 'Please don't be torturing yourself any more. It's over. It's in the past.'

Even though we'd never, ever mentioned Tom since that fateful day in Sullivan's Bar, I'd caught him so many times over the past two years lost in memories and lost in time, staring into space in deep thought. I didn't want to see him in any more pain, not when he was doing so well.

'I was selfish and so confused, Charlotte,' he said to me, as he sat before me in his dapper navy suit, white shirt and pale blue tie. He'd dyed his hair the most hideous yellow for the occasion, but it was a glimpse of his old character coming through again so we all loved it. 'I was an arrogant prat, to be honest, but I was also very much besotted with a man I knew I could never have. I don't think I could ever go through that again.'

He gulped back tears.

'Oh, Matthew!'

I didn't want to interrupt him too much. I knew how difficult this must be for him, yet therapeutic at the same time to get it all off his chest.

'My attraction for Tom was a huge wake-up call that my sexuality wasn't as straightforward as I'd hoped it would be, pardon the pun. But I should have got over myself and given you both a chance. He didn't want me, he wanted you. I know I'm way too late in saying this, but I'm so very sorry.'

I clasped his hands in mine and rubbed them to warm them up, always feeling that unconditional urge to protect and look after him. The evening was creeping in and the temperature had dropped substantially also. That's the thing about Irish weather – four seasons in one day and all that.

'I appreciate you saying this,' I told him, looking into his eyes which were a mirror image of my own. 'But we don't have to keep living in the past, so let's keep focused and move on to a great, great future. Look at where we both are now, eh? You have Martin, I have Jack. We are—'

'*Are* you happy, Charlotte? Really happy?'

I paused. I smiled. I tucked a strand of hair behind my ear and I breathed out.

'Of course I'm happy,' I told my big brother. 'It's my wedding day so of course I'm happy. Now don't worry about me ever again, and let's keep going forward.'

He looked away and then back at me, holding his head up high.

'I'm not going to be in this wheelchair forever, you know,' he told me with tears in his eyes. 'I feel like such a loser, not being able to dance with my sister on her wedding day.'

I shook my head, willing my own emotions not to show. 'You're going to ruin my make-up if you keep going, you rascal! Don't go making me cry, now! You *will* walk again. You're too stubborn not to.'

Matthew gripped my hands when I went to let go. He wasn't finished.

'I hope I didn't ruin your life, Charlotte,' he whispered to me, his face etched in agonizing pain. 'You rarely sing and you never write, do you? Tom Farley believed in you and even possibly loved you, but I couldn't get past my big fat ego to let it happen. I hope you are telling me the truth and that you're really happy with Jack.'

I felt my nose itch and I sniffled, which told me I was on the edge of letting go of a burst of emotion, but I couldn't. I breathed out.

'I *am* happy,' I assured my brother. 'Now, let's hit the bar and celebrate your little sister getting hitched. I need a gin and tonic. A large one! And I think you do too.'

Emotions were high, but I held it together knowing that fate was playing its part in my life and I reminded myself I was the luckiest girl in the world.

It was my wedding day. Of course I was happy.

'So, eight o'clock then at the new steak house?' I say to Sophie, who is now on a roll of examples of how habitual and boring our husbands are fast becoming.

'Yes, see you then,' she says, still on her rant. 'Did I tell you he is growing a *beard*? It's the most hideous thing I've ever seen! I swear he's losing the plot, never mind his hair!'

My head, on the other hand, is still full of arithmetic and spelling rhymes from my day at school. My new job is 'different', let's say, and after two full months in, I'm just not totally convinced I fit the bill. I don't think I've ever been so glad it's Friday and I can't wait to get home into the warmth of a bubble bath in our new dainty cottage.

With an authentic thatched roof, whitewashed walls, red ornate sash windows and two floors of country-inspired living designed by Jack's long-time friend Rick, whose impeccable taste gave it the wow factor, it's a world away from the buzz of city life. It reminds me in a way of the pace of Loughisland where everyone knows your name and your neighbour lives across the fields, rather than next door. I've even started an Instagram page for interior design lovers and my followers are growing rapidly, way quicker than I ever anticipated. It's the closest thing to heaven and is slowly beginning to feel like home.

I say goodbye to Sophie, smiling at her observations of married life, and reflect on the past few months which have been progressive and exciting in so many ways, yet hugely challenging as I do my best to adapt to a whole new approach at Holy Trinity.

I wasn't even going to apply for the post, but Jack found it in the newspaper and almost broke his neck to get it to me, insisting it was just the step up I needed. A fresh start to go with our new life as a married couple.

'They're going to love you!' he told me on the morning

of my interview. City life was busy and fast, and I still enjoyed every day at St Patrick's where I'd cut my teeth as a teacher and was so attached to the pupils and parents who were now so familiar, but he was right, I needed a challenge. I needed a change. I'd tried to pour some energy into writing songs in the evenings, but it just wasn't happening, so instead of forcing it, I decided to take a crack at a fresh start in a new school. When I got the job, my family were absolutely over the moon, but I was devastated when it came to leaving St Patrick's. Although I know it's early days and a big change, I'm still not sure if I've done the right thing for me.

'I do believe if you fell into manure you'd get up smelling of roses,' my sister Emily said when she came round to celebrate my news of moving to a 'very posh school'. 'Mam and Dad are wondering if they could announce your news in *The Times* just like Jack's parents did when you got engaged! You're definitely going up in the world!'

There was no doubt about it, life was moving on really fast for our family, with Matthew and Martin now settled, not in Dublin, not in Loughisland, but across the country on the west coast of County Galway where Martin had taken a career break in dedication to seeing Matthew walk again. It was a bold and brave move but, just like me with my new job and new home, I could see that Matthew also needed some fresh energy to allow him to really shift his life up a gear.

'You're playing a blinder,' Jack reminded me this morning when I left for work, nervous again about a whole new day ahead. 'Plus it's Friday and we'll have some fun tonight.'

I'm so glad it's Friday.

I sing along to Ed Sheeran on the radio, then the familiar voice of the DJ who accompanies me on my journey home most days announces his next track with news that makes my ears prick up as I approach the rainbow-coloured village of Ardara.

'Next up it's the latest from one of my favourite bands of the moment,' says the DJ in his usual upbeat, eager tone. 'They've just announced a long-awaited new arena tour which will get all you fans up and close with them at last! They just keep getting better and better! It's Blind Generation, with their new single, "Move Into Me".'

I slow down a little as the tick-tock drum beat opens the song but instead of panicking, then switching channels as I've often done when I've heard or seen any reference to Blind Generation, I turn the radio up and put the windows down. I'm determined to shift my mind-set and Tom Farley's wondrous voice fills the car.

It's a clever melody with a catchy hook and by the time I pull into the stony driveway that leads to our cosy cottage, I'm singing along without any of the old anxieties, fears or regrets that I once associated with the first person who truly broke my heart.

I am a mature, successful, independent, talented woman

who is proud of who I am now and of who I was then. I'm over him. I've forgiven myself once and for all, and to prove it, I do something I should have done a long time ago. I open my emails and, right then from the driveway of my new home, I send Tom Farley a message to acknowledge his massive success, and to give myself closure from the ghosts of my past.

Dear Tom, I write quickly.

You mightn't even use this email address any more, but I just heard your new song on the radio and thought I should send a long overdue message of congratulations from one friend to another. I know I'm about three years late, but better late than never, I hope!

I'm so delighted for you and all you've become, Tom.

I only wish I'd had the courage and maturity to say it before now, but sometimes it takes the heart a bit of time to catch up with the mind.

I hope you're enjoying every moment of your wonderful life which I've been following from afar as your star keeps rising. Keep pumping out those hit singles, you talented sod! You deserve every bit of success that comes your way – I'm rooting for you, and always will.

Most of all, I'm so, so proud of you Tom Farley.

With all my love,

Charlie x

I quickly delete the 'x' and press 'send' before I change my mind. Then I let out a very deep breath and I smile from the inside out when I see my husband through the window, bopping around the kitchen as he makes a cup of tea. He may be predictable, he may be a creature of habit, but we've created a very beautiful, very safe and very wholesome life here as a married couple.

I get out of my sparkling new car and close the door shut, feeling the sun on the back of my neck and hearing the sweet sounds of summer from above.

'Honey, I'm home,' I call out with a giggle as I make my way through the yellow door of the cottage. I kick off my shoes in the hallway, feeling the cool of the stone floor under my feet, and then I hear what my husband is listening to in the kitchen.

'Have you heard this band, Char?' he asks me, dancing around with a mug of tea in his hand that says, 'World's Best Husband'. 'They're freakin' awesome. Now, that's what I call a tune!'

It's Blind Generation of course and the song is the one I just heard on the radio. Looks like Blind Generation is everywhere.

Jack puts down his mug and takes both my hands, forcing me to dance with him whether I want to or not. But I *do* want to dance with him. I want to laugh with him and dance and sing in a way I've been waiting to for so long now.

The sun streams through the window onto the floor, making tiny sparkles of dust look like fairy magic between us, and before long we're both singing together to the chorus of Tom's big hit single.

I never thought I'd see the day when I'd be able to do this, when I'd totally feel free of hurt, guilt and regret, but that day has come, and it feels even better than I'd hoped it would.

I'm dancing with the lightest of hearts and a free, open mind. I'm dancing with my husband, the man I love, and it feels so good.

Chapter Twelve

Sophie and Harry arrive fashionably late as always, armed with craft beers and crisp white wines that make my mouth water at the very thought. After a long soak in a bubble bath just as I'd planned, I feel relaxed and ready for the weekend in my cool red slacks, pink blouse, flat sandals and loose ponytail.

'It's so good to see you!' I say to Sophie, who looks like she's casually stepped off the cover of *Vogue* magazine in her cropped white trousers, nautical T-shirt and wide-brimmed straw hat. Harry looks like he's just got out of bed with scruffy hair, jeans and wrinkled shirt, which is nothing unusual, but it's why we all love him so much. As usual, he carries a Yorkie dog under each arm – no matter how many times I meet Milo and Jess, I don't think I'll ever know how to tell the difference.

'Get the wine open asap,' says Sophie, unloading her bag of goodies. 'I've had the week from hell and I need alcohol!'

Jack comes to her rescue, handing her a large glass of

chilled Pinot from the fridge, and we make our way outside into the evening sunshine.

We opted for a change of plan, thinking the weather was too fine to sit in a stuffy restaurant, so we're having dinner al fresco at our place, our first time firing up the barbecue since we moved in six weeks ago.

'So, how's the new job going?' Harry asks me when we're settled on the decking, looking out onto nothing except miles of greenery and a pale blue sky.

Sophie wasn't joking when she mentioned her husband was growing a beard. Its ginger tone gives him a very royal look (I've always jokingly called them 'the royal couple' but this is going to give me more ammunition for some playful banter), but it suits him, even if Sophie doesn't like to hear it. Harry will do what Harry wants to do and, no matter how much Sophie pretends to think she's boss, she won't change his mind. But she loves him just the way he is, beard or no beard.

'My new job is . . . well it's . . . let's just say it's very different to what I was used to at St Patrick's,' I say to him, popping an olive into my mouth. Jack has prepared a table of nibbles including sun-dried tomatoes, small cubes of feta cheese and mixed olives with a delicious Italian dressing, and as we sit here in the garden with the smell of the barbecue and the view of the sun going down in the distance, we know we've made the right decision to dine at home.

'Posh little bastards, I bet,' says Harry, laughing then

swigging his beer. 'I used to be one of those nasty little buggers too, so I feel your pain. We gave our teachers hell in primary school. I don't envy you at all.'

Sophie rolls her eyes. 'He isn't joking about being a spoilt brat at school!' she says to me. 'Harry went to *the* most elite primary school in Wales and made his mark on the place forever. You know the type where they wear a hat and blazer as part of their school uniform? And his mum tells me he tormented the teachers every day he was there.'

Oh dear. I have about twenty versions of mini Harry at my new school then, I think to myself. It's just going to take time to settle in, at least that's what Jack keeps telling me.

'Do you hear Miss Head Girl, here!' says Jack, sticking up for his male companion and joining in on the banter. 'Sophie, you were a right little climber at boarding school, always licking up to the teachers, not even satisfied to be a class prefect, oh no. Head Girl was what Sophie wanted to be and that's what Sophie was.'

'I call it ambition,' laughs Sophie. 'I wonder where the hell all that fire went to sometimes when my clients are boring me to tears. You all right, Char?'

I sit up straight.

'Huh? Yeah, I'm fine,' I mumble, taking a drink of my cold wine, then another just for luck. If Charlie is my common, girl-next-door nickname that is forbidden by my parents, then 'Char' is the polar opposite, a reflection of the upper-class teacher in the upper-class school, with the upper-class friends in my ever-so-fancy car and upper-class home in the countryside. How the hell did I get here?

'I bet the parents are stuck-up assholes too,' says Harry, reinforcing my reluctance to relate to my new job and all that comes with it. I can't help recalling my carefree, more casual approach to teaching at St Patrick's where the children loved to hear me make up stories and sing my 'lucky number' song at the drop of a hat.

At Holy Trinity it's the opposite. We have a strict curriculum to adhere to, with weekly reports to be filed, so, in the eyes of rich, paying parents who want only A grades on their child's records, there's no time for spontaneous creativity.

'I can't say I have much in common with them,' I say to Harry, trying to be diplomatic, but experiencing a twist in my stomach that feels like homesickness. 'They're definitely a world away from anything I've ever been used to.'

Jack has gone to check on the food, uncomfortable, I guess, with my indifference to a job he encouraged me to go for, while Sophie realizes it's time for a subject change.

'Anyhow, never mind boring work chat,' she says, sensing my discomfort and coming to the rescue as always. 'We spent the journey here talking about a new band we've just discovered. They've a song that's never off the radio and I absolutely love it. What did I say their name was, Harry? You know me, I'm bloody useless with names. Blind something?'

'Blind Generation!' Jack and I say at the same time, and then Jack comes back out from behind the barbecue, leaving a stream of smoke behind him.

'Their new song is awesome!' he says. 'I'd love to hear them live one day! We were dancing like two eejits round the kitchen to that song earlier and singing along at the top of our voices. It's a great song.'

My tummy leaps.

It's on the tip of my tongue to say how I know the lead singer, how he has been such a huge part of my life, how he was in my brother's band, how my conversation about him with Matthew caused that now infamous life-changing accident that led me to Jack, how I feel like I'm now over it all at last . . . but I don't. I keep it to myself. That's all in the past and it really doesn't matter any more.

I don't want to talk about Tom Farley. I want to keep those old wounds well and truly healed over.

'Sing us a song, Char! Go on!' says Sophie, a few glasses of wine and four full bellies later. Jack is next to me on the sofa indoors now, while Sophie and Harry lounge on an armchair each. It's dropped dark and our evening, as always with the Darlings, has been fun, relaxed and full of laughter and stories.

'Yes, I'd love that,' says Jack, squeezing my hand a little for encouragement. 'I've always wished I could play a musical instrument, it's such a gift.'

'Did you never play music, Jack?' asks Harry. 'I was a mean spoons player back in the day, but my music teacher always said I'd a voice that would scare dinosaurs. Did wonders for my confidence, old Miss Boot. Boy, was she aptly named or what?'

I chuckle at the very thought of it.

'You know, my poor mother spent a fortune on piano lessons, but I just didn't have it in me,' says Jack, 'which is why I'm so in awe of the talent the Taylor family have. Matthew should have been a huge star and Charlotte is hiding her voice somewhere, but I wish she could find it. I'd love to hear you sing, babe, and I don't mean hearing you sing in the shower or along with the radio. I mean sing your own stuff.'

I push back my hair and set my wine glass on the little wooden coffee table in front of us, wishing I could find my singing voice and my writing confidence again too. I feel panicky at the thought, so I focus on my surroundings, just like Jack taught me when I confessed one day after a difficult time in my new job that I felt out of breath, overwhelmed and anxious.

The coffee table was left here by the previous owners and is one of my favourite pieces of furniture in the cottage, while a huge seascape painting sits above the fireplace, a housewarming present from Emily and Kevin who know how much I love the ocean. There's a bookshelf containing everything from my childhood collection of

Enid Blyton to Jack's eclectic taste, including Seamus Heaney poetry and Paulo Coelho's latest offerings. I breathe in and out, reminding myself I can say no. It's just a friendly suggestion. I don't have to sing if I don't want to.

'Do you think Matthew will ever sing professionally again?' Sophie asks me, unaware of my brief inner anxiety. 'That song he sang at your engagement party was something else, wasn't it?! It's such a shame to let a talent like that go to waste.'

'I hope that when he settles into life in Galway, he'll take a few gigs over there,' I say, wishing my words to come true. 'In fact, I secretly think Martin was encouraging him to go there for that very reason. You know, a fresh start, a new beginning. Sometimes we all need that.'

Jack puts his arm around me.

'I have to say I totally agree,' he says, pulling me closer for comfort. 'Matthew will thrive with all that new energy there and Martin has his head screwed on for sure. He knows if Matthew is to walk again, and I truly believe he will, then positive change, lots to look forward to and lots to keep living for is the answer.'

The room goes silent as we ponder the idea of my brother ever getting out of his wheelchair – I've pictured the scene over and over in my head, willing for him to make it one day. It hurts me so deeply to think that it's how people know him now. *Poor Matthew. The one in the wheelchair.*

The one who was depressed. The one who could have made it, but didn't.

'He was always so full of life and fun, you know,' I tell my friends with a smile, trying to recall some of Matthew's real character before the accident. 'You should have seen him on stage back then when Déjà Vu were on the way to the top! He had crowds of people eating out of his hands, a real showman people couldn't get enough of. It's all he ever wanted to do with his life, and we were all right behind him. I still can't believe it was all taken from him so cruelly.'

I always get such a buzz when I think of Matthew in his heyday, but my lip trembles at the thought of how he is now.

'You must have been so proud of him,' Sophie says, softly. 'You still are proud of him, I know that. What on earth happened for it all to go so wrong for him? Didn't I hear they had a record deal and were going places?'

I try to speak, but I can't even go there. I can't tell any of them how my love for another man, the same man my brother loved, the very man who is the singer in the band they were all just so excited about, is what made Matthew spin his car into a ditch . . . It's all too much. I can't tell them.

'Just creative differences, I suppose,' I say with a shrug, hoping that they won't probe me any further. 'Matthew always described it as a break-up, and he never got over it so it's not something he likes to go into much detail on.'

Jack knows I struggle with talking about Matthew, even though he's never been told the full story. He can tell when I'm struggling, be it a conversation about work, friendship or even something that might come between us. He says he can tell by the quiver in my voice, how I play with my hair or my eyes dart around the room. He knows I'm struggling now.

'Matthew's a strong, decent, super-talented guy and he has a great future,' says Jack, his upbeat tone changing the mood instantly, in a way that only he can. 'So, Charlotte love, what do you say we get this party started and you give us a song? Find that voice again, I know you can.'

I want to. I really, really want to, but I just can't. I can't sing for them. Not now. Not yet.

'I will someday, love, I promise, but would you mind if we put on the iPod instead?' I ask, my eyes pleading for understanding. 'I don't think Sophie and Harry have heard the sound system yet? It's awesome.'

Jack is fully supportive to me as ever and immediately drops the subject without a fuss. He gets up from the sofa and to lighten the mood he does his best embarrassing dance, a quick step mixed with a moonwalk, which has us all in stitches.

'OK, ladies and gentlemen!' he says. 'I'm now taking requests for the cheesiest tunes you can think of. What do you fancy? Speak now or forever hold your peace!'

'Steps!' says Sophie without even having to pause for

thought and Harry lets out a groan which comes from the very tips of his toes, but Sophie is already on her feet, poised and ready for action with her glass in her hand.

'Oh mate, what have you started?' Harry asks, rubbing his head as if in agony at the thought of it. He pretends to block his ears seconds later when the bouncy sounds of '5,6,7,8' pumps out through the speakers, but before long he's on his feet too, full-on 'boot scootin' baby' joining in on the fun, and the four of us line dance around our living room with the coffee table pushed back to make extra space, where we belly laugh and dance our legs off into the wee hours of the morning.

I'm with my favourite people who know and love me, I'm laughing and having fun, and any thoughts of Tom Farley are finally fading away as time passes by.

I want to be nowhere else but here, right now, loving and living in every moment.

Chapter Thirteen

Sundays have always been my favourite day of the week, but I'm fast coming to realize that summer Sundays spent outside the beautiful town of Ardara are going to be even more special.

Waking up to the sweet sound of silence, as opposed to the hum of traffic and horns in city life, then taking it easy over a locally produced breakfast on the deck where the sun hits your shoulders is the stuff of dreams and I inhale every moment.

'I'll get some more coffee,' I say to the three pale faces before me.

Sophie and Harry vow to leave after breakfast, but each are nursing hangovers from hell so a delay is inevitable. All four of us are still full of giddy laughter about different parts of the night before, with the highlight being Jack's attempt at stand-up comedy after too many gin and tonics. It meant the only person who understood his jokes was him, due to his fits of hysterics every time he tried to reach a punchline.

'My jaws are sore laughing,' says Sophie, as she attempts to tackle the sausage, egg and bacon on her plate. 'I wonder how much longer we can get away with acting like teenagers on the weekends. I mean, if some of your patients heard the shite you come out with at the weekend, Jack Malone, they'd run a country mile!'

Jack seems to agree. 'I'd run a country mile from me on any given day, never mind the weekends,' he jokes. 'Ah, we'll all grow up someday, especially when we have our twins, isn't that right, Charlotte?'

I roll my eyes at the ongoing joke we have between us about starting a family, but I do feel a pinch of pressure now when it's mentioned. It's assumed to be the next step in life after marriage, isn't it, but just like Sophie, I don't know if I'm ready for it yet.

'Triplets,' says Harry. 'That would put manners into all of us. A good old set of Irish triplets each.'

Sophie almost chokes on her breakfast. 'Triplet boys,' she says, 'just to make it even more craic. Yes, that's what we need to stop these Sunday hangovers. Gosh, my mother would think she'd died and gone to heaven if we'd even just one baby, never mind three. She's still dropping hints like a punch in the face every time I see her.'

Jack and I exchange a knowing glance. 'Marjorie is the same,' he says, referring to his own mother. 'She's itching to hear the pitter-patter of tiny feet and makes no bones about it. We just ignore her, don't we, Char? We'll do things at our own pace in our marriage and not how others think we should. God, my head is banging!'

I bring him over an Alka-Seltzer and he touches my arm and smiles at me in appreciation. I have to say, one of my favourite things about living with Jack is how we always know when the other one needs a bit of looking after, and we do little things to show we care. Like the many times I've been crucified with period pains and he'll bring home a load of chocolate, fizzy drinks, crisps and sweets, knowing I need to binge on the sofa watching telly while he cooks dinner. Or at more serious times, like when he recently arrived home from work after one of his patients, a young single parent called Jenny, had tried to take her own life and it had floored him. I knew he needed quiet comfort and no stress, so I ran him a bubble bath and lit the fire, then gave him some space to get his head around it.

Marriage can be hard work, but it's also extremely rewarding and I know that what Jack and I have here in our lives is what a lot of people dream of.

'This place is so *deceiving* from the outside, isn't it!' says Marjorie Malone in a voice that would break windows as she examines every room a few hours later. There's simply nothing like an unexpected visit from the in-laws to ruin any given Sunday, is there? 'Would you look at that view, Dad!' she continues. 'It's like something out of that comical old John Wayne movie, *The Quiet Man*! And so much space for children to run around safely and not have to worry about traffic like we did when ours were young.'

Jack makes a face behind her back at her very obvious mention of babies and I try not to laugh. He loves his mother dearly, but she really has no idea of how to be subtle.

'You won't get much trouble from the neighbours, anyhow,' says Jack Sr. 'Ah, this is my idea of heaven, it really is. It's just a slice of perfection. Well done, you two. You work hard and you deserve such a beautiful home.'

I often forget what Dr Malone Sr sounds like as he doesn't really get much opportunity to speak when his wife is around, but one to one he's a very kind, gentle soul and I can see where Jack gets his exceptional bedside manner in his job from. He certainly learned from the best.

'Who fancies the pub, then?' asks Jack, eager to give his parents something to do rather than skulk around the house passing comments, and to our surprise they agree. 'We could grab a bit of a late lunch when we're there. Come on, my treat.'

We walk for just over a mile past fields full of sheep and cows, scarecrows and strawberry fields and I feel like pinching myself to think that this utter tranquillity is on my doorstep. Jack's father is right, we have worked hard to own our first home in such a beautiful place and, as annoying as Marjorie can be, it's lovely to have visitors to share it with.

'Jack, Charlotte, so good to see you!' says Peter the barman when we stoop under the low red door into the darkness of the little country pub. 'Nice to see some new faces too. You're all very welcome.'

We decide to make the most of the lasting fine weather with a drink in the beer garden at the back of the pub, where we revel in the wonderful atmosphere that always greets us here. Traditional Irish music lilts in the background, couples, families and groups of young singles enjoy a lazy Sunday afternoon drink and even Marjorie seems to enjoy it as she laps up the view with some people-watching.

'Everyone is so friendly around here,' says Jack to his parents. 'I think we're going to love it here.'

'I already do,' I tell him, and he takes my hand under the table.

Marjorie orders a coffee as she is designated driver for the afternoon and manages to get another poke in when I opt for a glass of white wine.

'I suppose you may as well enjoy lazy Sundays like this while you can,' she guffaws, watching every mouthful I take. 'My Caroline has her hands full running after her twins day in, day out. She probably wouldn't remember the last time she got to kick back and relax like this during the day, but then she is just *so* committed to her children! She had them young too, in her twenties, so she has still the energy to enjoy them.'

Ouch. My eyes widen in Jack's direction for help.

'Caroline texted me to say her big weekend with the girls

is coming up soon,' he says quickly, coming to my rescue. 'You know the one she takes every six months or so? It normally takes them all a week at least to recover when they head off to – where is it again? Marbella? Long way to go without the children for someone so dedicated, but she deserves a break like the rest of us. We all have to live life how we choose to ourselves, don't we?'

I have to excuse myself to use the bathroom to avoid the look on Marjorie's face but, as always, Jack knows how to floor her, hook, line and sinker when she starts. To my relief, by the time I get back his parents are already talking about how they really need to go soon.

'Chill out for a while,' Jack says to them. 'What's your hurry? I thought you were going to have some lunch?'

Jack Sr rolls his eyes and finishes his pint of beer. 'God forbid that we'd leave that damn cat for a whole afternoon!' he says to us, swallowing his drink like he's swallowing nails. 'I swear our Tiddles has more say in what we do every day than I do! It's time I took up golfing again.'

I feel sorry for Jack's dad a lot of the time. In fact, seeing the two of them together is a gentle reminder of how lucky we are that Jack and I are so compatible. He makes me laugh, he knows when to push me and when to back off, and I still get a rush when I see him every evening when he comes in from work.

Marjorie looks around, trying desperately to get another jibe in before she leaves but she's struggling as there really isn't a lot to ridicule around here. The staff are a delight, always greeting us by name and making us so welcome to the community, as are the nearby villagers who have gone way beyond the call of duty to let us know where they are if we need anything. Everyone we met on our short walk down the hill to the pub had a smile and a wave, which is a far cry from the anonymous city life that Marjorie is used to. It's killing her not to have anything negative to say, I just know it. I'm so glad she is leaving. Truth is, I can't bloody stand her and never could.

'Early start tomorrow?' she says to me as she puts her Burberry clutch bag under her arm. 'I'm sure the children are much more disciplined at Holy Trinity than they were at St Patrick's. Much easier on the head after a busy weekend, yeah?'

Boom, she got me after all. Boy, I'm so glad to see her go.

'She reminds me of the parents at school,' I tell Jack as we stroll back up the hill towards the cottage over an hour later, our hangover well settled with the hair of the dog. 'Always looking down on me, always reminding me how I'm not one of *them*. I'm different, I'm working class, I don't really belong but they're giving me a chance to try and fit in because of . . .'

He stops in his tracks.

'Because of me?' he says, looking very offended.

'Yes. Because of you and your family,' I tell him. 'They accept me, or tolerate me should I say, because of the fact I'm Doctor Jack Malone's wife. There's no way I'd have even got an interview at Holy Trinity had I still been plain old Charlotte Taylor who grew up in Loughisland on a housing estate and you know it, Jack.'

He shakes his head, his forehead creased into a furrow. 'No, Charlotte, please don't ever say that!' he pleads with me. 'You got the job in Holy Trinity because you were the best candidate for it, not because of anything to do with me or my parents. Don't think that way, it's not true.'

I may be a little tipsier than I thought because I can't stop now. I'm on a roll.

'I hate it there, Jack,' I say, falling into his chest now. 'I totally hate it and I'd give anything to be back in St Patrick's singing my songs to children who appreciate me, instead of stuck-up little brats who would rather give snide comments on my clothes than show me some respect. I hate it.'

Jack looks like I've stabbed him in the heart, but I had to say it. I can't go on pretending any more, even though it had been his idea I went for the job in the first place and I hate to hurt him. It was a step up the ladder, that's for sure, but it hasn't turned out that way for me inside. I want him to tell me it's not worth all this stress, I want him to tell me to jack it in and be myself, the type of teacher I used to be, the type of person I am deep inside.

'You'll—'

'Don't say I'll settle in, because I don't think I ever will,' I say to him, hoping for him to support me so badly. 'I dread every day in that school, you've no idea how much I do. I love everything about our life, absolutely everything apart from my job.'

He lifts up my chin and looks into my eyes. 'And my mother,' he says with a smile. 'You couldn't possibly like her either?'

I manage to laugh through my tears. 'OK, I'll admit I'm struggling to like her too, but that's not a new thing and I can cope with her from a distance.'

He tilts his head to the side and kisses my hair, making me feel better already. It's moments like this that I'm so glad I have Jack to lean on every day.

'Come on, let's go home,' he says, putting his arm around me. 'We'll have a good chat tomorrow when we're perfectly sober and after we've had a nice early night. We'll make some plans because there's no way you're working in a job if you hate it that much. Life's too short. But in the meantime I have plans for you this evening, Mrs Malone, and I can't wait to get you home.'

There's no way you're working in a job if you hate it that much.

I couldn't have asked for a better response. Jack knows me, he loves me and he has my back on every decision I make.

I get a whoosh of butterflies in my tummy, longing already

to be snuggled up beside him in our kingsize bed with its cool linen sheets and cosy, duck down duvet. So I push the dread of work tomorrow to the back of my mind for now and we stroll up the hill at our leisure, me leaning into him, loving the familiarity of his smell and the feel of his jumper.

I will give it another week in that school, and then I'm making up my mind once and for all. Jack's right – life's way too short for feeling this sickness in the pit of my stomach every Sunday evening and I don't need to keep going through this hell.

'Are you sure there's nothing else bothering you?' he asks me as he turns the key in the front door. 'You would tell me if there was, wouldn't you Charlotte?'

'Of course, I would,' I tell him honestly. 'It's just the job. I'll give it one more week and we can talk about it then.'

It's just the job.

Isn't it? Yes, of course it is, I convince myself, but deep in my heart I've an awful inkling that things mightn't be as secure in my life as they seem on the outside. I don't like this feeling at all. It's like a gut-wrenching anxiety that when things seem too good to be true, they probably are.

Is it Matthew? Has something happened to him in Galway? Or Emily? I hope it's not Mam or Dad – or what if something happened to Jack? I feel like a beautiful bird, gliding along a beautiful lake but beneath it I'm paddling for all I'm worth and no one can see it. It's like a fear in the pit of my stomach, like I'm waiting for all I have to go belly up just like my life did on the day of Matthew's accident. It's like I'm preparing myself for the next trauma, whatever that may be.

I know my life is perfect to the outside world, yet my mood is slipping and I don't know why.

It's probably the hangover kicking in again, I repeat in my head like a mantra. Things will be easier in the morning.

Chapter Fourteen

June 2018

'Mrs Malone? A chat please in my office?'

My class of twenty-five eight-year-olds are engrossed in 'library time' and I'm using the silence to catch up on marking some homework when the school principal, Miss Jean Brady, interrupts with a sentence that rises in pitch with every word, and a smile that tells me she's about to lynch me for something I've done wrong again in her prissy, stuck-up prison – I mean, 'school for rich kids'.

I nod to Paula, my classroom assistant, who has gone fifty shades of white at the very sight of our very own version of Maleficent and mouths to me 'Good luck.'

Two more weeks to go until summer, I repeat inwardly as I follow the click of her heels down the corridor, and then make the swift turn left into her office. It's more like something you'd see in an inner-city law firm than a south Dublin primary school with its highly polished floor, stripy rugs and splashes of greenery.

A framed photograph of a smiling boy and girl sit on her desk, which shows that maybe somewhere in her hollow make-up is a heart, but I don't believe a witch like Brady could produce such innocence and beauty. In fact, I'd put money on it that the photo was cut from one of those cute French kiddies' fashion catalogue and is all for show.

She sits down and exhales so exaggeratedly that I already want to attack her in a very violent manner. It's so not my nature, but Miss Jean Brady brings out the dark side of me every time she invites me for 'a chat'.

I wait, preparing my armour for another dig. What will it be this time? Could it be another reminder not to take a cup of tea or even a glass of water into the classroom for health and safety reasons? Or maybe she still has a problem with the way I sometimes don't fully pronounce my '*ings*'? (Yes, seriously.) Or could it be that I've gone and deeply offended one of the eight-year-olds in my class by mispronouncing the surname Althorp again, saying it as it's written and not 'Awltrup' as it should be? That was a biggie.

I wait, wincing inside but trying my best to be brave and thick-skinned.

'James Leicester,' she announces, as if I should salute or bow to attention at the sheer mention of a sprog of one of the wealthiest families in school.

'Yes?' I say. My face is a blank canvas of expectation. 'He's in my class? Lovely boy.'

I use the term *lovely* very loosely.

'I had a call from his governess this morning and to be honest I've been trying to get a chance all morning to interrupt your class, but I'm at my wits' end at this stage as to what to do or say to you this time,' she says to me.

This time? Jesus, this must be bad. I try and think of what the hell I could have done *this time*. Did I swear in front of the little shit? Call him a brat to his face when I was thinking it? No, I definitely didn't. I wait . . .

'You do know that our children have after-school activities to further enhance the strong focus on core subjects we teach here during the day?' she continues. She stares at me for a response.

Ah, Jesus, I know what she's on about now. I feel my hands start to tremble, not with fear as they usually do when I'm sitting in this leather chair of doom, but with absolute frustration and bad temper at what's coming.

I nod slowly. I've an urge to roll my eyes and sigh but I remain poker-faced as I've trained myself to do by now. This must be the fifth occasion I've been called into her office, but this is the most pathetic and insulting reason so far.

'You brought a *guitar* into school yesterday?' she says, raising one perfectly arched eyebrow above her black-rimmed glasses. 'Is that correct? A guitar?'

I open and close my hands, feeling the fizz of adrenaline

pump to my fingertips, and then I breathe through my nose, trying my best to control the string of expletives that are lining up on my tongue.

'Do you have an answer to my question?' she asks, drumming her shiny French manicured nails on the pretentious leather mouse mat in front of her. Everything in this hell hole palace is branded with the precious school logo, which is gold, of course, and says something in Latin that nobody even knows how to translate.

'Yes, I did bring my guitar into school, Mrs Brady.'

'Miss!' she corrects me.

Whoops.

'Yes, I did,' I repeat, feeling my voice shake. I think of Jack's words to me when we last discussed my job here. *Don't take any more shit, Charlotte. Not one more ounce of her nonsense. If that witch insults you again, stand up to her and tell her to shove her job where the sun doesn't shine. You're far too talented and smart to be treated like that. Don't take it ever again, not for one more single day.*

'Why?' she asks me, lifting a pen now to make some notes on her branded, lined block of paper. I have an overwhelming urge to tip the desk and its entire contents over and storm away, but I'd probably end up in jail for assault if I did, so I contain myself.

I breathe in and out, counting quickly the days I have to endure to get to the end of term when we'll break up for summer and I'll hold onto a full two months of pay from the pockets of the rich who send their silver-spoon-born offspring here. Ten more teaching days, that's all I'd have to last if I can just hold back and not react to this nonsense.

'I don't have much more time to waste on this matter, so if you don't mind, maybe you could answer me *why*?' she says to me.

I twist my mouth, trying to decide on my reaction.

'I thought it might be fun to sing some songs with the class,' I try to explain. 'We were talking about some items in the news and I thought The Beatles' classic "Let it Be" might strike a chord, pardon the pun, and—'

'The Beatles!' she says, her head about to spin full circle on her narrow shoulders. 'You thought it would be fun to sing The Beatles to eight-year-olds whose parents pay thousands of pounds a year towards your salary!'

I blink, trying desperately to know where to start to explain my reasoning. I've so much going through my head, but I can't decide whether to go all soft and creative in my explanation, or whether to eff her off to the highest degree.

I choose soft and creative.

'You know something, Miss Brady,' I say to her in my best country accent, which I know to her ears sounds like nails running down a blackboard. 'There's nothing more beautiful than hearing children sing, be it in the morning, afternoon or evening. Did you know that children's heartbeats synchronize when they sing together?'

She looks genuinely baffled at my reaction.

'You sang another song, I believe?' she says, not even listening to what I just said. 'A song you made up yourself? I don't even know the lyrics to The Beatles, never mind a song you decided to present to my children from your own mind, and I forbid you to take a decision like this behind my back in future!'

Soft and creative, soft and creative.

'Singing makes people smile from the inside out, be it in the shower, in church, on a stage or in a classroom,' I say to her. 'It releases endorphins, it makes us move and dance, it creates a bond and it also creates wonderful memories. It—'

'But it's not *your* job here, Mrs Malone!' she interrupts me. 'We have a *classically* trained music teacher, a real-life composer from the orchestra who comes in once a week to tutor children whose parents have chosen to educate their children in this manner. It's not up to *you* to sing The Beatles or some of your own nonsense to them! How dare you!'

Whoa, I can't deny that hurts. Some of my own nonsense? I feel my lip tremble. I will not cry in front of her. No way.

But I don't know what to say right now because I honestly can't think of anything more uplifting than a teacher singing with their young pupils, and as I recall, they all seemed to enjoy it at the time, even that stiff little so-and-so James Leicester whose 'governess' reported me.

'No more singing in class,' she tells me, still writing on her horrible note paper. 'It's as simple as that. Leave any musical notions you may have off your job description, because it wasn't on it in the first place.'

I won't cry. I won't.

'But I thought I was . . . I thought I was their class teacher,' I say, gulping back tears now. 'Isn't it my job to nurture the children here, to make them feel happy and relaxed in their everyday life, not just through following a strict curriculum? Am I wrong?'

I blink, hoping to disguise the pools that are forming in my eyes. Her words have hit me hard and she knows it.

'No more singing in class,' she repeats, as hard as a stone. I clasp my hands together, I twiddle my thumbs. I can feel my heart thumping and perspiration breaking through onto my navy blouse. My dress sense was also deemed inappropriate so I had to 'tone it down' and wear only black, navy or other suitably muted colours in case a flash of colour might poison the poor children's minds.

'Can I ask you a question before I go?' I say, taking from her silence that she has now finished chastising me. She puts her pen down, pushes back her glasses and tilts her head to the side, waiting.

'Go ahead,' she says. 'Quickly. I don't have all day.'

I've wanted to ask her this for so long. I need to know the truth.

'Why did you hire me in the first place?' I ask her, looking her right in her steely grey eyes. 'I genuinely would like to know, because all I've ever done here seems to be wrong in your eyes. I'd like to know how on earth you thought from my application and interview that I would fit into your establishment?'

I can't even bring myself to call it a school. It's like an institution, like a military operation, a horrible place that people actually pay for. I didn't even think such ancient, right-wing places existed any more.

She puffs out a snigger and takes off her glasses.

'Oh, I think you already know the answer to that question, Mrs *Malone*,' she says to me, emphasizing my husband's surname.

I knew it. I bloody knew I was hired because I'm a doctor's wife and not because of my own credentials or what I could bring to the job. I'm humiliated, I'm insulted and I'm hurt right to my very bones.

I stand up tall, willing myself to hold my cool, but the adrenaline pumps within me, as does my pride, my intellect and everything I have worked for since I left Loughisland to study in Dublin, a world away from my family and the place I called home. I think of my father's face the day I graduated, his cheeks pink with pride and a tear in his eye he couldn't hide and didn't care to.

I think of how my mother went round the whole village telling everyone who would listen that my name would be in the paper on the graduation list of honours and how she showed my photo to everyone who came into our modest home.

I think of how they saved their hard-earned cash to put me and my two siblings through a third-level education, of how much time and effort they put into Matthew's music and of how my family is bursting with more talent and have more soul than the woman in front of me will ever know.

I think of how I got my first job in St Patrick's and how the principal heaped praise on me at every turnaround, mostly for my music, and how I proud I was to finally make my mark in my family when I'd to follow in such fine foot-steps as my big brother and sister.

How dare she hire me for a name I married in to? What an insult to me, my family and my whole being!

Then Jack's words come back to me. I hear his supportive voice in my mind.

Tell her to shove her job where the sun doesn't shine if she ever bullies you again, I mean it. You're better than that. You're Charlotte Taylor from Loughisland and I love you. Everyone loves you. Don't ever let her bring you down.

She puts on her glasses, shooting me a glance of disdain.

'You can go back to class now,' she says, looking at her computer screen now. She lifts a file and stretches her arm out towards me, without looking my direction. 'Can you give these to Rosemary at reception on your way past? Actually, never mind, I'll do it myself.'

I clear my throat.

'I haven't finished,' I say to her, my knees actually

knocking under this horrible straight navy skirt I bought just to try and fit into her ridiculous, boring dress code.

'I beg your pardon?' she says, taking her glasses off again. Her eyes meet mine.

'I said, I haven't finished,' I repeat.

Here I go.

'You know, for such an educated woman, you sure do lack soul, as does this excuse for a school you are running,' I tell her. 'So, you can stuff your job, stuff your "*ings*" and your ridiculous standards and your skinny stiff upper lip, Miss Jean Brady!'

'Mrs Malone!'

'It's Charlotte *Taylor* actually,' I correct her. I never wanted to use my married name in my professional life and I won't ever again. 'You'll be singing my songs one day when they're on the radio and you'll be telling people I used to teach here. Yes, *used* to because I'm out of here right now. Oh, and tell James Leicester's glorified babysitter from me to go listen to some of The Beatles or even Guns N' Roses and let her hair down. Even headbang a bit if she feels like it! She might even learn a thing or two! I'm out of here at long last. Go stick your job and your shit-hole of a school where the sun don't shine! Goodbye!'

I turn on my prissy kitten heels and march out of her office, down the corridor and into my classroom where I hug Paula and wish her luck.

'Where are you going?' Paula asks as the children stare at me open-mouthed.

'As far away from here as I can find,' I tell her. Then I gather my belongings, say a quick farewell to the children (it's not their fault their parents are assholes) and I make my way out to the car where I call Jack and put him on loudspeaker as I reverse out of my parking space and out through the gates of education hell.

'I did it!' I say to him, hearing the fear in his voice when he answers. We never call each other during the day unless it's an emergency so I know I've probably frightened him to death. 'I told the bitch where to go and I've left Holy Trinity once and for all.'

'Jesus, Charlotte, did you really?' he asks, his voice half trembling, half laughing. 'Wow, that's my girl! Don't let anyone ever walk over you! I'll see you when I get home and we'll have a party. You can burn those stupid clothes they made you wear too. It's their loss, Char!'

I turn down the car windows, turn up the radio and sing my heart out all the way home, thankful as ever that my darling husband understands me the way he does. I'm tired of pretending to be another me just to please everyone else. From now on, I'll do what's best for my soul and I'll never, ever let any notions of pleasing others get in the way.

Chapter Fifteen

'Oh my goodness, Emily, what on earth have I done? I think I'm losing my mind.'

My sister and I are sitting on top of a powdery sand dune looking out over the picturesque blue seas of Brittas Bay the morning after my resignation. Despite my kick-ass attitude and big display of 'I don't care' the night before, I'm not so confident now with the realization that, for the first time since I graduated, I'm actually jobless.

Jack left for work in the hospital just after six this morning, leaving me plenty of time to roll around our big bed feeling lost and alone in my thoughts. To be honest I'm terrified of what the future holds. I'll never get another teaching job in Dublin once news travels of how I pissed off Miss Jean Brady and told her to shove her shit-hole job where the sun doesn't shine. She has friends in high places, or so they say.

'She's like the Simon Cowell of teaching, and I'm screwed, Em.'

My ever so supportive sister Emily can't stop laughing.

'Do you know how many people would murder their mother for a job at Holy Trinity School, and you tell the principal to shove it?' she says, with a loud cackle. 'I bet if you did a survey of teaching graduates and asked them their dream job on the east coast of Ireland, you'd be sure that Holy Trinity would be right up there. But fair play to you, Charlotte, you left in style! She sounds like a right old wagon though so you did the right thing. It's just so typically you!'

I really wish she would stop laughing. It *was* a little bit funny last night when Jack and I were fantasizing about a voodoo doll version of Miss Jean Brady, but now, in the cold light of day with a long summer ahead and teaching jobs in Dublin being like hen's teeth, it's not really a laughing matter at all.

'I wonder would St Patrick's have me back,' I say in a daydream, staring out at the sea. 'I think I'm in shock. Do I look pale? I really do think I've got post-traumatic stress from all this.'

Emily pretends to roll around in the sand now, slapping her hands off her bare legs and then kicking her ankles up in the air. She looks like a baby elephant being tickled but I daren't say that out loud.

'Oh, stop being such a drama queen!' she says when she comes out of her fit of hysterics. 'You'll get another job, don't panic. You've always been a lucky sod, so no doubt you'll come out of this one bigger and better too so no need to fret. Teachers need cover all the time and you might even pick up a maternity leave between now and September, or sick leave or something. You did the right thing, sister. Chill out and enjoy – oh my God I really can't believe you actually quit!'

And then she is off again. The whole morning is basically a repeat of this, and Sophie's reaction isn't very different when the news reaches her.

'My mother just rang me to say you called Miss Jean Brady a witch to her face!' she howls down the phone. 'She's on the board of that school and she is over the moon because she hates her too! High five, Charlotte Taylor Malone! You just said what hundreds of people in Dublin are thinking! But what the hell are you going to do with yourself now?'

I didn't exactly call her a witch, but Chinese whispers and all that . . . plus I have absolutely no idea what I'm going to do now but I can't bring myself to say it out loud. At least I agree for once with Sophie's mother – now that's a turn-up for the books.

When I ring her that evening to break the news, my own mother is equally as shocked as Sophie, but much less impressed.

I must admit I actually contemplated telling Matthew first to soften the blow, knowing that he wouldn't be able to hold back on his daily phone call from Loughisland to Galway (my parents call him religiously every evening after the six o'clock news). But I realized that would be unfair and I should really be a big girl and own up.

'What on earth did you have to quit for?' she keeps saying, over and over again, no matter how many times I give her examples of how Miss Jean Brady has been treating me since I first set foot in the school. I tell her about my clothes (big mistake, she agrees), my pronunciation (she's a bit offended because she couldn't afford to send me to elocution lessons) and finally about my music (again, she doesn't see the big deal in that one).

'I just couldn't take it any more,' I say with my eyes closed, getting a flashback to when I was a teenager caught skipping school and knew I had to admit it, hoping when I opened my eyes the whole problem would have disappeared and be forgotten. But no matter how much I try and explain, it doesn't seem to cut the ice with my mother.

'Have you lost your whole assertiveness, or have you forgotten how to stand up for yourself without packing a good job like that in?' she asks me in despair. 'This reminds me of the time you were suspended by the nuns in second year of grammar school for wearing those silly-looking Doctor Marten boots to school instead of the black patent slip-ons I bought you that cost me the price of a week's groceries. I just don't understand how you achieve so much, Charlotte, and then just throw it all away in a whim. Not everything in life is disposable, when will you realize that? Why can't you just be more like—'

My ears close over at this point and I actually start to hum to myself to block out the noise.

Why can't you just be more like Emily, is what she's going to say but I will let her rant and rave until she gets tired of her own voice or realizes she's only repeating herself.

I've disappointed her, I've let her down again, just when I'd earned so many brownie points by becoming a teacher in the first place, marrying not only *a* doctor but *the* doctor who is credited for making such a difference to Matthew's mental stability and overall recovery, then bagging a job in a school so far removed from my old life that we didn't even know it existed until I miraculously landed the job.

I pinch my eyes as old familiar feelings of failure creep over me, reminding me how I've always been perceived as the rebel child, always the one who just couldn't quite keep up with the rest or just keep in line for that matter.

'I'm sorry, Mam, but I couldn't stay in a job I hate just to please everyone else,' I say to her when I eventually get a break in the conversation. 'Jack is totally behind me on this so I hope you and Dad will be too. It's not as simple as it sounds. The place was horrendous, please believe me. I didn't just do this on a whim or to disappoint anyone.'

She goes off again until I hear my father interrupting. Once again it brings me back to my teenage years when I was always the one who caused rows between them, be it because of my grades at school, which my teachers often described as 'inconsistent', or my choice of company from friends to boyfriends, or my unique ability to make an absolute mess of everything I turned my hand to, from part-time jobs to whimsical hobbies that got me nowhere.

The only thing I was good at was writing songs, but my parents hadn't a clue about that as they were so wrapped up in Matthew and his big dreams of being a rock star, and in Emily's solid and steady progress into accountancy then marriage (and soon babies no doubt) without as much as a whimper from her.

I finish the phone call and go to bed, even though it's only just five in the evening and Jack will be home soon, starving and probably hoping for a nice dinner ready for him just like he would have ready for me if I wasn't working.

I'm a shit wife, I'm a shit daughter and I'm a shit teacher. I'm a shit musician too as I haven't been able to lift my guitar to sing anything more than simple songs (and The Beatles) to eight-year-olds.

I put my pillow over my head in a bid to stop the noise in my mind and will myself to switch off and go to sleep so I can forget about it all.

I'm so exhausted.

'This is not a crisis,' says Jack later that evening over dinner, which he made before he woke me up from my pity-party slumber. 'Please stop beating yourself up, Charlotte. It's really not a big deal so try not to overreact to other people's reactions. You have to be yourself and you did what's best for you, it's that simple. You can't live in misery just to please your mother or anyone else.'

I push my food around the plate in front of me, knowing that my husband is talking total sense as usual, but I'm still bubbling from my conversation with my mother and I just can't shake it off.

'Why does it always have to be *me* who upsets her?' I ask him, as if he has the answers. Luckily, he didn't know me when I was the rebel child of the family so he has no idea how many times I casually messed up. More importantly, he doesn't know that I hold a lot of responsibility for why my brother is in a wheelchair and I hope he never finds out. No one knows that except for me, Matthew and, of course, he who should never be named, Tom Farley.

Speaking of Tom Farley, he never did reply to my email wishing him well on his big hit song, but hey ho, that's the least of my worries. I need to get my head together and work out what on earth I'm going to do with my future now that I've messed up my teaching career.

'Don't worry, love, I'm just feeling a bit low in myself, but I'll get over it. I just feel like I've thrown all I worked for away and I've let my family down. Again,' I say to Jack, who I know is worried sick about my state of mind right now.

He clears the table and when I go to help him he pulls me closer for a hug.

'I'm a big believer in things happening for a reason,' he says to me, his voice as soothing and comforting as ever. I look up into his stunningly beautiful midnight-blue eyes that manage to make me go weak at the knees even when I'm feeling a bit dead inside like I am now. 'Yesterday is just part of your history, Char, but it's not going to stop your future. Take this time to reflect and plan for the next step in your life, whatever direction that will take you. You've the world at your feet and any school in the country would be foolish not to give you a chance. Miss Jean Brady and her team of sharks are only big fish in a very small pond.'

I can't help but giggle, which I think was Jack's aim with his big speech.

'You really love throwing in a metaphor or two just to drive your message home, don't you, Doctor Malone,' I laugh, and he ruffles my hair playfully.

'You love my metaphors,' he says, giving me one of his million-dollar smiles. 'It works on my patients, so I kind of hope that someday it will work on my beautiful wife.'

He wraps his strong arms around my waist and pulls me closer to him so that I'm touching a part of him that tells me what's on his mind.

'I've a dreaded feeling your mother is going to really step up the baby pressure now that I'm officially unemployed,' I say to him as he nuzzles my neck, forcing my eyes to roll back in my head with pleasure. 'She'll think I've no excuse not to fill this house with little people since I've no pupils to take up my attention any more.'

Jack's attention is most definitely on other things and

he's driving me that way too as his hand slips down below my waist.

'We can always go and practise,' he says, gently tugging my hair with his other hand and kissing me, taking my breath away. 'What do you say?'

For the first time I allow myself to visualize what it would be like to have our very own little family here in Ardara. The thought of a mini Jack or mini me gives me an unexpected glow. Maybe the time to think about it isn't so far away, after all.

'I say we need to practise at every opportunity we can,' I agree, feeling dizzy and hot in anticipation. 'Let's go upstairs and do our best.'

Chapter Sixteen

Wicklow, August 2018

July, thankfully, went by in a blink.

My days of unemployment shouldn't really feel as low as they do as technically, if I was still working, I would be off school now anyway enjoying one of the great perks of teaching: a very long summer.

Yet knowing that doesn't seem to ease the pain I've been feeling as each day rolls into another and I can't seem to see any hope ahead. I'm afraid to admit it to anyone else, but my self-confidence is on the floor and I feel my mood slipping deeper and deeper into a darker place. I'm totally unsure of who I am, of who I want to be, and of where I'm going next.

Kirsty came to stay with us like a bolt out of the blue, which both delighted and exhausted me at the same time, but there's only so much of a person's ever changing love life you can keep up with, and I was soon dizzy with names of dating *apps*, never mind names of actual dates. So by the time she left you could say I was more or less glad to see her go.

I then spent a luxurious two weeks in the South of France with Jack where we enjoyed long, lazy days exploring vine-yards, museums, cities including Cannes and Nice, but since August kicked in, this summer seems to be just dragging on and on and on.

My mother made a list of alternative jobs for people with a degree in teaching, thinking it might spark me off in a new direction since my entire reputation as a teacher had gone down the drain. I know her intentions were good, but her execution was exasperating.

'How about tutoring?' she said one day at the start of a random phone call when I was lying in bed. 'Maggie Farrell's sister's daughter does it and makes a clean fortune. Or is it her son? Anyhow, Maggie Farrell's—'

'I have no idea who Maggie Farrell is, never mind her sister's daughter's son or whoever is making a fortune, Mam,' I told her, getting off the call as quickly as I could and burying my head under the duvet.

'Keep busy,' said Jack. 'Something will come up, love. You'll see.'

But as I waited for something to come up, my mind-set kept slipping further down. I lifted my guitar one day and sat in the living room as the sun burst through the window. I tried to strum a few chords, searched desperately in my head for some words to come but my mind was totally blank. In frustration, I tested myself to see if I could get through a full version of James Taylor's 'Sweet Baby James', one of my all-time favourites, but it just wasn't happening. I had to really fight the urge to throw the guitar into the corner, then I sat there alone and cried for what I'd let this darkness do to me. Is this how Matthew had felt when he had been battling with his sexuality and it led him into depression? Am I depressed? Am I facing some sort of identity crisis?

Jack would know and would help me in a heartbeat if I spilled it all out to him, but he is struggling with a few heavy cases from work as it is, and I'm his wife after all, not his patient. So I hide it from him, only revealing my impatience at not being able to find work, when really I know my issues run a lot deeper.

Visiting Matthew in Galway managed to distract me for the short time I was there, but it also served to stir up some old raw emotions when I saw him in his new environment. His determination hadn't waned since he left for pastures new, even though he's been stuck in that chair for almost three years now, and it just breaks my heart every time I see him in comparison to the way he was, so handsome, vibrant, full of craic and music and song. His old spark is still there somewhere, ironically much more so than it was in the years just before his accident, but I put a lot of that down to Martin and how he has stuck by him every single day since it happened.

The weather was glorious while I was over in Galway and we spent our days in Matthew's back garden with its sea view, drinking cold beers, reminiscing and putting the world to rights as we listened to music that brought us way back to our youth, not to mention the memories attached to every song.

'Remember the time you got suspended for clapping along in choir practice, pretending to be someone out of *Sister Act*,' Matthew reminded me, much to Martin's amusement. 'You were always getting into trouble; innocent trouble, but enough to put the nuns into a spin, not to mention our poor mother who was convinced it was front-page news every time. I don't think she'll ever get over you being caught smoking on the school bus. She was reminded of it every time she went to the post office!'

'Oh, you little minx, Charlotte Taylor,' said Martin as he sipped his glass of Malbec. 'And I thought that butter wouldn't melt in your mouth.'

I sighed in a bid to defend myself.

'It was actually an after-school detention for my *Sister Act* clapping in the choir, not a suspension if you must know, Matthew, so don't exaggerate,' I corrected my brother. 'And by the way, I'm so glad I'm not depending on you for a job reference now that I'm an out-of-work teacher!'

Martin agreed with me. He shuffled up in his seat.

'He'd sink you, Charlotte! He does the same to me all the time!'

Matthew was enjoying the attention and stirring the pot.

'I can assure you that any of my blips in school were minor, Martin,' I said, keeping it going. 'So don't listen to him. He always did love to spin a yarn when he'd an audience, didn't you Matthew? All I can say is, once a showman, always a showman.'

And speaking of audiences and being a showman, they went on to tell me with great enthusiasm how they'd now secured two gigs a week in the city as a two-piece act under the tongue-in-cheek name of 'Wonder Wheels', playing cover versions of popular songs to tourists, students and whoever passed through some of Galway city's finest bars, pubs and nightclubs.

'It's a full-time job keeping up with artists like Ed Sheeran,' said Matthew, unable to hide his elation as he told me all about his latest repertoire. 'And to be honest I was very out of touch with the music of today, but I've quickly learned how to please the variety of people who turn up in the melting pot that is Galway.'

'It's a hive of music,' Martin told me, his eyes joyous too at his own recollection of how immersed in the local scene they'd already become. 'We're just starting out but I've no doubt we'll get even busier soon.'

My heart soared when they then brought me up to speed with Matthew's new rehabilitation programme and how his medical team were constantly setting targets to build muscle and were encouraging him to work on various equipment and exercises to try and reconnect his brain to his limbs. Matthew was full of vigour when he talked about walking again, which lit a fire inside me too as I fed off his enthusiasm.

'It's a guessing game,' Martin explained, equally as dedicated to my brother's rehabilitation as Matthew was himself. 'It could be months, it could be years, but a lot of it is down to a positive mental attitude and that's what we're working on every day, isn't it, Matt?'

I caught them smiling at each other just as I had so many times before, like they shared a code that only the two of them knew, and I had to fight off so many mixed emotions as my tender state absorbed every move of Matthew's happiness.

I gulped back a bitter taste in my mouth which caught me unawares. Matthew's life with Martin was full of new beginnings and opportunity, whereas mine had been steamrolled down a path I didn't choose, just to help Matthew. I reminded myself I wasn't in a great place and forced myself to be happy for my brother.

I also looked, as I always do, for Martin's halo when he spoke with such passion about Matthew, reminding myself that they'd only just met before the tragedy that changed their lives. Yet here he was, still dedicated, still totally committed to Matthew, and I knew that things would have been so very different for all of us without him.

That's love, I told myself. That's absolute true love.

'I bet Jack has words of wisdom for you when you feel panicky, Charlotte,' Martin said to me over dinner when I explained my whole work dilemma in greater detail. Once the subject came up, there was no hiding my low mood, even if I'd managed to escape showing it most of the time I was in their company.

'Jack is as awesome as he always is,' I told them, and that was true of course. In fact, Matthew and Martin reminded me of me and Jack in many ways. Our bond is strong and pure, unconditional almost, and I know that we care for each other in equal measure. 'He keeps reminding me of how I've nothing to worry about, that better things are round the corner, but I feel like such a failure, you know? I feel like I've let everyone down. I was a teacher in a top-class school and now I'm nothing.'

But just as I was about to really open the floodgates and get going, Matthew brought me back to earth with a bump.

'I know, let's walk the prom tomorrow and you can bitch to me for the whole time about how shit your life is being a fully qualified, unemployed teacher with years of experience and loads of talent to boot,' he said.

My eyes widened at the extent of his point. Ow.

'I don't think it's fair to say that as if it's my fault,' I said to him, that bitter taste hitting the back of my throat again.

Martin tactfully excused himself from the table. One thing I've noticed about him is that, despite his deep love, he takes no shit from Matthew and is also careful enough not to get involved in family domestics.

'No one ever said it was your fault that I can't walk,' Matthew told me, sipping his wine as if I should just forget the twinge in his earlier comment. 'What I mean is that you're married to a doctor, you've a few years of teaching behind you, you live in a spectacular home with no health concerns whatsoever. I just don't get what you have to complain about when you say "now I'm nothing".'

Ah, now we were getting somewhere.

'So you think that just because I have it all on paper I should automatically be ecstatically happy?' I questioned him. 'Why do you always think you know what's best for me, Matthew? You've no idea how I feel or what my ambitions once were or what they may be now. Being a doctor's wife with a nice home I worked hard for doesn't define me. I'm more than that, so please don't judge me. I don't cast the same judgements on you.'

Matthew rubbed his forehead.

'Don't tell me you're going to say how you could have been off living a high life of fame and fortune with you know who.'

'Tom!' I said, knowing that just by saying his name I'd hit a nerve. 'Tom Farley, yes, sometimes I do wonder! You know, I pressed pause on my life and the path it was going on to stay at home and help you get better, so don't pass idle comments about how I "should" be happy with my lot when sometimes I do think that things could have been so different for me.'

Matthew took a deep breath.

'I see him on posters everywhere I go,' he said, more sternly now. 'Do you think it doesn't hurt when I see how he's tasting all the fame and fortune I once dreamed of? But that's where it ends, Charlotte. I'm over him in every other way, but I'm not sure I can say the same for you.'

Martin came back to the table and we both went quiet.

'And I'm not saying you should be happy with your lot,' Matthew continued moments later when we both had simmered down. 'I just hope you're being honest with your-self because, otherwise, the only person you're fooling is you.'

He poured me more wine and Martin picked up the cue to change the subject, choosing instead to ask me how I was settling into life in Ardara and asking if I knew Peter who runs the bar there and Mary who runs the art gallery. I took the bait. I didn't want to fight with my brother, nor could I stomach hearing what he had to say to me about Tom. I'd hoped we had crossed that bridge and burned it. I didn't want to go back to that conversation again.

Despite that minor blip, all in all, I was delighted to see how Matthew's new life in Galway suited him and even though I did manage to complain a bit, it did fill my heart to see him try his best to stay positive. His never-ending determination to get out of the chair one day was inspiring and humbling to say the least, and so with all that in mind, I didn't mention my work worries, or dare to tap into any hidden angst over Tom Farley again.

Matthew, as assertive and perceptive as always, wasn't going to let me get away just so easy when he had me all to himself, though.

'You're allowed to feel the way you need to feel, Charlotte,' he told me as I was leaving to go back to Ardara that Sunday evening, totally contradicting his joke about walking the prom, but I know why he said it when he did. 'I have days when I want to scream at how unfair it is that I'm *so* determined to get on my feet again, yet my stupid, sorry excuse of a body doesn't have the power to keep up.'

I sat beside him on their front porch, wondering how the hell we created this mess between us.

'I look around at people with other problems, much more extreme than mine,' he told me, 'and I try to remind myself how I could be so much worse off, then I also try to give myself a metaphoric kick in the behind to make me grateful for what I have in comparison.'

He almost acted out his words, so dramatic and visual. He was definitely born for the stage.

'But then I think no,' he announced. 'I'm allowed to feel miserable when I need to. Society reminds us to be grateful, to be thankful and to be happy but some days you just have to give in and feel shit, and that's OK too! It's OK to have a day when you feel sorry for yourself and all your own struggles, because those struggles are real to you, right here, right now, and you have to feel them in order to deal with them.'

I couldn't have agreed with him more.

'High five, brother,' I said to him, and we did a hand-shake that we'd made up as children, which made both of us smile.

Before I left, I tried to think of how to explain to him how I've been feeling but I couldn't find the words. I knew on paper my worries weren't even remotely comparable to what many were going through, but the truth was, I was going down and I knew it. The light in my life, no matter how things might look to the outside eye, was slowly being dimmed by a black curtain that was closing in my ever-darkening mind. I knew I'd love to give myself a kick, but I wasn't so sure my resolution was as simple as that.

'I do have days when everything feels like doom and gloom,' I admitted to my brother who looked back at me tentatively after our handshake. 'I won't lie to you, I do.'

He nodded in return. If anyone knew how that felt, it was Matthew.

'Because of what you could have been?' he asked.

'I don't know, Matthew,' I said honestly. 'I don't know if I can explain what's going on in my head but some days I don't feel like getting out of bed. Just some days.'

'And that's fine, Charlotte,' he said, more concerned this time. 'But it's when every day feels like shit that we should be worried. Are you sure it's just some days? Look, if every day is bad, you maybe need to talk to someone? It's OK not to be OK. You know that already.'

I shook my head and plastered on my smile again.

There was no way Matthew was going to be left worrying about me on top of everything else he had going on in his life. He had bigger and better things to be focused on, like learning to walk again for a start, not to mention his own history of mental health problems.

'No, I'm not like that every day at all, I promise,' I told him, squeezing his hand. I lifted my keys but, before I headed for the car, I gave him a quick peck on the cheek. 'I'm proud of you, you know that, Matthew? I'm so proud of you and everything you stand for. You're my big brother and I love you. You're making all of us so proud every day that you struggle and battle to get back on your feet again. And you will. I just know it.'

Matthew looked away, his eyes shining, and in my mind I got a glimpse of him in his navy apron that day three years ago in the corner shop, shying away from my attempt at a hug when I went there to tell him of my news about Tom Farley.

But he didn't shy away this time. In fact he turned right towards me and extended his arms, inviting me to lean down and embrace him. It took my breath away and made my eyes a bit glassy too.

'And I love you too, little sister,' he whispered. 'Maybe

you'll pick up that guitar of yours soon and show us all what you're made of.'

I could only nod as I fought back tears of happiness and sadness rolled into one.

'Just try it, Charlotte,' he continued. 'I know your confidence was knocked by that snobby school principal, but you're way better than that. I know you are.'

I got into the car, put the window down and started up the engine. A blast of country music startled us, making us both laugh at the welcome distraction from the emotions that filled the air around us both.

'It's nice to see your taste in music has stayed the same, anyhow,' he shouted across at me. 'Start singing again, sister! You don't know what you're missing! It's good for your soul!'

'I will very soon!' I call back at him. 'I'm working on it, I promise.'

Chapter Seventeen

I'm in bed when Sophie calls unexpectedly at the door just after eleven a.m., springing me out of my dream in which I was tutoring children who were speaking a different language and I couldn't understand a thing they said. Their words were right in my face as they spoke mumbo jumbo and they laughed at me with toothless grins, pointing and mocking, telling me how useless I was and how I'd never be a real teacher.

'Thank God you're here!' I tell Sophie. I realize I'm shaking. 'Oh Soph, I was stuck in the most horrendous dream! Why are you even here? It's so good to see you. Come in.'

I say 'Come in' but by the time I say it, Sophie is already in the kitchen filling the kettle.

'Nice pyjamas,' she says. 'Do you actually wear those in bed with Jack?'

I glance down at my Disney pyjamas, realizing they are now about nine years old and are as tattered and torn as my mind is at the moment.

'Sentimental value,' I say, 'and no is the answer to your question. Of course I don't wear these in bed with Jack! I sleep naked!'

'Eugh,' says Sophie as she flicks the kettle to boil. 'Too much information.'

We take a mug of coffee each outside and Sophie lights up a cigarette, much to my bewilderment. She never smokes. It looks funny and doesn't suit her at all.

'What on earth are you doing?' I ask her. 'You don't smoke. Give me a puff.'

She glances at me and shakes her head. 'No, you can wait,' she says. 'I'm being rebellious. I'm never rebellious so I thought I'd take a drive out to see you and smoke a cigarette when I'm supposed to be working. And you don't smoke any more either so don't even think about it.'

We both sit looking out at the spectacular views ahead of us with only birdsong for company, when I let out a deep sigh that makes Sophie almost choke on her cigarette.

'Do you think we're having a mid-life crisis, Sophie?' I ask her, in a very serious tone. 'I mean, I feel like I'm cracking up a bit inside. Maybe I'm just bored. Can you crack up from boredom?'

Sophie lets out a noise that sounds a bit like 'pfttt'.

'I'm perfectly in control of my life,' she tells me, blowing out a stream of smoke that tells me this isn't her first taste of nicotine. 'Plus, we're too young to be having a mid-life crisis. You, however, really need to get your shit together and deal with what's going on in your head, Char. Emily is worried about you, even your fair weather friend Kirsty is worried about you, and your mother is going round the bend. Tell me what's going on with you, darling. You know you can tell me anything.'

I dig deep as I cradle my coffee mug but, no matter how much I try and search my mind for a deeper problem that might exist, I can't find anything bigger than the actual truth, the trigger that started my low moods that have lasted all summer.

'I just need to find my purpose again,' I tell Sophie. She puts out her cigarette at last. 'I just need to find out who I am and where I'm going because right now I can't seem to find another teaching job, I can't find it in me to write songs like I used to, I can't do anything that makes me feel worthy. I just need to find my "reason to be" again.'

Sophie looks at me with great pity.

'Just being yourself is a good enough "reason to be" if you're not feeling up to much else,' she tells me. 'Sometimes we put ourselves under too much pressure to be this or be that. Sometimes we have to just "be", to sit still and collect our thoughts. Don't be so hard on yourself, please.'

I breathe out and lean back on my chair, wondering how much longer I can just sit still and think about things. That's part of my problem. I've had way too much time to think.

'You know, Sophie, when we were growing up in Loughisland, it was the happiest time of my life, even though it was simple and we didn't have much,' I say, not knowing where my words are coming from or where they're going. 'The sound of the ice cream van coming into our estate was like our own little version of Disneyland, a bit of snow in winter gave us a whole new playground and we'd use coal bags as makeshift sleighs to slide down hills, and we could tell what day of the week it was by what Mam was making for dinner.'

Sophie smiles but I know my childhood was several light years away from what she experienced. I'm not saying it was better or worse, it was just different.

'I wore my sister's clothes when she had grown out of them and I longed for the day when I could wear my own things, instead of depending on Emily's growth spurts,' I say with a smile. 'I'll never forget the time I saved enough money from picking strawberries at the weekends to buy a whole new outfit of my own. A denim jacket with patches on, a full-length floral tea dress to go underneath it and a pair of boots that made my mother's eyes water. I was fifteen and it was my first sense of self, my first expression of who I really was inside. I'll never forget that feeling.'

I know that Sophie is trying desperately to think of something to say, but she can't relate at all, can she? From what she has told me, as a child she was showered with ponies, violin lessons, speech and drama tuition, designer clothes. Her weekend entertainment was the opera whereas mine was going for a bag of chips with my friends. She knew exactly who she was and where she was going in life from the day she was born.

'Charlotte, you're one of the sweetest, funniest, most caring and talented people I know,' she says to me gently. 'You're an out-of-this-world teacher, but most of all, you're my best friend in the world, even more than Harry sometimes. I'm serious about that.'

Her gentle words make me lose my breath.

'*Really?*'

'Yes, really,' she nods. 'I'd be lost without you, Char, and the laughs and words of wisdom we share. You're such a special person, so unique that even my mother likes you – and that's more than what she feels for me!'

I manage to laugh at that one but it *is* true. I've gone way up in Sophie's dragon mother's estimations since I walked out on Miss Jean Brady.

'Maybe you don't see it now, but you are so special, and being a teacher at Holy Trinity doesn't define you – in fact I didn't like to say it to you before, but you're so much more than that place,' she continues. 'You're deeper than the people associated with places like that, you've got more soul.'

'Ah, thanks Soph. That's nice to hear.'

'Believe me,' she continues. 'I've known Jack Malone for a very long time now and he doesn't suffer fools. He never did. Everyone who meets him salivates when he walks into a room and yet he only has eyes for you, Charlotte. You'll get your mojo back, babe. Give your head a break and hopefully you'll see the bright side again soon.'

Sophie is right but I wish it was easier to get my head out of this tangled mess I'm in. I know I need to switch off, or at least control the noise that's battering me from inside, to calm the claws that are dragging me down, telling me I'm just a girl from Loughisland who doesn't deserve to be here in Ardara with a handsome husband who I adore.

The words in my head whisper that I don't deserve Jack Malone and the beautiful life we have together. A part of me still dreams of a life on the road making music like I could have with Tom, even though I know nothing now about him. All this confusion makes me worry that someday, very soon, I'll mess all I have up in style and then I'll lose Jack too.

'I hope my mojo comes back to me soon,' I whisper.

Sophie reaches across and takes my hand, swinging it slowly and closing her eyes. Maybe she *is* having a mid-life crisis? Maybe we both are. Can you have a mid-life crisis at the age of almost thirty-one?

'You're going to be fine,' she tells me. 'You've got a great team around you, everyone loves you. This is just a phase.'

'Or a phrase, as my aunt Bridie calls it,' I laugh lightly. 'She always gets her words so terribly mixed up and it used to get on my nerves, but now it's just funny. She once told my mam she had Matthew up on a peddle stool.'

Sophie laughs her head off. 'A peddle stool!' she repeats.

'Oh I'd love to see her again, dear old aunt Bridie. She was such fun at your engagement party. You do make me laugh with your stories, Charlotte. Don't ever lose that spark. I'd miss it terribly if you did.'

I smile sincerely at that. Sophie and I are opposites in so many ways yet we just work together as friends. Maybe I am where I'm meant to be after all. Maybe I do deserve this beautiful life I've been given, even if I did pack in my job and throw my whole reputation up in the air.

'Look, I don't know if you're even up for it, but on a totally different subject, I've got some tickets for September twenty-third to see that band we all seem to like in Dublin,' Sophie tells me, her eyes brightening with excitement.

A band? That does get my interest actually. Maybe hearing some live music would shift me up a gear and perhaps help me get the courage to start writing again. I loved hearing live music in Galway with Martin and Matthew. It lit a spark in me, even if that spark went out again like a damp squib as soon as I got into bed when we'd left the pub.

'Maybe it will be something to look forward to instead of the usual seafood restaurant or hanging out here when we get together next month?' Sophie says. 'What do you think? You don't have to answer now, but have a think about it, talk to Jack.'

I let go of Sophie's hand and tie my hair back up into a loose bun, already decided that whoever it is or wherever it is, I'm going, hands down.

'Who's the band?' I ask her, and then the penny drops in my head as I realize exactly who the band is. My stomach does a somersault. Oh no.

I'd seen posters around the city, in fact I'd seen them everywhere, even in Galway when I was visiting Matthew.

'You mean, Blind Generation?' I squeak, not even recognizing my own voice when I speak. 'Is that who you mean?'

'Yes, that's them,' says Sophie, and then she goes off in another ramble as to how she still can't remember their name no matter how many times she's told it. 'One of the girls at work says her husband has some sponsored tickets to give away and she asked if I fancied it. She'd heard me singing their song one day, bless. Anyhow, no big deal but I have them if you want to go. Ask Jack.'

'I will,' I mutter, feeling rushes of energy surge through me like I've haven't felt in a long time. 'Sophie, would you mind if I had a quick shower? We could go for lunch?'

She turns right round to face me.

'Well, that perked you up no end!' she says, with sheer delight on her face. 'If I'd known the suggestion of going to see Blind Generation would shake you up, I'd have told you the minute I got here. You go do your thing, Char baby. I'll have another coffee, this time without the cigarette. What on earth was I thinking, smoking? I actually feel a bit sick now.'

But I don't hear a word she's saying. I make my way to the bathroom and, as I stand under the hot streaming water, all I can think of is that I've just agreed to go and hear Tom Farley sing live, in actual person. What the hell am I thinking agreeing to such a mad notion? I'm going to see him in the flesh for the first time in three years. I'm bringing my husband. And I'm going with my best friend who has absolutely no idea that I even know him – or knew him, should I say – in the first place.

It's just a night out, I tell myself. It's just a concert. And Tom Farley is just someone I used to know. It's not going to change anything. Is it?

Chapter Eighteen

'Are you sure you're going to be OK while I'm away?' Jack asks, as he packs his bags for his journey to Montreal. 'Ten days feels like a long time to leave you on your own when you're not yourself at all.'

I hand him an extra two folded shirts I've ironed for him and get a wave of panic at the thought of being here for so long alone, but there's no way I'm going to let him see my true feelings. This research trip to Montreal has been in his diary since the beginning of the year, and I know how much he has been looking forward to it. His father did it, his grandfather did it, and now it's Jack's turn to take the baton and continue the fascinating neurological studies his family are known for.

'I've a stack of books to read, two more jobs to apply for and, who knows, I might even take up painting while you're away,' I say to him. 'All those days skulking round the art gallery in Ardara have piqued my interest and I could do with something creative to feed my withering brain. The lovely lady who works there, Mary, is very inspiring and keeps urging me to give it a go, plus I spent a fortune on materials the last time I was in.'

Jack sits down on the bed and pats the space beside him, so I join him and lean my head on his shoulder. There's a knot in my stomach that won't go away and it tightens every time I think of him leaving, not to mention the madness of going to the Blind Generation concert tonight. I could always back out, fake a sickie and no one would bat an eyelid considering my recent frame of mind, but part of me wants to get closure on whatever fears still exist within the depths of my head about Tom Farley and all he represents.

'Or you could use the time to take up singing and writing songs again?' Jack suggests. 'I know you miss your music so badly, Charlotte, and I often wonder if it's me who has held you back in some way from expressing that side of you.'

He looks deep into my eyes and his familiarity fills me up with such a glow of warmth and safety that makes me miss him already.

'It's definitely not you,' I tell him, and I mean it. 'You are everything that's good in my world, Jack. The way you make me feel, the life we have together, this beautiful home we've made, and all we have to look forward to fills me up inside. You're the best thing that's ever happened to me. I just sometimes fear that you could do better than be with someone like me. I'm not sure what I have to offer you any more.'

Jack pushes my hair back off my face and shakes his head.

'Oh Charlotte, don't ever say that again, you eejit!' he says, kissing me on the lips. 'You are everything to me. You're my whole world and I still adore you as much as I did when I first laid eyes on you. Everything about you is what I need, and what I want. I just fear there's something stuck in you. You're holding back. And I think it's something to do with why you don't play or write music any more.'

I swallow hard. There are many perks with being married to a very clever, very handsome doctor but there is always the fact that very little gets past him when it comes to matters of the heart and mind.

I so want to tell him how I feel responsible for Matthew's accident by getting involved with Tom Farley, and how those feelings of guilt never seem to go away.

I want to tell him how I hope that by seeing Tom in real life tonight I can finally put his ghost to rest in my head. I want to tell him how Matthew and I were both madly in love with the same man who will sing tonight on that big arena stage, but I can't. I just can't. Jack is right. It's stuck in me and I can't get the words out.

'Are you sure you're OK to go tonight when you've such a big journey ahead of you tomorrow evening?' I ask him.

'We could come up with some excuse to Harry and Sophie. They'd understand.'

Jack stands up and stretches out his arms high into the air. He looks good enough to eat with his tanned, muscular torso, the runway of dark hairs on his belly that lead down to the top of his blue jeans that always turns me on. I often look at him in awe and wonder of how someone could be blessed with such a caring nature, brains to burn and looks of a movie star. It's no wonder his patients often fall in love with him (thank God Matthew didn't!) and we sometimes have a laugh about how he has to professionally resist the clutches of women of all ages when they become attached to him. He is my husband and he is an absolute gift. I wish I felt good enough within myself to stand beside him.

'You look hot, missis!'

Sophie greets me as usual with a compliment, just like she does every time we meet up for our monthly night out together. She hands me a cocktail and whoops with excitement as the crowds build up in the bar next to the arena where Blind Generation will take to the stage very soon. The sound system blares out their new album, which includes the number one song 'Move Into Me', and I try and distance myself from any connection to the voice that everyone sings along to.

'It's so good to be dressed up and get out of the house instead of skulking around in my jammies!' I say to Sophie, admiring her efforts also. I opted for all black in a bid to blend into the background (not that I think I could be spotted amongst almost ten thousand fans) and I've scrunched up my hair into messy curls which actually make me feel a bit like my old self again.

'You're a bit like Sandra Dee,' jokes Harry. 'The nice-looking version at the end of the movie, I mean. Not the boring, frigid version.'

'Well, thank goodness for that!' jokes Sophie. 'I'm sure you're delighted, Char! And since we're all being so complimentary: Jack, you look delicious as always, you big ride.'

I put my arms around my husband's waist and swoon at the feel of his touch when he does the same back. It's not often Jack dresses down as he's mostly in a suit for work, but tonight he looks super sexy in his black jeans and T-shirt. I suppose together we do have a bit of a Danny and Sandy look about us.

'Er, what about me?' asks Harry, pointing at himself. He looks, as always, just like Harry. 'I don't hear any compliments coming my way.'

He rubs his chin, dropping hints to what might be a bit different about him.

'The beard! It's gone!' I exclaim, patting his arm as I finally notice. 'What on earth made you shave it off? I have to say you look ten years younger without it, Harry boy, but you did look good with it too. Now, *that's* a double compliment.'

Harry looks pleased and goes back to sipping his pint.

'It was just a *phrase* he was going through,' whispers Sophie, imitating my aunt Bridie and we laugh while our husbands look baffled. 'Now I can put him back up on his peddle stool!'

I go into stitches laughing and enjoy my drink and the music, not to mention the company I'm so lucky to share. By the time it comes to take our seats for the concert, I've distanced myself as well as I can from any connection to the man who will be on stage tonight.

Maybe this *is* step one to letting go of the ball of guilt that has sat within me for far too long. I feel quite upbeat and positive; much better than I have since I left my job. So far, it's looking like it *was* a good idea to come here tonight after all.

The lights go down in the large arena and the crowd's applause builds into a deafening crescendo as Blind Generation take to the stage with the rousing opening chords of one of their mounting collection of hits. I can feel my heart beat in my chest with anticipation to the beat of the bass drum, as everyone waits for the main man to take to the stage with the opening lyrics of their big hit.

'You don't fool me any more.'

His voice . . . it's his voice.

'Wow fucking wow!' says Sophie, almost spilling her beer

from her plastic cup as Tom Farley's lyrics echo through the giant speakers and fills the vast space of the arena over wild screams and applause. The audience jump from their seats. I take a gulp of my beer too as the most surreal moment I've ever experienced unfolds before me. There he is before me in three versions – in real life beating on a guitar and twice more as giant images of his face fill two huge screens at each side of the stage. My heart beats faster. He hasn't changed a bit to look at. Still the same touchable, tousled hair, still the dimples, still the same turquoise, almond-shaped eyes, still the indescribable sex appeal, still the same man I—

'Jesus Christ, he is something else!' says Sophie, interrupting my train of thought.

'I heard that!' says Harry from beside her. 'But I get what you're saying. He's a cool dude for sure.'

Jack stands to the other side of me, his hands drumming a beat on his legs to the rhythm of the song, and I link his arm, wanting the feelings of betrayal I have within me to go away.

I'm not doing anything wrong by being here, am I? Tom doesn't even know I'm here. If he'd cared to, he could have emailed me and invited us all along, but he didn't. I'm very much a part of his past as he is mine. It would be different if I'd planned it, or if I'd set this up as an excuse to see him again, but it was all Sophie's idea. It's just a night out and it's what we need before Jack goes away tomorrow. I've nothing to feel bad about. Jack is enjoying himself. We all are.

But no one is enjoying themselves as much as Tom Farley is on stage and when we take our seats again for a slower number, my heart rate finally settles and the rush of excitement that rippled throughout the whole crowd seems to simmer a bit.

Now I get to look at him properly and inhale this moment. I think of the day we said goodbye in Howth, how we used to talk on the phone for hours from my little flat in north Dublin where me and Kirsty lived. I think of how I watched him for years on smaller stages with Déjà Vu and of how proud I am of him right now, even though our lives are worlds apart. I feel a tiny tug of regret, that old feeling of 'what if' again, but mostly I feel happy for him. This is what he wanted. This is what I wanted for him too and now he's living it.

'How's it going out there, Dublin?!!!' his raspy voice calls into his microphone and it's enough to put the crowd into hysterics again. The audience is a mixture of men and women, of young and old, and Tom Farley has every single one of them eating out of his hand. He wears a faded, grey, low V-neck T-shirt, ripped at the neck, which says 'Dublin, Ireland' written in white. His arms sport leather wristbands and are more tattooed than I remember them ever being, and his shiny red electric guitar is slung over the front of his pale blue jeans. He looks like he has been sent from above. Being the front man of a band suits him so much more than being hidden behind a drum kit, never mind bluffing his way in a real estate office. He was born to do this. He's a true star.

'You might not know this,' he announces, and again everyone goes wild before they even hear what's coming next, 'but I used to live here in this place known as the "Fair City".'

'Wow!' says Sophie. 'How the hell did we not know that!'

'I came here when I was seventeen,' he continues over the cheering crowd, 'and I left only a few years ago to follow my dream. I was one of the lucky ones. I followed my dream and I caught it big time, but it was a bit of a bumpy ride to get this far.'

He strums on his guitar as he speaks and I notice his accent has changed just ever so slightly. The Irish twang that once put such a lilt on his native American tone has mellowed, but his voice still sounds like he's smoked too many cigarettes with its husky, deep mood that could make any woman faint at his feet.

'I had a band when I was here,' he says, rubbing his forehead like he used to when he was in deep thought. 'They were a bloody great bunch of guys.'

Oh God. Oh God, what's he going to say next? Don't name the band. Don't name the band, please, Tom.

'They were called Déjà Vu but I'm not sure anyone here

is old enough to remember them? We were shit-hot if I do say myself.'

The audience erupts. Of course, they remember Déjà Vu. Local radio loved them. The Irish media courted them. They were almost a household name all over the country.

I feel Jack's eyes on me, and then Sophie's, and then Harry's. I casually look up, trying to look as surprised as they are.

'I think he was their drummer?' I stutter, doing my best to sound like I don't care.

'That's so cool!' says Sophie.

They seem to have bought it. Thank goodness. But the worst, or the best, I'm not sure which, is yet to come.

'I loved living in Dublin,' he says. 'I stayed in a place by the sea where the beach was on my doorstep and the living was easy. But I have to say, I left here broken-hearted when it all went wrong for the band. I had to swallow my pride and head for pastures new,' he says. 'I had to start again.'

The audience sounds drop to a whisper as they listen to what he has to say next.

'But my broken heart wasn't only over the band, of course,' he says, strumming his guitar again. 'There was, as in most stories of heartache and loss, a beautiful lady who I also left behind.'

The crowd goes silent, making the sound of my heart thumping feel even louder.

'She's married now, I believe,' he announces. 'And I'm engaged to be married now as well, so life goes on.'

I have no idea where this is going. I think I'm going to be sick. What is he doing? What is he going to say? He's talking about me. Oh Tom.

The audience erupts and cheers now and my head starts to spin.

'But shit, it hurt!' he says, strumming a little louder. 'This is a song I wrote about that time of my life. In fact, I put it down one night in London a few months after we said goodbye. I was still missing having her beside me, I was pining for her. The song is simply titled "You" and I think it says it all. You guys can sing along if you know the words.'

He plucks the strings of his guitar, introducing a haunting, heartfelt melody that hits me straight in the gut from the very first moment I hear it. The arena goes dark and fans light torches on their phone, making me feel like I'm looking down onto thousands of tiny fireflies that move to the light, gentle rhythm and the sounds of his husky voice.

And at that Tom Farley and about ten thousand people burst into song, while I sit there dumbfounded, drinking in the words, and trying not to look as stunned as I am from deep inside.

Kept up, by the night rain
And the wind
Blowing through the cracks in the window frame

There's little else to do
I'd be sleeping if I could, instead
Of thinking about you

I double back, down the back roads
of my mind
Retracing every step, every wrong turn and every
    crossed line
Memories running through
Wide awake in a dark room
Thinking about you

The verses trickle into a chorus that stings my heart and tells me how much I was on his mind for such a long time. I'm floating . . . I'm drowning in his voice.

In my heart I've made a pact
Promised myself I won't look back
But it's never long before I do
Oh how I wish I could stop
Thinking about you

It's beautiful, it's heart-wrenching, and even though there are rows and rows of people between the two of us who know every word, I feel like I'm locked into a moment with him and there's no one else here. He doesn't know I'm in this vast arena, yet he's singing it just for me. I know it.

I close my eyes and feel every word he says, remembering the pain of saying goodbye and how much we didn't want to let go but didn't feel like we had much choice.

Again and again, I swear blind
That I've let you go
Turned out the light, locked the door, walked away
    and said goodbye
But that's never been the truth
And to lie does me no good
Thinking about you

In my heart I've made a pact
Promised myself I won't look back
But it's never long before I do
Oh how I wish I could stop
Thinking about you

I feel my chest tighten, my head drops and I'm so glad that Sophie's reaction is as emotional as mine as it takes away any spotlight I feel might be on me now, even though no one else in this huge place knows who he is singing about. No one knows, only Tom . . . and me.

'So, so bloody gorgeous,' says Sophie, wiping her eyes at the end of the song. 'I'm actually crying. That was so amazing.'

The song comes to a gentle finish. Whistles and cheers

erupt around me while Tom Farley takes a step back on stage and laps it up, shaking his head in appreciation as the claps and cheers get louder and louder around him.

'Wow, looks like even rock stars have their hearts broken!' says Harry. 'That's a hit! I bet whoever she is comes running back to him now!'

They have no idea. Except for Jack, perhaps, whose eyes I can feel on me. Oh God, he must know something is up with me right now . . . but how would he? I've never mentioned Tom Farley to him, ever. I've deliberately never mentioned him. Jack often says he can tell what I'm thinking by the expression on my face. He knows me better than anyone.

I can't believe I'm here. I can't believe this is happening.

Tom takes the microphone in his hand again and addresses his audience.

'Man, I spent a *very*, very long time thinking about her,' he says. 'I hope she's doing OK now, and that she's happy now. OK, band, let's go! Let's rock this city!'

With four beats of a drum, the band kicks into the next track with a total mood change but I'm still paused in thought at what just happened. The lyrics of 'You' still echo in my head.

In my heart I've made a pact
Promised myself I won't look back
But it's never long before I do

I'm too afraid to look around me in case my husband or my friends have made the link or can see the pain in my face, and I feel panic arise within me. Tom didn't say my name, that's one good thing, but God that was close. I had absolutely no idea that song existed but his fans knew every word. I can't believe he wrote those words about me. I realize that just like Sophie, I'm crying too, but for so many different reasons.

For lost love, for regret, and for the aching I have right now in my heart and the confusion in my head.

I feel perspiration soaking the back of my neck and I'm finding it hard to breathe. I look around me quickly to see that Jack, Sophie and Harry are thankfully way too excited as finally the sound of the big song they've been waiting on, 'Move Into Me', makes the set list next, so they aren't noticing my build-up of anxiety. I manage to excuse myself, pretending I desperately need the loo, and I interrupt the entire row to get out past them.

'You all right, love?' Jack calls after me, craning his neck as I shuffle past the others in our row.

'I'm fine!' I say, giving him a smile and a thumbs up. 'Just need the loo!'

I hate telling lies, especially to Jack. I hate everything about this, except the song. I love the song. Is that wrong? The lyrics and melody are stuck like a carousel in my mind.

Oh how I wish I could stop
Thinking about you

I climb the steep steps that take me into the cool light of the tunnel-like corridor that runs around the arena, thankful to be out of the heat of the sticky crowd.

Again and again, I swear blind
That I've let you go . . .
But that's never been the truth

I need water. I need to calm down. I need time to myself to digest that I'm in the same vicinity once again as Tom Farley, that a song he wrote is actually about me and that he has no idea I'm even here.

He hopes I'm happy. He's met someone he wants to spend his future with at long last. In another world, in another life, that could have been me. I could have been another me.

I think I'm going to faint.

Chapter Nineteen

'That was out of this world! Just incredible!' says Sophie as we make our way out of our row of seats and shuffle along in the crowd to exit the arena over an hour later. Below our tiered seating, a crew of techies come crawling out from every angle of the stage. Dressed in black T-shirts and combat shorts, they start dismantling the instruments, sound equipment and lighting that made up the Blind Generation show. And what a show it was.

Tom was on fire and never dipped in energy once as he sang hit after hit. He even threw in a cover version of The Pogues 'Dirty Old Town' which had everyone bouncing and singing along as a grand finale.

I did my best to show some enthusiasm, to pretend that I was as indifferent and as intrigued as everyone around me, but inside my stomach was sick. I couldn't wait to get away from it all so I could just think and digest all I'd seen and heard.

Part of me still longs for him, or for the idea of him at least. I can't deny it and I'm angry at myself for feeling that way when my own husband is by my side, so oblivious to the crazy map of my mind. I feel like I'm cheating on him with the goings-on in my head.

'I think I'm in love with Tom Farley,' I hear a voice behind me say as we take baby steps to get through the crowd. 'I can't believe he lived here in Dublin!'

'Me neither,' says another voice. 'I wonder who the girl who broke his heart was. I bet she's kicking herself now. I would be!'

They laugh and change the subject but I'm sure they aren't the only ones thinking that way and wondering who the girl he left behind was.

'Did you see his new girlfriend?' I overhear another fan say. 'I heard she was in the bar across the road earlier with some of his family. She's the Swedish supermodel, Ana Andersson. Lucky girl!'

'His fiancée, you mean,' said her friend. 'They're getting married in December. I follow her on Instagram.'

Jack puts his arm around me protectively as we follow like a herd of sheep, out towards the door, past a huge merchandise stand where revellers are still queuing up to buy souvenirs of Blind Generation, until at last we step outside into the cool of the September night.

I don't think I've spoken much since we left our seats. I can't. Even though I can't wait to escape, I strangely feel like I've left a part of me inside the arena and that part of me doesn't want to go home yet. I was hoping for closure, but instead I've ripped open a gaping wound inside me that I thought was tightly sewn up and well healed. Maybe if I'd seen him properly it would have helped? Or if I'd spoken to him?

I look back at the arena as we drive away into the night, across the hum of the city and onto the motorway on our way home.

It was the song. I was doing really well until he sang the song.

'I can't believe you didn't mention before that the singer was in Matthew's band?' says Jack as he slows down on approach to a toll bridge. 'That's pretty awesome! Does Matthew know one of his guys made it so big? I've never heard him mention it. Strange that he wouldn't.'

I search in my purse for loose change and hand it to Jack, who gives it to the cashier and drives on through the toll. A Blind Generation song comes on the radio and I quickly change the channel. Too quickly, perhaps.

Jack glances at me.

'I didn't make the link until he said it, either,' I say to Jack, kicking myself for lying to my husband. I don't want to talk about this now. Jack is leaving tomorrow to go to the other side of the world for ten whole days and I can't bring this up before he goes. It's all too complicated. I don't want to hurt him, and I don't want to hurt myself any more than I'm already feeling now.

'It might be hard for Matthew to see his former drummer taste such fame when he missed out, I suppose,' Jack says, totally oblivious to the bigger picture. 'It's so sad to think it could have been him up there, but instead he's playing pub gigs in Galway.'

I look out the window onto the darkness of the road that flashes past us.

'Maybe that's why he hasn't mentioned it,' I mutter, trying my best to think of something else I can say to change the subject.

We zoom on down the road home and I even pretend to be asleep for part of the journey, but all the time my head is scrambled as feelings I don't want to acknowledge race through my mind. I want to tell Jack and just come clean but I've left it too long now. I've lied to him and I hate myself for it. I really wish we hadn't gone to the concert tonight. One day I'll learn to listen to my gut. One day I won't be so reckless. I really feel I was playing with fire tonight, and I got close to being burned.

I lie in bed as September rain pitter-patters on the window pane of our cottage and turn around on my pillow, reaching out to touch Jack. But my hand just meets empty sheets.

I open my eyes, wondering what day it is, and my stomach drops as the memories of the night before come flooding back. The concert, the noise, the screams of the crowd, the look on Jack's face when Tom said he was in Matthew's band, the sick feeling in my stomach as I watched him perform, the song . . . oh my God, the song. And now the web of lies I've created.

'Jack?' I call out, untangling myself from the sheets. I get up and put on my dressing gown, then make my way out to the top of the stairs where I can hear music coming from downstairs and the smell of frying bacon wafting up the stairs. Jack is listening to and singing along to The Police. Sting is singing one of my favourites, 'Every Little Thing She Does Is Magic', and Jack knows every word, which makes me smile. He sang that to me on one of our early dates. I feel like I've woken up to a second chance, so glad that all my secret past with Tom Farley wasn't revealed last night. I hope that it's over. That it's never mentioned again, though I know that the next time we see Matthew, Jack will mention it innocently, not knowing the history and the mess attached to his name. And then Matthew will lecture me even more about how I need to get over Tom Farley and be honest with myself, once and for all.

I make my way down to the kitchen where I'm surprised to see Sophie at our table, dressed for work in her grey pinstripe suit and red lipstick. She looks tired, as if she'd rather be in bed than en route to nearby Arklow for a meeting. I remember she told me about going there last night.

'I desperately needed a coffee so thought I'd swing by,'

she says in apology as if she's interrupting us. 'Sorry if I disturbed your morning.'

'No, you're not a bit sorry,' laughs Jack. 'You knew well I'd be cooking breakfast while Princess Charlotte sleeps and your belly was rumbling at the thought.'

I hold up my cheek as Jack kisses me good morning and pull out a chair at the table across from Sophie.

'You have him well trained,' says Sophie. 'Never in my wildest dreams did I ever think I'd see Jack Malone being so attentive in the kitchen. He couldn't boil an egg when we were at college, and that's no exaggeration.'

I rub my eyes and yawn. 'He is spoiled as well,' I tell Sophie. 'He gets breakfast in bed most Sundays, don't you, honey?'

Jack is too busy singing along to one of our favourite songs to notice.

'You tired too, Char? I'm bloody exhausted,' says Sophie. 'I don't know what I was thinking, planning a meeting this morning after rocking my socks off till so late last night.'

'Try flying to Canada like I have to,' says Jack, flipping bacon in the pan. So he is listening then. 'I've approximately three hours left here before I go to the airport and I still need to grab some stuff from the cleaners.'

'I'll do that,' I say to him. 'At least I'll feel useful for something.'

Sophie tilts her head briefly in sympathy for my sense of unworthiness while they both busy around after their careers, but before I can indulge any further, she lights up when she recollects the buzz from last night's gig. Ah, here we go . . .

'Before you go any further, missy, can you please explain what that sex god singer was talking about last night on stage about being in the same band as your brother!' she exclaims. 'How could you have missed that? Do you actually know him?'

Shit. A direct question. Do I *know* him?

'Of course . . . well, I knew him at the time,' I say, feeling my heart skip. A hot flush creeps over me. 'He was their drummer for a while. They didn't last long really, just less than two years, so I didn't get to know him very well, but yes, I probably did meet him a few times.'

Sophie spreads out her hands in disbelief and bewilderment.

'So, you're telling me that if you'd wanted to, you could have got back-stage passes for us all last night?' she asks like a teenage girl with a crush on a boy band. 'Ah man, I'd love to have met them! Next time, you need to be on the ball, Char. That's quite a claim to fame!'

I wish she would stop.

'So, would he still remember you?' she asks. 'Gosh, I wonder who the girl in Dublin was who broke his heart. I bet she's kicking herself now.'

I squint at her briefly and glance up at Jack but she doesn't get my hint to shut up.

'I heard someone behind us say exactly the same thing last night,' says Jack as he serves up our breakfast. I pour some orange juice into each of our three glasses. My hand is shaking. I heard it too, of course. 'He did say she's married though, didn't he? And he's on the same path himself. I suppose life does move on. Nice of him to acknowledge her.'

Sophie tuts in disagreement.

'If I were his fiancée I wouldn't think it so nice!' she says, grabbing a slice of toast before the toast rack even gets to the table. 'It was a bit personal, wasn't it? The newspapers are all over it today.'

I cough. I almost choke. I quickly take a drink of orange juice to try and disguise my shock at what Sophie just said. The *newspapers*? Jack sits down at the table, lifts his knife and fork and tucks in, while I almost have a heart attack beside him.

'What – what do you mean, the newspapers?' I ask Sophie.

'Entertainment news, online and in the usual papers in the shops,' she says. 'They're really going to town that a big megastar like Tom Farley had his heart broken by an ordinary Dublin girl and wrote a song for her. They say the song has hit the number one spot overnight.'

Jesus.

'I suppose they're just making a story of it, trying to find out who she is, but it's great publicity for the band, and the song,' she says. 'Makes me think it was a set-up for that reason. The poor girl is probably just a normal woman on the school run this morning who doesn't want or need the attention. Can you imagine? I'd die!'

My stomach is going round like a washing machine and I don't know how on earth I'm going to manage to eat the lovely breakfast before me. Jack glances at my face and then at my plate.

'Charlotte, you are really pale,' he says. 'Did you sleep OK, or are you feeling unwell? I'm not sure I should be leaving you like this. You're not yourself at all.'

I shake my head and lift my knife and fork to try again but I can't do it. I just can't. I think I'm going to be sick.

'I'm probably just tired,' I say to him. 'Sorry, babe, but I'll pop this into the oven and have it later if you don't mind. You know me, it takes me a while to come round in the mornings and I'm just not ready for it yet.'

Jack doesn't seem to mind at all and continues to eat his own food, but Sophie is watching me and I've a feeling the penny has dropped with her. I feel her eyes on me as I open the oven and put in my plate, close the oven and fill a glass of water from the tap. I know she is still watching when Jack starts talking about the crowds of people at the concert, the pain in the ass it was getting parked, the price of the cocktails compared to what you'd get in Ardara for the same cost, the way everyone was scrambling for merchandise. Sophie isn't listening at all. Sophie knows.

'I'm going to sit out on the deck and get some fresh air,' I say to both of them. 'Maybe I am coming down with something after all. I'll be back in a few minutes.'

'Do you want me to sit with you?' asks Sophie.

'No,' I tell her. 'I won't be long.'

My head is thumping and the blast of fresh air helps clear it a little as I let the wind and cold wake me up and shake me out of my zombie-like state. I need to just come clean and let us move on from this messy link to Tom Farley. Matthew is bound to let it slip next time we see him and what if the media do track me down? It would be so humiliating for Jack and for the whole Malone family to see little old me plastered over the newspapers as the one who broke the heart of one of the most famous singers of our time.

'I'm going to head off, Charlotte,' says Sophie, popping her head out through one of the patio doors. 'Are you feeling any better?'

I nod quickly, glad to hear she is going even though I desperately want to tell her the truth.

'OK, I'll talk to you soon, Soph,' I tell her. 'I'll give you a buzz later once Jack gets on the road.'

Her eyes look at me with deep longing and fear. 'It's no big deal,' she whispers to me. 'Well, it is a big deal but only just because of who he is. I'll chat to you later. Chin up.'

I can see now why she's so good at her job, but I don't respond.

I stand up straight and follow her into the kitchen again and out towards the hallway, past Jack who is now reading the paper. My sickness returns.

'Cheers for breakfast, Jack,' says Sophie, hugging him where he sits at the table. 'You keep safe in Canada, you old clever clogs. We'll miss you.'

Jack gets up and comes with me to walk Sophie to her car at the front of the house.

'You'll keep her company when I'm away,' he says, as if he's talking about a pet or a young child. 'She gets bored easily.'

I nudge him playfully. 'We'll be busy partying day and night, won't we, Sophie? No time to get bored round here!'

Thank goodness for friends.

'Oh, I miss you two being together already!' she says, getting into her black, sporty Mercedes-Benz. 'It's like Ant with no Dec, or Bill with no Ben.'

'Get to your meeting or you'll be late, you rascal!' says Jack. 'I've bags to pack and need to say goodbye to my wife, wink, wink!'

Sophie skips off to her car, then zooms out of the driveway and beeps the horn as we wave her off. I'm smiling on the outside but on the inside I'm in pieces.

How can I keep on pretending that nothing happened last night? I shouldn't be feeling this way about someone else when I've got the world at my feet right here. Jack lights up my whole life, Sophie is great fun and I've so much going for me. So why am I still feeling like I've a huge weight in my gut that just won't go away?

Do I still love Tom Farley? Did I ever even love him or know him well enough in the first place? I'm torturing myself with guilt, anger, regret, lust and utter confusion, and it has to stop. I just don't know how to make it stop.

'I'll nip out shortly to the cleaners now and grab those two suits,' says Jack. He chats on about how much he has to do and how he'll do it when he finishes one more coffee and reads the paper, but I can barely concentrate as I follow him back into the kitchen.

Why am I holding onto the past like this when I've so much in the present and a wonderful future in the palm of my hand?

'Sophie's right,' he says, straightening out the newspaper with a flick of his wrist when he sits back on his perch. 'They're really going to town wondering who the mystery lady is who inspired this new number one hit by Blind Generation. Must be a slow news day. Surely you'd know, Charlotte? You should call them up and ask them to make you an offer to reveal all. Make a fortune.'

He laughs to himself, thinking it's so funny, but I'm not laughing at all. I tighten my dressing gown at the waist and close my eyes for a moment and when I open them, Jack has stopped laughing too.

His face drops.

'Charlotte, what's wrong?' he asks. He gets up quickly

and comes to me. 'Charlotte? You really are scaring me. You don't look well at all.'

I gasp, like a child does when they're crying sore and can't get their breath.

'No,' I tell him. 'I'm fine.'

Tears stream uncontrollably down my face. My mother is right. I work so hard for everything and then I ruin it. I just can't stop myself. I ruin everything.

'You're not fine,' he says to me. 'You're not fine at all. I can tell.'

Of course he can tell. The man knows me better sometimes than I know myself. He knows everything about me, except for this one big weight that I've carried around for so long. He knows everything about me except that I was once in love with a man who I couldn't have and who I still don't know I'm completely over yet, no matter how much I deny it to myself.

I take a deep breath. I avoid his eye. I need to get this over and done with, once and for all.

'Look, there's something I have to tell you,' I say, my voice trembling. 'I've lied to you and I need to come clean, but please don't be angry with me, Jack. I should have told you earlier and I don't know why I didn't.'

Jack's face falls and he leans his hand on the back of one of the kitchen chairs. He is ashen, he even looks older than he is and I am so afraid of breaking his heart. I'm so afraid of losing him. I don't know where to start.

293

'Charlotte, are you sick? If you're sick, we'll get you all the help we can and leave nothing to—'

'No!' I tell him, wishing now he would just be quiet and listen. It's hard enough to know where to start without him guessing.

I need to start somewhere. I start with the song.

'The song Tom Farley sang last night,' I say to him.

'What?' He looks totally confused. 'What song? The girl in Dublin?'

His eyes blink as it begins to ring clear. He actually looks relieved at first.

'I know who he was singing it for,' I say, not even knowing if I'm making sense. 'But he didn't even know I was there, I swear. Oh, this is going to sound so bad, Jack, but I wouldn't even have gone to the concert, only Sophie said she had tickets. I shouldn't have gone because now it looks like I was lying when I said I didn't know he sang in Matthew's band.'

Jack is sitting down now, a mixture of fear and utter confusion on his face. I don't want to hurt him. I don't love Tom. Oh, I don't even know myself any more.

'Charlotte, I'm lost here,' Jack says to me in bewilderment. 'If it's so important that it's made you look sick and pale, you're going to have to slow down a bit and tell me this in some sort of chronological order. The song? What about it? Was it for you?'

I take a deep breath through my nose and then exhale

long and slowly through my mouth, just like Jack had taught me to whenever I was feeling panicky or shaken at work.

'Yes, Jack. The song he sang about missing someone and trying to get over them was about me,' I tell him. 'I was the one who broke Tom Farley's heart, Jack, and he broke mine at the time too.'

Again, he looks like he is somewhat relieved at first. He exhales as if I've just lifted a ton of bricks from his shoulders.

'Wow. Really? Is that it?'

I keep going.

'Not really,' I say. 'The day of Matthew's accident in Loughisland . . . remember I told you we had been discussing a mutual friend and how Matthew flipped? Well, I'd told Matthew how Tom and I were planning to be together. Turns out Matthew was in love with Tom too at one stage and it drove him crazy. Jack, it's my fault that my brother is in a wheelchair.'

'It's what?'

'Mine and Tom Farley's,' I continue, 'and I've been living with the guilt ever since. I stayed here for Matt and I let Tom go, but I never wanted to, Jack. He didn't want to leave me and I didn't want to leave him. And, ever since that day, I've wondered if letting him go was the right decision.'

Chapter Twenty

J ack sits with his head in his hands. The clock ticks on the wall behind him, making a poignant yet eerie sound to break the silence as I wait for him to speak.

'You know, at first I wasn't even upset about this,' he says, every word already sounding like glass breaking on my ears. 'There's no big issue at all that you've a past with this man, or even that he wrote you a song – because let's face it, he's pretty darn good at that. It's his job.'

I know there's a 'but' coming.

I'm right.

'But what really *is* eating at me right now is how you went along with us going there last night knowing you had this pretty big history with him and you didn't even say. It's like you've something else to hide?'

For a split second I thought that Jack was going to just shake this all off, but of course he isn't. I've made a fool out of him and a liar out of me.

'How did you put up such a front, Charlotte?' he asks me. 'How did you not say when you first heard that song on the radio that you knew him so well, when we danced and sang along to it here in our own kitchen, when Sophie suggested going to hear him sing in a massive arena? There were so many times when you could have told me about his big love story with you and the link to Matthew's accident but you didn't! Have you something to tell me about the two of you? Is there something you don't want to admit still going on in your head with him? I don't get it. I just don't get it, Charlotte. You're a really good actor, I'll give you that.'

And I'm also a liar and a cheat with my sneaky ways of staying silent.

I knew I didn't deserve someone like Jack. I hear my mother again reminding me how I earn so much and then throw it all away.

'I mean, who even *is* this guy?' he asks, his eyes widening now as a million thoughts go through his head. 'How did you get ready here last night, all dressed up for our night out, knowing all along that the singer in the band "broke your heart" and was a catalyst in your brother's accident and you didn't even mention it? I can't understand it and I don't know if I ever will! That's messed-up shit, Charlotte! Why didn't you just tell me? Do you still have feelings for him? Do you?'

I feel tears coming, but there's no point crying now. In my silence over Tom I managed to create this big web of lies and now I've hurt my husband, the person I love more than anyone else in the world.

'I didn't know where to start,' I say to him.

'How about just with the truth?!' he says, his voice rising up a few notches, louder than I've ever heard him speak to me before. 'How about telling me that the lead singer in the band we spent all of last night listening to was in fact your ex-boyfriend and that his history with your family is so complicated that he had to flee Dublin and make a new start rather than hang around and mop up the mess he helped to make here?'

He paces the floor now while I stand here feeling dumb and stupid in my dressing gown.

'He didn't flee,' I tell him, in a monotone voice, like a school kid caught playing truant who has given up and pleaded guilty as charged. 'He got an audition in London. He wanted me to go with him but I didn't want to leave Matthew. We drifted apart . . . and then I met you.'

Jack's face shifts from an expression of deep wonder to sheer frustration as he tries to make sense of this all. He keeps pacing the floor. I am jumpy and nervous but I need to feel what he is going through. I need to feel what I am putting him through.

'But why not just *tell* me at the time?' he asks me. 'Why the big secret? All you said about that row in Loughisland was that it was over a mutual friend and that Matthew stormed off. Why didn't you tell me the rest? It's because you still have feelings for him, isn't it? You just said it yourself that you've always wondered if you made the right decision by letting him go. Did you make the right decision?'

I can't answer that. And I can't say I've feelings for Tom because I don't know that for sure. I don't know what to think any more – only that I wish we hadn't gone to the concert.

'Matthew was in love with him,' I try to explain, shouting a bit myself now. 'I didn't know it and it's why they broke up. I mean, it's why the band broke up. But Tom was in love with me and . . . I was going to tell you all this, Jack. I should have, but—'

'But nothing!' he interrupts me. 'We weren't even together at the time so why complicate it all and leave it till now when we're married, when I'm about to fly off to Canada to do something that means the world to me and my family, and when I'm just after sitting through two hours of music including a song that I'd no idea was about my wife!'

Ouch.

'Can you imagine how that makes me feel?' he says, looking right into my eyes now. 'It's like I don't know you right now, Charlotte! I've no idea what is going on in that head of yours any more! No one does! Do you still talk to him? Or do you still love him, Charlotte? Answer me! Do you?'

I purse my lips tight as tears burst out of my eyes and I shake my head quickly.

'I love you, Jack,' I whimper, but his eyes tell me I haven't answered his question.

He storms out of the kitchen and I try to catch my breath. Deep, uncontrollable gasps come from the pit of my stomach and I make my way into the living room where I crawl into a ball, wondering how the hell I managed to create such a mess. Jack is an educated, intelligent, understanding, beautiful man and yet I couldn't bring myself to tell him one of the most life-changing moments that ever came my way. And I can't even think of a reason why.

Instead I tangled everything up and went to a concert looking for some stupid closure on an issue that should be long dead and buried in my head. Why am I still haunted by Tom Farley? Why can't I just let him go forever? Why can't I be straightforward and live in the present instead of wondering about the past? I can't stand myself right now. I can't interpret my own feelings, never mind explain them to my husband. I'm such an idiot. I'm about to ruin the best thing I've ever had and I've no idea how to stop myself.

I'm so utterly confused and twisted up inside from my head to my toes. I've no clue what to do or what to say to my husband who is upstairs getting ready to leave me for the first time since our wedding day. The thought of him being so far away is enough to spring more tears in my eyes but I can't go on feeling sorry for myself.

This was my mess in the first place, and it's time I dealt with it once and for all.

*

'I have to go now,' says Jack when he comes back downstairs over an hour later. 'I need to clear my head before I go to the airport.'

I must have cried myself to sleep because my eyes are sore. When I look at the clock I realize Jack has been upstairs for longer than I realized. He's probably been to the dry cleaners and back again. I drag myself up off the sofa. I feel sticky and dirty and I'm so afraid right now. I'm scared stiff of losing the one person who I never wanted to hurt.

I was meant to be driving him to the airport. I'm not even dressed yet. I'm an absolute mess.

'But you've another hour before you need to leave,' I say to him. 'Let me get ready quickly and I'll drive you there. Jack, please. Please don't leave like this.'

He can't even look me in the eye. He looks exhausted, drained and deflated, not like my intelligent, handsome husband at all. How could I have been so stupid? Emily's words ring in my ears from the day in our apartment in Merrion Square when she warned me that I should let Jack go if I still had feelings for Tom Farley.

But I've no idea if I do or not. All I know right now is that I don't want to lose Jack. Am I being selfish? Do I still have feelings for Tom, deep down? Why did last night affect me so badly? I can't think straight. I'm panicking and I can't think.

'There's a taxi on the way for me now,' he tells me, busying himself in the mirror, fixing his hair and pretending to adjust his tie. Anything to appear distracted so he doesn't have to look at me. 'Maybe this time away from each other will do us both good, yeah? Who knows, it might help you finally make up your mind as to what you want from life, or even if you want to be married at all.'

Oh God, no, I don't want to hear that. I feel like I'm being smothered by a flurry of words and feelings that have got way out of hand. I clench my fists and then stretch my palms, wanting to physically cling to Jack in desperation and beg him not to leave me like this.

'Jack, this is all wrong,' I tell him, trying to get him to look my way even though I feel hideous and ugly for making him so upset as he's embarking on one of the highlights of his whole career. 'Please just listen to me. Let me take you to the airport and we can talk along the way.'

He shakes his head.

'You don't seem to have anything to add to what has been already said,' he reminds me. 'I've asked you why you didn't tell me before now but you don't seem to want to share the big secret. I even asked you if you still loved him and you couldn't say yes or no. I'm also wondering why you made me endure that shit show last night while you sat there pretending how you might vaguely remember him. *I think he was their drummer?* Why the lies, Charlotte? You've got nothing to say to me!'

I try and think of why I lied. I try and make my brain work and remember why on earth I didn't tell my own husband of the part I played in Matthew's accident and how I've been trying to bury it since.

'I was afraid, Jack!' I finally spit out to him. 'I was afraid to tell you because every time Tom Farley's name is brought up it seems to cause huge trouble in my life. I was afraid to tell you how it was me and my ex-lover who upset Matthew so much that he drove his car into a ditch and was almost killed because of it. I was afraid to bring it up. I've never discussed it with anyone until now. I was trying to forget it!'

He just looks at me like he's seeing right through me. He isn't buying my explanation for a second and, when I say it out loud, I realize it sounds like I've been holding onto a dream of a younger me, someone who had no idea of the realities of life or the challenges that it can bring. I didn't know love, I'd only just tasted it. I need to shake this off, but I've an awful fear I've left it too late.

I hear a car pull into our driveway and I feel like stomping my feet like a spoilt child who isn't getting her way. I want to scream and cry and beg him to stay and talk this through more. Today was meant to be cosy and romantic as we said our heartfelt farewells, not rushed and gut-wrenching like what we're going through now.

'If you were afraid of ever mentioning his name again,'

Jack tells me quietly, 'you wouldn't have gone to hear him in concert last night, would you? If you were so afraid to face up to your history with him, you certainly wouldn't have stood beside me pretending you didn't know him when you knew him inside out.'

I touch his arm in desperation as the taxi driver sounds the horn outside but Jack walks away. He lifts his suitcase and I try to stop him but he doesn't look at me until we get to the door.

'I have only ever loved you, Charlotte,' he says to me sincerely. 'I worry about you, I care for you, I put you first in everything I do. My main concern in going to Canada to do something that I feel passionate about was if you were going to be OK here because you have been so low for such a long time now.'

His lip is trembling and he looks me in the eyes as his own fill up with tears.

'You have plenty to think about, Charlotte, and plenty of time and space to do so while I'm gone,' he says to me. 'It's about time you were honest with yourself. It's about time you decided if you want to be with me and if you're capable of being mature and honest in our marriage. You're not that carefree young girl any more. You're my wife. Maybe it's time you remembered that and started acting like it, instead of some ditzy fan girl with a crush on someone you don't even know any more.'

The taxi driver sounds the horn again. I open the door

to let him see that Jack is on his way, wishing I could tell him to go away and let me drive my husband to the airport.

'I don't need to think about it!' I plead with him in desperation. 'I love *you*, Jack! I love you and everything we have together. I messed up and I'm sorry but I won't ever be so foolish again.'

Jack laughs a little, not in a joyous way but in a way that looks like he is realizing something for the first time.

'You know, Charlotte, it's a bit ironic, this whole thing,' he says to me, his mouth bitter and twisted and sad. Yes, mostly sad.

'How do you mean?' I ask him.

He pauses. 'Matthew's decision to get into his car that day was his own decision, no one else's,' he says to me. 'Yes, you upset him with your big announcement about your relationship with Tom, but his reaction to that was all his own making. It's about time you let your own involvement in that go, but maybe you don't want to?'

'What?'

'Maybe it's the only thing left that links you to Tom Farley and you don't want to ever let it go?' he continues. 'Have a really good think about it. We can see where all of this – our marriage, our home and whatever future we have – stands when I get back, but I won't tolerate lies, Charlotte. You mean more to me than that, and I thought you felt the same way too.'

I watch him walk away from me without glancing back. I urge him to look back but he doesn't.

The taxi driver opens the boot of the car and Jack puts his case in, then goes to the back seat and takes out his phone, using that as his focus until the car drives off and our cottage here in Ardara is far out of sight.

I close the front door and scream into the silence.

Damn you, Tom Farley. And damn my weakness for you too.

What on earth am I meant to do now?

Chapter Twenty-One

I ignore several phone calls from Sophie as I lie in bed later that evening, contemplating the stretch of ten days ahead with no Jack, no job and no clue of where I'm going in my life.

I haven't eaten all day, I haven't showered and, in true self-destruction mode, I make the mistake of going on social media where I come across photos of last night's gig, multiple shares of the song 'You' and thousands of comments from fans drooling over Tom, still wondering who his mysterious Dublin girl once was.

If only they knew the very unglamorous truth. If only they could see me now, lying here alone with my tear-stained face and my relationship in tatters.

Pictures of Tom and his fiancée Ana are everywhere I look so I throw my phone to the side and don't bother charging it when I hear the battery dying. Ana is as beautiful as her status as a supermodel suggests. Tall, willowy, blonde and with cheekbones like razors, she's almost too beautiful to be true. And she's young. I'd guess about twenty-three to

Tom's, what . . . thirty-five? Not that bad, I guess, considering the world he lives in. It's hardly a stereotypical rock-star age difference.

I think of Jack, making his way to his hotel in Montreal, his head mangled with all sorts of theories as to why I've chosen to keep this all from him for so long. Does he really think I'm still in contact with Tom? Does he think I'd planned to go there last night in some sick, sneaky way to feel close to him again? Why the hell *did* I go to the concert? What's happening to me? I can't understand why I'd even contemplate it when all of my life, well, most of it, is going quite smoothly – apart from the big issue of being unemployed, of course.

I hate how I do this to myself. Why can't I ever feel complete with my lot? Why am I always the one wanting what I don't have? It's like a disease and it's eating me up. Maybe I do need to talk to Tom. Seeing him on stage just made me worse, but if I spoke to him? Oh my God, why am I still thinking of him?

I need to clear my head. I just don't know how.

I get up at seven, having barely slept a wink, and I stand under the shower for as long as I can, trying to focus on how I can sort my life out. I call Jack as I sit on the edge of our bed twenty minutes later, wrapped in a towel, but he doesn't answer, then I realize he is five hours behind and he's either still travelling or sleeping.

'Jack, it's me,' I tell his voicemail. 'I wanted to say . . . well, I don't know what I wanted to say. I suppose I just needed to hear your voice. I miss you.'

I hang up and rub my face with my hands. Then I get dressed, go downstairs and put on a warm coat and hat, and set off for a walk hoping that some fresh air might help me get focused. I walk down past the pub which is preparing to open for another busy day when tourists and locals will avail themselves of the finest food and hospitality. Peter, the barman and co-owner, greets me as he puts out his chalkboard with today's offers and specials: 'Traditional roast of the day – seafood chowder – fresh cod and chunky chips'. The very thought of food makes me nauseous.

'Jack off to Canada, then?' says Peter in his usual smiley, cheery way. 'You'll be missing him, so.'

'I sure will,' I reply, pretending everything is as it should be. Pretending . . . how much of my life have I spent pretending?

'It will go in fast, wait and see,' says Peter. 'And sure we'll all keep an eye on you – if you need anything, even a chat, you know there's always a welcome in here for you. Don't be a stranger now, Charlotte.'

I go further but can't resist stopping by the window of the art gallery with the little yellow door and thatched roof. I never can seem to pass this place. A rather odd-looking still life of the poet, Oscar Wilde, is Mary's 'painting of the week' and just seeing him raises a smile from within me as

I remember my engagement party and how my father became obsessed with him after seeing the statue in Merrion Square where we used to live. Strangely, I really like the painting and I make a mental note to tell my dad about it the next time I see him, since we are both now super fans of the man who wrote about the importance of being yourself.

Jack and I really have come so far since our time in Merrion Square. Never in my dreams did I think I'd find a place I loved more than Dublin city, but here I am, mesmerized by every little corner of the new place I now call home.

I wave solemnly through the window at Mary, the jolly owner of the art gallery, who sets down her coffee cup and comes out to say a quick hello.

'So, have you painted me a picture yet with those lovely materials you bought last time?' she asks me, folding her arms under her generous bosom. Her cheeks always have such a weather-beaten, rosy glow and just looking at her makes me smile. I know nothing about Mary, only that she always uplifts me and that she makes a mean cup of tea, but she always seems to be able to read my mood like a book.

'I'm going to make a point of it now that Jack is away on business,' I say to her, trying my best to echo her cheery disposition. It obviously doesn't cut the mustard with Mary.

'You look sad, girleen,' she says to me, using the old Irish

endearment that reminds me of my grandmother's generation. Mary is nowhere near that age, but her sentiments are
so old-school and gentle that she never fails to give me
comfort. 'Is there something bothering you? It's not good
to bottle it up, but tell me to mind my own business at the
same time if I'm prying. You just don't look yourself at all.'

Mary is in her early sixties, I'd guess, and though her
views are often simple and straightforward, she runs a
gallery that people travel to from miles and miles away, so
I've learned to take her humble words to heart when she
says something that she believes in.

'I'm grand,' I reply to her, using another familiar Irish
term that can mean one thing or another depending on
how you say it. My deep sigh, in this instance, gives my
game away.

'You know the door is always open here if you ever need
a chat,' she tells me, seeing right through to the depths of
my pain. 'We love having the two of you here in Ardara,
but I know it can't be easy settling somewhere so far from
home. You'll mind yourself, now, won't you, Charlotte.'

This time I do smile sincerely in response.

'I will, Mary,' I tell her, 'and I'll get painting very soon
too.'

Mind yourself, meaning 'take care', is one of my favourite
everyday Irish sayings and hearing it reminds me once again
of how much I love living here, and how much I love to
bump into people like Peter and Mary. Yes, I know I'm an

313

independent, educated, fully grown woman who is more than capable of looking after myself while my husband is away on a brief work trip, but I do think it's nice that the people around us care enough to look out for each other. I've never experienced community spirit like it and probably won't ever find it anywhere else.

I walk further into the village, not knowing where I'm going but only that I need to keep moving and keep my mind busy. 'We are hiring' says a sign outside the grocery shop, which makes me think of Matthew and how he was so happy that day in Sullivan's corner shop back in Loughisland in his little apron and with his regular customers popping in and out, enjoying his easy come, easy go arrangement with Angela in the bar.

I wish I could go back in time and change everything about that day. I wish I'd just listened to him instead of divulging all about Tom to him. I should have just waited to hear him out, let him have his moment of glory with his revelation about his sexuality and his idea of a family holiday to raise my mother's spirits that Christmas. If I hadn't been so quick to jump in with my information, how different would all our lives be now today? Matthew had been doing so well after his battle with depression but that was all ruined by me and my big mouth.

Maybe if I'd waited . . . if I'd approached it in another way? If I'd let him settle into his relationship with Martin, get his confidence back fully, knowing everyone loved and accepted him for who he really was, I could have introduced the whole Tom thing in a different, softer and more appropriate way.

And where would I be now had I done that? Would I be with Tom still? Would I have met Jack? Probably not. It's crazy to think the whole path of my life, and of Matthew's, Tom's and Jack's was determined that day with that one conversation. It was all shaped by that one decision to go home to Loughisland, just all in that one moment.

And I still can't stop thinking of the alternative, of the other, parallel version of me – would I be happier? More content? More successful? Would I be surer of who I am? I'm torturing my already troubled mind by even thinking that way.

I need to eat something before I collapse.

Jack calls me when I get home and the sound of his voice is enough to ground my nervous energy just a little. I lie down on the sofa and close my eyes as we chat about our day, each skirting around the tension in his voice that still exists over how we left things between us. He's a decent man. He loves me, but I've hurt him deeply.

'Jack, I'm missing you like crazy here,' I say to him, wondering what on earth else I can do to make him feel better. 'But you know, I think you're right. I need to really get my head around everything and all the changes that have come with leaving my job and not being able to find another one so far. I think this space will be good for us both and if it's all too much for you to trust me again, I'll totally understand. I just hope I can prove to you that I'm worth it.'

He seems relieved to have bypassed any more awkward small talk about weather, flights, time differences, hotel room décor and what the food is like in Canada. I waffled a bit about bumping into the village gossip, a fuzzy-haired, eccentric lady called Monica who locals call 'The Town Crier' as she always has her finger on the pulse when it comes to the latest beat on the street, and he laughed when I told him I'd fed her a load of exaggerated lies just to get her tongue wagging. But now it's down to the serious stuff, and there's no way I'm letting it roll into an uncontrollable snowball. I have to talk this through with him.

'I just want you to be honest with me,' he tells me, which I think is very fair of him. 'I need you to be honest with yourself and with me. That's all I'm asking, Charlotte. Please don't live a lie. Life's too short and you know it.'

I feel pins and needles set in as the pinch of anxiety looms within me.

'I promise I'll be honest,' I say to him. 'Thanks for giving me the chance to prove it to you. I know I probably don't deserve it.'

He laughs a little and I imagine his face, his pin-up looks and come-to-bed eyes that have everyone he meets mesmerized.

'You're my wife,' he reminds me softly. 'I won't give up on us that easily, but I don't want to be with someone who isn't sure if she's in the right place in her life. Or with the right person. Only you can decide that, Charlotte. I'll respect whatever it is you want to do or where you want to be. It's kind of out of my hands.'

I want to hold him, to feel his warmth against me. I want him to be back here in our cosy home, making dinner, chatting about a box set we've been watching together and guessing the plotline. I want to be going to the dry cleaners or ironing his shirt when he's in a hurry to get to an appointment. I want him to pour me a glass of wine, or surprise me with my favourite wild flowers he gathered when out on a walk to the shop. I want to be in the pub with him on a Sunday afternoon, sipping our beer and planning our next night out with Sophie and Harry. I want to listen to his worries and fears about his patients, swearing me to secrecy as he opens up his heart to me. I want to pretend we've no chocolate in the house when he gets a craving and then surprise him with a secret stash I bought just for him. I want to lie on the sofa and catch him looking at me, his blue eyes smiling, as I cry at something silly on the TV.

But most of all I want to know that by the time he gets home from this trip, I'll never give him reason to doubt our marriage or how much he means to me again.

And to do that, I need to put some old ghosts to rest.

I need to find Tom Farley.

Chapter Twenty-Two

Trying to track down someone you used to know who is now a famous rock star isn't as easy as I thought it might be. Despite several attempts to get in touch with Tom Farley, I find myself hitting brick wall after brick wall.

Firstly I send a message to the email address I used to use regularly to communicate with him. I'm guessing that since I didn't get a response the last time when I sent my hearty congratulations, I might be going down the wrong path once again, but it's worth a try and my most obvious first port of call.

I cuddle up on the sofa, take a deep breath and decide to take the bull by the horns.

Dear Tom, I type into my phone then quickly delete it. *Way* too formal. I'm obviously becoming much too used to writing job applications.

Hi Tom.

That's better.

*Congrats on a great gig in Dublin at the weekend! I
was there with my husband and my friends who are
big fans of your music*

Always nice to set the pace – I've got a husband. We're
cool. We like your music . . . a compliment, yes. That's a
good way to start.

*Oh Tom, I'm so, so happy for you on so many levels
and it was really cool to hear the song you wrote
called 'You'.*

I'm getting a bit gushy and personal but it's not like I'm
talking to a complete stranger, even if he has been catapulted
into the stratosphere of fame since I last spoke to him. I
contemplate writing 'the song you wrote for me' but I get
a last-minute panic in case it wasn't even about me in the
first place. I know it was. I'm just nervous. Anyhow . . .

*I was hoping maybe, if you're still in Dublin, we
could have a quick catch-up just to say hello? It
would be lovely to meet you and your fiancée Ana.*

I immediately delete that line. It would *not* be lovely to
meet his fiancée Ana. Not one bit. In fact right now I can't
think of anything worse than meeting her. I couldn't give a
monkey's about his fiancée, no harm to her. I'm sure, being

a supermodel, she's drop-dead gorgeous and a lovely person all round, but that's not what I need to be faced with now. Call me insecure, it's just not.

I've put my number below - no pressure, but if you're about, give me a call or text and I'll do my best to come see you before you head off on your travels again.
I'm so proud of you, Tom. I think I've said that before, but I am.
All the best,
Charlie x

I press send. And then I wait. And then I wait more.

The hours tick by and I finally realize that staring at my phone while horizontal on the sofa is not going to make him reply any quicker, if at all.

So I make tea. I watch some trashy daytime television. I have a bath. I scour the internet for jobs. I even apply for a job that is too geographically far away for me to contemplate, but anything to keep my mind busy and my fingers from checking my phone or refreshing my emails.

In the evening I watch back-to-back soap operas. I haven't watched soap operas since I was living at home in Loughisland where it was like some sort of religion to keep up to date with all in soap-land, but I find myself catching on to the storylines and characters like it was yesterday. My aunt Bridie would be proud of me.

Emma Heatherington

I binge-watch Netflix. I go to the shops and stock up on food I don't want and will probably never get round to eating, and that I'm not even sure I like. The early evening turns into night and I eventually lie in bed, wondering what exactly I'm hoping to gain from this meeting, should it ever miraculously happen.

Closure, I decide. And answers. Yes, answers to all the questions in my mind so I can finally let him go. But what if I do actually meet him and he's still all I ever dreamed him to be? What if those feelings I've buried inside of me rise to the surface and what if . . . what if he still feels the same about me, too? Then what would I do? Would I actually leave Jack for him?

Can I even compare him to Jack? No I can't. They are totally different people, who move me in totally different ways. With Jack I feel comfort, laughter, friendship, a deep and meaningful love that I know will last forever, yet there's this itch I just cannot scratch. With Tom all I feel is an empty hole inside me that I'm convinced only he can fill. But what if this all backfires and I'm left broken-hearted over Tom all over again while he moves on with his gazelle-like fiancée? I'd be left licking my wounds while Jack sails off into the sunset telling me to, quite rightly, stuff our marriage and all our plans for the future.

I toss and turn all night, and reach for my phone the minute I wake up the next morning. Still nothing.

I go for a walk around the village. I have tea with Mary

322

and pretend that I'm fine, even though she repeatedly tells me that I don't look one bit fine. I admire Oscar in the window to try and divert the conversation. It doesn't work.

'You've bags beneath your eyes that would carry a Kardashian's luggage, and every time I see you, you resemble a ghost with your pasty white face. You're not fine, but all I can do is look out for you. That's all.'

On Mary's advice, and in a bid to 'rest my head and heart', I sit out on the deck at the back of our house and paint a picture. It's meant to be some horses in a field but it more closely resembles two Womble-type figures with noses that are way too pointy to be any animal I've ever seen in real life. I should stick to teaching and singing, I decide.

I even pick up my guitar, hoping the angst I'm feeling right now might spur on some magical melodies and words of wisdom, but it doesn't. Instead I find myself once again playing songs that even my brother is probably tired of singing to students and tourists in Galway, just for the sake of playing something.

Sophie rings to see if I'm OK and if I want some company. I tell her I'm tired and going to have an early night. Emily rings to tell me she did a pregnancy test and it was negative again. She's broken-hearted so I forget about my own troubles for half an hour and console my grieving sister.

I call my mother. I just need to hear her soothing voice, even if I know she will only want to talk about the latest teaching jobs she has found in the newspaper, or give me detailed updates on Matthew's medical progress when I'm already up to speed with how my brother is doing. He is so close to fulfilling his dream of learning to walk again. Even the thought of him standing tall once more makes my eyes almost spill over. I think that would be the happiest day of my life if it ever comes to pass.

Jack messages me from Canada. He's had a liquid lunch and is enjoying a tour of Montreal with some of the other delegates on the trip. Thinking of him enjoying himself makes me happy but also makes me miss him more, and when he says he's met up with an visiting group of Irish doctors my mind races wondering if his ex, Ursula, is one of them. He mentioned bumping into her one day at one of his clinics and my stomach turned at the thought.

I ask him directly if she is there. He tells me she is. I go to the bathroom to be sick.

I need to get my life back on track. I need to see Tom and settle my racing mind, but I'm running out of ideas of how to get in touch without sounding like the raving lunatic I fear I'm becoming.

Later that night, I Google Tom's record company and contemplate writing them an email. But when I type the address into my phone I realize I've no idea what to say. *Hi there multi-national record company people, I'm one of Tom Farley's thousand or so ex-girlfriends and I'd really like to get in touch?* They'd probably file my name under 'stalker types' in their office, tell me to join the queue of super fans and block me from getting in touch again.

I look up his management and ring their office in London but chicken out when their answerphone asks me to leave a voicemail.

What the hell am I doing?

My fingers hover over Twitter and Facebook, knowing that the person on the other side of the social networks probably is someone employed to be, not the band, and certainly not Tom himself.

I go to bed and lie awake again, staring at the ceiling feeling empty and lonely inside at all I have to lose if I don't get my act together. I'd be nothing without Jack, as much as it's not cool to admit it. Yes, I've a career to pursue and I know I'm a great teacher, and yes I will probably find the courage someday to write down some songs that actually make sense to others and that they might even like to hear, but I love my life and I love my husband. I don't need to find myself or love from within, thank you very much self-help books. I want my husband but I need to prove to myself and to him that I can do this, and then walk away guilt free and lock the door of Tom Farley in my mind forever.

I close my eyes, roll over and put my hand on Jack's cool empty pillow, feeling a raw grip of fear in my stomach as the thought of losing him becomes real.

And then my phone bleeps, making me turn over in the bed to reach out for it. I check the time. It's after midnight so I know it can be only one of two people – either it's Matthew wanting me to hear one of his latest compositions that just can't wait until morning, or it's Tom Farley in some last-minute miracle.

Charlie! Here's my number, gorgeous. Call me.

Oh Jesus.

My whole insides leap and I sit up on the bed, staring at the seven simple words on my phone screen.

Charlie! Here's my number, gorgeous. Call me.

I can hear him say it as I read his words. There's no signature, no telling who it is, but of course there is no need to. It's him. He called me Charlie.

This is it then. I feel weak.

I lie back and hold my phone to my chest, wondering if I can pick up the courage to actually go ahead with what I'd planned. This is what I've been waiting on for two whole days. Hell, no, make that years and years. I can't pull out now. I need to see if being face to face with the man I used to love will shake off the cobwebs of the past once and for all.

I press call on my phone and I wait to hear his voice with my eyes closed and my heart thumping. I'm going to speak to him at long last. This is what I've been waiting on, isn't it? I can't back out now.

The phone rings, and rings and then I hear his voicemail.

'*Tom here. Shoot me a message and I'll get back to you. Cheers!*'

I gulp. I try to speak. My voice squeaks.

'Hi Tom, it's me, Charlotte. I mean Charlie. It's Charlie Taylor. I just got your message so I'm giving you a call to see about, um, maybe meeting up? Anyhow, this is my number. Oh, you already know that. Um, it's late. Maybe chat tomorrow, yeah? Bye.'

I hang up the phone and plunge down onto my pillow, cringing and without a clue of what I just said or if I made any sense. I put Jack's pillow over my head and will myself to sleep. It's going to be a long night.

It's five p.m and two days after my message to Tom Farley.

I'm in my car after torturous waiting for a reply which finally came my way, but not in the form of a phone call as I'd been expecting from him. He didn't call me back, but instead sent a message to meet him in the bar in Howth at '7ish?' today which was enough for me to go full steam ahead with my plan to get him out of my system.

I drive towards the city with my head full of memories and scenarios of what the future might bring. I head out a little bit further east, making my way towards the little peninsula of Howth where Tom and I spent so many magical moments, and my mind is racing overtime. Did he choose to meet me there for old times' sake? Is he trying to be all nostalgic by bringing me here again? Why is he still here? Was he hoping I might get in touch? Was the song like a smoke signal to me? He knows I'm married so it's not like he could blatantly reach out, but is this fate giving us a third and final chance at testing our destiny?

I turn the radio up, and then I turn it down, then I turn it off and then on again. I can't concentrate when I've music playing, yet I feel panicky and alone if I don't have some noise to distract my troubled mind as I see through the last minutes of the two-hour journey up to Howth. My fondest memories of my brief time spent with Tom are from this area of Dublin and I well up thinking of how emotional our reunion is going to be. The sights and smells fill me up and bring me back to those days of hopes and dreams. I feel excited inside. I've waited a long time for this.

But what will happen when we finally come face to face again?

Do I hug him when I see him? Is he planning dinner and drinks or just a coffee and a catch-up? Will our conversation flow like it used to or will it be stilted and distant like the years between us?

I wonder what he's wearing. I imagine he'll wear jeans and a T-shirt, dark grey or black to show off his bulky arms and manly chest that makes all the ladies swoon.

Whatever it is he has planned, I hope I look OK for the occasion too. I scooped my hair into a messy bun before I left, carefully applied some mascara and blush and a sweep of pale pink lipstick to match the muted tones of the maxi dress and pale blue denim jacket I'm wearing in hope that the rain stays away, which is always a gamble in Ireland at this time of year.

I chose comfortable shoes, thinking how we might take the famous Cliff Walk together again beneath the moonlight, reminiscing about how much we'd planned when we last met up in the same place. We'd talk about how time and fate wasn't on our side, but how we've found each other again for the third time in our lives. Third time lucky, he'll joke to me, and we'll share a moment knowing that this time, destiny is on our side.

My mind is running away with itself, I know it is, but this is the type of fantasy I've had for years and years, and now I'm about to face it head on to see if it all comes true.

I wonder will he think I've changed at all? I've so much to tell him about Matthew and how he's found happiness with Martin, about my job at Holy Trinity and how I told old Miss Jean Brady to stuff her job (he'll love that one!) and of my marriage to Jack of course.

Jack. I can't think of Jack right now. I need to stay focused.

I glance at my reflection in the rear-view mirror. I'm thirty years old now, not the dewy-faced twenty-two-year-old student he fell for when we first sang together, or the besotted young woman I was when we met that night in the December snow.

I've changed, of course I've changed, and I'm sure he has too. I've grown up in so many ways, yet part of me, the part of my heart that I've saved for him, has somehow stayed the same. Even though I saw him on the big stage a little less than a week ago, I still imagine him as the gentle, endearing, beautiful soul whose tragic background made me love him even more. I don't know what to expect when I see him up close again. I just hope I don't make a fool out of myself when I do.

I get a rush just thinking about seeing him in a mix of pure unadulterated nerves and excitement, but also fear. What if I do still love him? What happens then?

And then I'm here. Oh God, I'm finally here and I'm just about to see how this all unfolds at long last.

I park the car outside the pub, fix my hair in the mirror, spray some perfume and, just as I'm about to get out of the car, I think of Jack again.

What is he doing now while I'm on this wild goose chase? Is he too reliving old memories with his old flame in Montreal, far away from home where no one would ever know if they rekindled things just for old times' sake?

The thought of that makes me panic. What on earth am I doing here? This is madness. I get back into the car and turn on the ignition. I need to go home.

No, I need to see this through!

I get out of the car again and lock the door, and then I take a deep breath, bless myself just in case it helps in any way, and make my way towards the stone-clad pub and Tom Farley.

*

The wind from the coast blows loose strands of hair around my eyes as I make my way towards the bar with one hand clutching my handbag and the other holding onto my phone like it's my lifeline and minder. Tom didn't say to text him when I'd arrived, and he didn't tell me to wait for him in a particular place. He just said he'd meet me here around seven. All very casual, but enough to make me get my ass into gear and make this journey for my own sake, if not his. I feel like a teenager on a first date, or like I'm meeting my boyfriend's parents for the first time. Butterflies eat at my tummy but the rush of adrenaline pumping through me makes this all even more exciting and I know it's going to be worth waiting on.

A tall, willowy brunette who looks like she hasn't eaten in a fortnight stands outside the bar chugging on a rolled-up cigarette and she speaks in a foreign tongue in rapid bursts that tells she isn't a happy camper. She looks through me like I'm invisible, even when I say hello to her. A tourist, I'm guessing. Once you hit the coast of Ireland, no matter what part of the island, it's always packed with European and American tourists, trying to find the various sites and shores as they travel their way round in hired cars and camper vans.

I make my way to the door of the bar and once again get cold feet, but I can't and won't turn back now. This is the moment I've waited on forever. It's time I put my past to bed and realized exactly where I'm going in my future.

I push open the heavy door and step inside. This is it.

Chapter Twenty-Three

It's dark inside the bar and it takes my eyes a few seconds to adjust to the new lighting, a stark contrast to the bright, blustery evening outside in the harbour town of Howth.

The feel of the cold, cobbled floor beneath my shoes takes me back in time, as do the smell of beer and the noise of the TV in the background. I remember how we giggled as I manoeuvred across it in my heels from the night before, wearing Tom's Guns N' Roses sweatshirt and his jeans that just about stayed up round my waist.

Memories. This place is just bursting with memories of us. It's where we spent the most wonderful beginnings that December and it's where we tore each other apart with the most painful goodbye when he left for London just some months later.

I glance at the barman, convinced he's the same one as before, as are some of the customers who sit along the bar on stools, sipping frothy Guinness after work or taking time out from life fishing on the sea. It's a welcoming place, that's for sure, and I'm reminded of how I fell in love with it almost as much as I fell in love with Tom.

'Ah, you made it! Charlie, come and join us! The party's over here!'

The familiarity of Tom's voice makes me jump and I follow the sound to the same booth where we once sat huddled up by the fire on that cold December day, the day we made plans to run away together and live on love and music.

But, the *party*?

The fire in the hearth is out today, just a mass of grey and white ashes, and Tom isn't alone as I'd expected, which throws me. I thought it was going to be just the two of us. I must look like a rabbit caught in headlights as I stand clutching my handbag with about twenty pairs of eyes staring at me. Tom waves me over and I approach his table, the same one we sat at before.

'So this is your Dublin girl! Wow, I can see why she broke your heart, Tommy boy!' says one of his friends in a very strong and distinctive New York accent. I recognize him as the bass player in Blind Generation. If Sophie could only see me now . . . she'd probably murder me actually. As would my entire family, not to mention my husband.

I get dizzy looking around me, totally flummoxed at the gathering of people who I assume to be band and crew members, all merry and loud. It's hard to even find Tom amongst them. So much for our dinner and drinks . . . so much for our coffee and catch-up and moonlit walks on the pier.

I think I'm going to cry. I feel like such a fool.

Another two men, who I recognize as fellow band members, shuffle round to make room for me and I sit down quietly, unable to find my voice, which is lost in surprise that Tom has such vivacious company. I honestly thought I was meeting him alone, which makes me feel stupid and presumptuous, and maybe even regretful and silly that I made the trip this far. But I'm not doing this for him, I remind myself. I'm doing it for me and I'll just have to take from it as much as I can get.

I can feel his eyes on me now, smiling brightly. I manage to catch his eye and I smile briefly back. It *is* good to see him up close again even if this big reunion is absolutely nothing like I'd imagined it to be.

'Charlie Taylor, I can't believe you actually came all the way here! What a lovely surprise!'

A surprise? So he didn't think I'd turn up even though I thought it was what he'd planned? Or I'd planned? I'm confused now. I'm confusing myself to try and think of how I got this so wrong.

I can tell from the slur in his voice and the glassy look in his eyes that he's also very drunk. How wonderful.

'Charlie, meet Bosco, Lou and Steve,' he says a little too loudly, extending his arm dramatically as he points out each of the men around the table. By now they are more interested in their drinks and whatever conversation I just interrupted than they are in me, but they politely shake my hand and then get on with their own company. 'The rest of them can introduce themselves,' Tom adds. 'I'm too tired and pissed to even remember their names.'

He laughs, which means the others laugh too, and another group in the corner nod and wave my direction. I do the same back. They look as keen to see me as I am to see them. I feel like I've gatecrashed a wedding and everyone is too far gone to even be bothered I'm here at all.

I fidget, feeling my palms sweat as I grip my phone. I put it into my bag to stop holding it so tightly.

'It's good . . . it's good to see you,' I say to Tom, fixing my hair now. I have to say something and even if I'm working on a cringe factor that's off the scale, I'm here now and I need to make the most of it.

'You still do that to your hair when you're nervous,' he says, his eyes twinkling as they stare into mine. He really is drunk. 'You know, I used to think that was the cutest thing in the whole wide world. Man, you still are the most beautiful creature, Charlie Taylor, aren't you?'

Oh God help me. I can't deny it, but there's something about his voice. He may be drunk and amongst a heap of friends who don't give a shit that I'm here, but his voice could tame lions.

He hiccups then and excuses himself. I manage to laugh and roll my eyes as the moment, however beautiful, is gone.

I sit back in my seat, wondering why on earth I thought for even a second it was going to be just the two of us here today where we would reminisce and talk about where it all went wrong in our love story. I'd imagined us sitting on the bench where we had that last most wonderful day together, looking out at the sea, where he'd tell me how I inspired so much of his music, and how he never really let my love go all this time.

Is that what I'd hoped for? I'm not even sure it was, but I definitely didn't anticipate that I'd land in the midst of an afternoon party where the drinks, and God knows what else is going at this 'party', are plentiful.

I'm just about to ask Tom how he is, or attempt to indulge in other such small talk, when we're joined by a girl who goes by the name of Eva and who seems to be in a bit of momentary despair. It's the girl from outside, the foreign girl who was on the phone when I was coming in here, the one who looked straight through me when I tried to greet her.

'She is, like, totally lost,' she says, throwing her phone down onto the table. 'I give up on her. She just has simply no sense of direction, Tom, so you're going to have to send someone to go get her. The girl is clueless around that city. She's too hungover to concentrate and she says she spent the whole day crying because you won't answer your phone. Again!'

Tom grasps his hair in his hands and pushes it back so that his handsome face stretches, then he starts laughing. I assume they are talking about his fiancée, Ana.

'What the hell is her problem? I told you to tell her to get a taxi and come out here to Howth,' he says, his voice pinched and unnerving now. 'I don't know how much simpler it can be. We're chilling, here, man! She's really pushing me on this trip and you're not helping either, Eva. Give me a break, please!'

I stare at the table, totally lost and out of my depth in these unfamiliar surroundings. Eva, who I take it is one of Ana's supermodel buddies, is still to acknowledge I exist but I'm happy to sit here like I'm invisible. I also feel small, frumpy and ordinary next to her and no matter how many times I sit up straight and fix my posture, I know I'm totally way out of my comfort zone.

'So, tell me Charlie, Charlie, Charlie,' says Tom, singing my name, evidently having forgotten that his future wife is stuck in a hotel room in Dublin and can't probably spell the word Howth, never mind pronounce it to a taxi driver. 'You wanted to see me. How's life with you? I can't believe you went and got married and didn't even give me one last chance.'

You wanted to see me. I suppose that is the truth, but the way he says it makes me sound like some desperate fan wanting a 'meet and greet' at a time when he really could be doing better things.

He says all of this totally out loud but the band aren't one bit bothered by his big revelation that I should have given him 'one last chance'. If he'd said all this to me privately, I might have taken him seriously but to do so in company just seems jokey, like he is paying lip service.

Eva snorts in response.

'Ah, you must be another one of Tom's girls who got away,' she says, throwing her eyes up to the heavens and flicking back her long dark hair, all while texting on her phone. 'Aren't you the lucky one! Ask Ana. He can't even be bothered to help her find her way from the hotel in the city. Poor girl only got two hours' sleep and he should have waited on her, but no.'

The tension between Eva and Tom, who I'm unlucky enough to be sitting in between, is mounting fast but, when I look in Tom's direction, he doesn't seem to really give a shit. Could this have been me? Could I have been Ana, left behind in a hotel room in a strange city while he parties with his friends?

'Can you get my friend a drink?' he asks Eva, firmly and to the point, as if that's what she's here for. 'I'd like to buy Charlie Taylor a drink. Hey, by the way, how's your brother? I do think about him sometimes, you know. God, he really didn't get it easy, did he? Is he OK?'

His words and questions mirror those he asked me

that night outside Pip's Bar when he enquired about Matthew. I feel a little bit angry now when I see how different his life is and how indifferent to Matthew's he is with his casual question, but this isn't the time or the place to show it. Matthew certainly wasn't OK back then three years ago when he first enquired of him. He was crippled with depression, living back at home in our family home with Mam and Dad, his dreams of becoming a star like Tom crushed into oblivion. He wasn't OK then and now he is in a wheelchair trying to learn to walk again while he sings cover songs in tourist bars. I'm not sure there's a straightforward answer to whether or not he is OK.

But once again, just like the night in Pip's Bar, I won't let my brother down.

'Matthew is still as strong and resilient as ever,' I say. 'He's made a new life for himself over on the west coast and he's very happy. He's determined to walk again and we all believe he will.'

I don't honestly think Tom listened to even one word I just said.

I want to ask him for some time on our own, just so we can talk about . . . I feel tears sting my eyes again now that Matthew is in my head. I think of Jack and how strong a force we are as a family as we've worked so hard to get Matthew all the medical help we can find for him.

Actually, what on earth do I want to talk to Tom about? Another penny drops when I realize I know absolutely nothing about this man and he knows even less about me.

Would we talk about his family? I've never met any of them.

His music? I think I already can see how that's all been going.

His love life? Again, that's all pretty much right in my face when I see how he doesn't really seem too bothered that he has a fiancée.

I don't have anything to talk to him about. I don't know him at all.

He's been partying for days, he has a fiancée who is trying to keep up with him and evidently can't, and it looks like I'm just one of many women from his past who came and left while he followed his dream and left a trail of broken hearts in his wake.

Then, just when I'm coming to my senses and realizing that he really couldn't care less if I'm here or not, he reels me in with a statement that makes me very much the focus of everyone's attention.

'Guys, this girl could have been one of the most famous songwriters of our time,' he announces, finally remembering I'm beside him. Even Eva perks up her ears to listen and takes her eyes away from her phone. 'She sang her songs for me one day back in the Déjà Vu days and

I fell for her hook, line and sinker. Will you sing for us, Charlie? I'll get my guitar. Go on, sing us one of your songs.'

My heart starts to race.

'Let me get the girl a drink and give her time to relax,' says Eva. 'What do you want, Charlie? I'll shout the bar.'

But there's no way I'm singing here tonight. I can't even think straight, never mind remember words to songs I haven't sung in so long.

'What can I get you?' Eva asks again but I don't know if I want to have a drink or not. I have the car outside and I'd planned to go home after a chat with Tom on how we feel about each other, and to decide if it's really over.

The 'old me' would have loved this scene, a chance to kick back and get sloshed with a rock band in a cosy pub, but that's not me any more.

Have I turned into some sort of prude who can't just go with the flow? So many voices race through my head. I can still have some fun, though, can't I? I'm allowed to have fun. Jack isn't home for a couple more days and if I weren't here tonight, I'd only be sitting at home alone watching the hours tick by in Ardara, torturing myself. Maybe I could stay somewhere local and see how it goes? I did pack an overnight bag just in case. Maybe I owe it to myself to relax a little and turn off the voices in my head. Maybe I'm not giving Tom and his lifestyle a chance. Am I being too judgemental?

I've had a stressful few months. I'm not doing anything wrong by having a drink with an old friend, am I?

'I'll have a gin and tonic, please,' I tell Eva. I'm sure one drink won't blur my senses that much, will it?

Chapter Twenty-Four

Before long I'm sipping down the ice-cold gin and tonic, feeling it numb my anxiety more quickly than I could ever have imagined. Another one follows, and then another, and by now I'm a lot more chilled and in the zone which makes this whole set-up just a little more bearable.

Thankfully, Tom never mentioned me singing a song again.

He sits closer to me now as he serenades his audience with stories of life on the road, my arm touching his skin, and when he moves against me the feeling is electrifying. His arms are so strong and warm and I close my eyes wondering what it would be like to be sitting here as his girl.

Then I open my eyes, coming back to reality, and I try to focus on one of his tattoos to see what it says. I don't ever remember him having all those tattoos. They are marks and statements of his life after me and I want to see what they can tell me about the life he has lived since we parted.

'Forever Joanie', says one of them in big scrawling text down the inside of his forearm.

Joanie . . . yes, she's the girl he brought to that movie premiere, the one in the magazine that Emily showed me one day in my apartment on Merrion Square. The actress, that's right. She must have meant a lot to him if he got her name tattooed on his arm.

Wow. I got a song, she got permanent ink.

He also wears a short wrist sleeve of symbols like stars and hearts and a small American flag alongside an Irish tricolour, which I assume is representative of his family roots. A symbol of his birth sign Taurus blends into where his elbow bends, then a date which must mean something to him sits above it. Whoever tattoos his arms has certainly been busy.

The noise and chitchat around me fades like white noise in the distance and I feel like I'm reading the diary of his life just by following the inky patterns on his right arm. But then my eyes widen when I see that Joanie's isn't the only name on there.

Is that a 'Michelle'? And a 'Suzie'? Really? The figure of a scantily clad woman slithers down his bicep and underneath it says another name which I can't quite make out. Who is she? I feel a very brief pang of jealousy and then a whack of common sense hits me in the throat. He has an armful of women, quite literally!

I burst out laughing, cover my mouth and excuse myself

when both Eva and Tom glance my way. Is this what I could have been? A name scrawled as a memory or impression on his arm? Is this the modern-day equivalent of the old term 'notches on the bedpost'?

Tom leans across and whispers into my ear.

'This is all bullshit, isn't that what you're thinking, Charlie?' he says in response to my spontaneous giggle and moment of harsh realization. His breath smells stale, like my grandfather's used to when he came home from a day out backing horses. It makes me gag a little. 'I work damn hard, Charlie. I need to let loose every now and then but you're absolutely right. Most of this lifestyle is just bullshit. I don't even think Eva likes me any more. She used to *really* like me. Really.'

I watch as Eva snuggles up to one of the other guys whose name I can't remember. She pouts and purrs and flicks back her hair, and then straddles the man with one leg, all the while skirting across, vying for Tom's attention. I assumed at first she was Ana's friend, or maybe a girl-friend of one of the others, but now I cop on, no. She may be pretending to be Ana's friend but she's here for Tom's pleasure when it suits him – she's his casual bit on the side in some weird agreement that I can't under-stand.

I think I'm going to be sick. I've been such a fool. I don't belong here.

'You're right, Tom,' I tell him. 'This all stinks of bullshit.

But it's your bullshit, so maybe it smells a little sweeter from where you're sitting.'

He just laughs. Everything, it seems, is just a laugh when you're as famous and drunk as Tom Farley.

I excuse myself and make my way to the bathroom, regretting now that I've had three drinks and can't jump into my car and drive home to my lovely cottage in Ardara and prepare for my husband to come home. I need to get out of here. There's no way I'm hanging around here to join the queue and hope that Tom can fit me into his obviously very busy schedule. He didn't *want* to see me! He just more or less told me to come along for the ride and join in the craic if I wanted to see *him*! He has no interest in speaking to me in any other way or about anything more and I was a fool to think otherwise. All these years I've wasted, wondering 'what if' when he was busy ramping up his catalogue of Barbie dolls with plastic tits and Botox faces, pouting and purring like bitches on heat for his pleasure. No thanks!

I check the time. It's just after nine thirty in the evening. Still no sign of Ana, not that Tom seems to give a shit. Alternatively, I have two messages from Jack from the other side of the world who wants to know how I am, but I'm too afraid to respond, terrified he'll know I'm here in Howth with Tom even though I know that it's impossible he would. I've betrayed him enough by coming here. I've made a fool of myself, but I can't drive home now. I hate this horrible world of booze and strangers and I certainly don't want to be part of Tom Farley's harem. My brother was absolutely right when he said I'd always just be one of his conquests, even if he did bag a hit single out of our love story.

I make my way out of the bathroom onto a tiny narrow corridor that leads back into the main bar, when I stop, having come face to face with Tom alone at last. My heart jumps.

'Tom!'

I'm about to say I'm going to go home but he interrupts me.

'You having a good time, honey?' he asks me, swaying a little with a beer in his hand. He's obviously already forgotten our latest 'bullshit' conversation. 'Ana is here now. You'll probably hate her but don't judge her just because she's pissed at me. She's a good girl. She's just sometimes a bit misunderstood.'

He scrunches up his face and belly laughs at his own attempt at a joke.

'Look, Tom, maybe I made a mistake coming here and crashing your party,' I tell him, feeling like I'm speaking to one of my errant pupils. 'But I'm glad I did because I think I've finally got all the answers I need from you about us – not that of course there is an "us". I don't even expect you to understand what I mean, but I guess you duped me with your song. I was so stupid to think—'

Tom laughs even harder now.

'Charlie Taylor, what on earth *did* you expect from me?'

he asks me, spreading his arms out wide for effect. 'I loved you way back then, you know I did! Every word of that song is true. It's how I felt for you and it's one of the proudest things I've ever done, but I was wrong to try and get you to follow me into all of this when you were on track to follow your own dreams. You deserve so much better than what I could ever have given you. I mean, look at you! You're way out of my league! You're smart, you're beautiful, you would hate what I do when you see what it's like behind the scenes and when the lights go down. I hate it sometimes too.'

He's right, I do deserve better, and it's true, this was always his dream. It was never really mine. There's no way I'd want to be hanging around like Ana and Eva, waiting on my turn for his attention like a doe-eyed puppy. I'm much, much better than that.

'But you could change me in a heartbeat if you wanted to,' he whispers, leaning into me, almost catching me out again. 'I mean it, Charlie. I'd give all of this, every single bit of this, up for you.'

For a split second I believe him, but he's drunk and sentimental, I remind myself. And regardless, I wouldn't want him to give it all up for me. Ever. It's who he is and it's what he was destined to do, plus he's got names of women plastered all over his arms and he treats the one he's getting married to like dirt.

'You're the one, I always said it,' he says, holding my arm now. 'Kiss me just once more, Charlotte. Kiss me.'

I could choose to believe this. I could fall into his arms right now and believe every word he says, but there's no way on earth I want any of this lifestyle. I want Jack, my funny, sensitive, caring husband who knows me inside out. I want our home in Ardara with the deck outside where I plan to paint and sing again. I want our nights out with Harry and Sophie and my days strolling through the village saying hello to Peter and Mary, even if it's about nothing more than the fine weather we're having.

I even want my mother to keep telling me how hard I work for everything only to ruin it all. If it weren't for her constant reminders, I'd be tempted to throw my whole life away right now by being caught up in moments like this.

'That girl, Eva?' I say to Tom. 'It's absolutely none of my business, but is she your friend or Ana's?'

He smirks knowingly and nods his head.

'Ah, you're a clever little thing, aren't you?' he says to me. 'I knew you were smart. Charlie, do you have any idea how many Evas there are in my world? Hundreds, that's how many. But this is my life now, this is what I know. You and I had something absolutely way up there, but I could never be the man you wanted me to.'

'No, you're right. You couldn't.'

I think of Jack and how he puts our relationship first, even before his very high-powered career. I think of how everything to do with Tom Farley ruined my brother's life, whereas everything to do with Jack only ever tries to better it.

I think it's definitely time for me to go. Tom scrabbles in his pocket and finds a pen, then scribbles a note on the back of a receipt of some sort.

'Look, I still believe you could make a living out of your songs, babe. I never stopped believing that,' he says as he writes. 'You've got talent oozing out of your bones, so if you take one thing from meeting me here this evening, please take that. Sorry if I disappointed you. You're still the one, I meant what I said. It's up to you though. It's all up to you.'

He hands me the piece of paper, folded, and holds my fingers in his for a few seconds longer than he needs to. For just a moment, when I look at him, I see the man I once fell so madly in love with. His lifestyle has changed him in so many ways and by now I'm sure I don't like it but I know there's another alternative Tom Farley inside of him. A behind-the-scenes version, a man who away from the spotlight is still broken from the mess his parents left behind and a man who is longing for something he will never find.

Love.

Just as I thought there may have been another me out there, I know he can see another, parallel version of himself when he looks at me.

'Maybe we're all exactly where we're meant to be in life, Tom,' I say to him, putting the piece of paper into my handbag without reading what it says. 'Maybe you and I just weren't supposed to be together, after all. You're an amazing singer, a killer front man, and I meant it when I said I was proud of you. I really am. It was good to see you. Enjoy the rest of your celebrations.'

He leans in and kisses me on the cheek and I close my eyes, remembering how much I longed for his touch for so many years. I dreamed of this reunion, I savoured different versions of it in my head and spent so many nights thinking about him and what we could have had. But it's not for me. He's not for me after all.

I walk through the bar and, just like in slow motion, I see another version of myself sitting there. I see myself, in Ana's seat, waiting and hanging on Tom Farley's every word.

I see another me in her. I'm there in Ana, beautiful, stunning Ana as she stares into her phone screen, killing time, not knowing that the girl across from her is also staring into her phone and waiting on him too – a girl who is pretending to be her friend.

I was that girl for long enough. I waited for Tom Farley long enough. But now it's over.

I'm choosing love. I love my husband. I love my life. And it's time I got that life back, the life that was meant for me, not the one I dreamed about. I close the door of the bar and leave them to it.

Chapter Twenty-Five

I walk out into the fresh air and feel a spring in my step as I make my way down by the marina. I find our bench and take a seat, not only for old times' sake, but also to admire the view as I contemplate where I'll find a bed for the night. Howth is scattered with a few B&Bs so I know I won't be stuck. I just need a few moments to reflect before I settle down for the night and look forward to returning home first thing in the morning where I'll clean the house from top to toe and get ready for Jack coming home the day after tomorrow.

A cluster of boats of every colour sit in the bay in front of me. In the evening mist I spot red, yellow, blue and green as they bob on their anchors, with seagulls circling above and the lighthouse looking on. I inhale the fresh sea air, and when I breathe out I can't help but smile, knowing I'm finally free.

I tilt my head back towards the sky, feeling the breeze on my face, and a blanket of contentment wraps around me. I don't feel guilty any more. I know that Matthew is happy and that he'll be OK. I don't feel like I'm on the wrong path any more. I know exactly what I want in life and how I'm going to get it. I've spent long enough beating myself up in case I'd taken a wrong turn in life, but those days are now in the past. I want to concentrate on my future now, but most importantly my present. Yes, my present is what matters most and, with that in mind, I reach into my handbag to get my phone so I can respond to my husband.

I take the phone out and with it comes the piece of paper Tom handed me just moments earlier in the bar when we met outside the bathroom. I'd forgotten all about it. That in itself is a revelation when I think of how I'd longed for any sort of message from him for so long, always wondering what if, where he was and if I should have been with him.

I unfold the paper, noticing it's not a receipt as I'd thought but a small yellow flyer with the name and address of someone called Dianna Thompson at a record company on one side, but with Tom's message to me on the back.

Tomorrow, I read. *12.15 flight to London (chartered). Just me and you, Charlie. It's always been you. Meet me there if you want to try again, Tom xx*

I blink back shock as I reread his words. He is asking me to try again? He's asking me to go to London with him tomorrow?

No, Tom! No, no no! My head begins to spin and I scrunch up the paper into a tight ball. I'm just about to throw it, hoping the wind will catch it and take it away, but a dog barking at my ankles makes me freeze with my arm in the air.

'Get down, Bouncer! Down! I'm so sorry, love. He won't touch you!' says the owner over the dog's rough and aggressive snarls.

I always think it crazy when a dog owner says that as their pet sniffs and barks at someone. How does she know for sure he won't touch me? I lift my feet off the ground and curl into a ball. I stay that way. I can't move with fear.

And Bouncer? I could think of another name for him! He's a large, black, sheepdog type and if he wasn't barking at me like I'd just stolen his bone, I might find him a lot more endearing.

The lady struggles with the dog's lead and sits down on the bench beside me, which seems to work in calming old Bouncer down at last.

'There, there, it's OK,' she says and at first I think she's talking to me. 'No one's going to hurt you. There's room for us all, isn't there?'

I glance out of the side of my eye to see Bouncer, puffing and panting as his owner pats his head, and I realize I'm holding onto the edge of the bench for dear life. That was a lot more unexpected and frightening than I even realized. I go to get up from the bench, feeling like I've sat somewhere I shouldn't have in the first place. I'm still holding Tom's message in my right hand.

'No, please don't go on our accord, please!' says the lady.

I turn to look at her properly now. She has a very kind face, a familiar face that looks like I should know her from somewhere. 'You looked like you were so peaceful there. I'm so sorry to have disturbed you, but Bouncer thinks he owns this old bench. It's where we used to sit when there were three of us. It's just the two of us now, though.'

I have a new respect for Bouncer now and we look at each other having called a truce.

'Your husband?' I ask her. 'I'm sorry.'

She puts a gloved hand briefly on my arm.

'It's OK, my dear, he had a long and fruitful life and we enjoyed every moment of it,' she tells me. 'We sang, we danced, we laughed, we cried, we argued and we disagreed. We fell out a lot, but we never fell out of love. I think that's the secret.'

I think of Jack and how we hardly ever fall out at all. I think of Tom and how I didn't like what I saw right now, and of the message in my hand asking me to give him one more chance, once again throwing me into an absolute spin. Why am I even contemplating this? I've made up my mind.

'You know, life goes by in a blink and we spend far too much time wondering if we're doing it right,' the old lady goes on. She's on quite a roll now but I'm enjoying what she has to say. 'All that time wasted, wondering what if when we could be moving on and progressing, working towards our own destiny instead of always looking back.

Jack was a great believer in letting things be your history, but he always said to focus on your destiny. He used to remind me of that almost every day when I dared to let the little things from my past get me down.'

I do a double-take.

'My husband is called Jack too,' I tell her, feeling warmth in my belly that calms me down at the coincidence. 'I've spent far too long wasting time on wondering "what if". In fact, I came here to put some of my history to bed. I'm Charlotte, by the way.'

I reach out and shake the lady's woollen gloved hand.

'Peggy,' she says to me. She's in her late seventies, I'd guess, and her hair is covered in a bottle-green neck scarf tied round her chin. When I study her face I see lines that I know could tell tales that would make us all sit up and listen.

'Imagine if all the time you spent wondering "what if" had been spent on looking at what you already have, instead of what you haven't got,' says Peggy.

I straighten out the note from Tom and look at the words he wrote to me not too long ago. Another me would take the chance, thinking this was a message of fate. I don't know why, but I hand it to the lady beside me to show her what it says.

'This man is Tom? You said your husband's name is Jack?' she says, handing it back to me. Bouncer barks again at the sound of his old master's name. 'You still have a choice, you know, Charlotte. No matter how long you feel you have travelled in the wrong direction, you still have the choice to turn around. It's all up to you.'

I put the piece of paper back into my handbag and stand up, then let out a deep breath that comes from the tips of my toes. I yawn and cover my mouth with the back of my hand.

'I'm going to find a bed for the night,' I say to Peggy. 'Thanks for your words of wisdom and for your company. Oh, and sorry for sitting on Jack's bench.'

I say this to the dog and playfully ruffle his hair. He looks up at me with big sad black eyes, telling me that even though Jack's wife is trying her best to move on with her loss, they both still have a long way to go.

'I'm sure my Jack and I aren't the only lovers who sat on this bench watching the world go by and filling our hearts with hopes and dreams,' she says, with a twinkle in her eye. 'Maybe you sat here too with him?'

I bite my lip. I did, of course.

'I sat here with Tom three years ago,' I confess to her. 'It's probably why I wanted to sit here again tonight, just to make totally sure I'm ready to let him go.'

Tom and I spent a wondrous afternoon here. We stopped at this bench, ate too much ice cream and fed the gulls with wafers and bread. I look over at the bar in the distance where he is still drinking with his friends, masking his feelings and sacrificing true love for a life on the road that he knows will never truly fulfil him. I feel sorry for him now. I feel sad to finally let him go.

'Goodnight, Bouncer,' I say to the dog. 'You've given me a lot to think about this evening, Peggy. I'm going to try and get some sleep.'

She strokes the dog's head and looks up at me with eyes that have seen the world and all it has to offer.

'Don't beat yourself up about coming here to see your old friend again,' she says to me. 'Nothing, or no one, ever goes away from us until they've taught us all they were meant to. You've learned enough now to make your decision, haven't you?'

Her words fill me up. I feel so much better already.

'I have, thank you,' I tell her. 'Thank you, Peggy.'

The old lady bids me farewell and I walk towards a bed and breakfast in the near distance, which thankfully has a sign advertising vacancies. It has been a long, draining day and I know that I'll be asleep as soon as my head hits the pillow.

Tomorrow Tom will leave for London, having asked me once more to join him on his flight at 12.15. The note still lies in my handbag, not wanting for some reason for me to let it go, but I'm delirious from exhaustion and I'm emotionally drained. I check in to the bed and breakfast, climb the two sets of stairs with my legs dragging like lead beneath me and I fall into a much needed slumber.

I'm looking forward to tomorrow and all it will bring.

*

I awaken to a message from Jack with an update on his trip, sent to me a few hours ago while I was out for the count. His news makes me jump out of bed and I take the opportunity to spill out all my thoughts to him in return.

I open my heart and tell him all about coming here, about meeting Tom and how he asked me to go to London with him today. I tell him how I felt when I was coming here to see him in Howth, of all the anticipation and expectations I had of what a reunion with Tom might be like as I was driving here and how it reopened all the 'what if' thoughts I'd harboured since I last laid eyes on him three years ago in Pip's Bar. I tell Jack how I was met with a very different scenario, of how I found a man caught up in a very surreal lifestyle but one that he was born for and that I have learned now to respect for what it is and the person he has become.

I tell him how Tom gave me a note and how he reminded me of my talent and that I should start writing again, even if I was never to be with him. I tell him of the sadness in Tom's eyes, how I could see behind his façade and how I know that inside he is just the same as all of us. He is just an ordinary human being longing for someone to love and to love him in return.

I know that Jack won't pick up my messages for another while, but I know that when he does receive them he will read them through with the patience and understanding he promised me. Before he left he asked me to be honest, so

I tell him what I've learned about love from seeing Tom again.

I tell him how I've learned that true love doesn't have to be a strong, fiery passion that makes us wail from the pits of our souls in pain. It can be calming and deep, unconditional and pure. I've learned that love can be feeling comfortable and safe with someone, but still going weak at the knees when they look at you in a way that only you know. I've learned that love is knowing someone's imperfections, their weaknesses and their failures, but still wanting to be with them more than anyone else in the world. I've learned that when two people are meant to be together, nothing and no one can come between them. They might get lost along the way, they might make mistakes or the wrong decisions, but in the end, two people in love will always be together.

I've a new understanding of what love is, and I'll never doubt it again.

Then I get dressed into my jeans, trainers and jacket and I head for Dublin airport.

Chapter Twenty-Six

When I went to bed last night, my plan for this morning was to go home and turn on some music, change into my comfy clothes, open the windows and get ready for Jack coming home tomorrow but all that has changed now. I'd planned to shop for some of his favourite foods, maybe steak and chips and a bottle of Merlot, and to welcome him home wearing something special.

We'd spend tomorrow catching up and making plans, we'd talk about all the usual things we like to discuss, like work and food and drinks, like his parents and mine, of Matthew's progress, of Emily's pain, of Harry and Sophie's latest escapades, and we'd snuggle up on our very own sofa in our own little world as we locked the rest of the world outside.

Instead I'm standing in a terminal at Dublin airport, trying to find my way round through the hustle and bustle of students heading off for a new term at university, families and couples taking last-minute deals on September holidays and in the distance I see a commotion that can only mean one thing. Blind Generation have been spotted and a mob of fans have circled round them to try and get a glimpse of their musical heroes.

Tom is here, just like he'd told me, for a chartered flight at 12.15. My stomach is in knots.

I don't see Ana or Eva with them but then I didn't expect to either. It's not like Tom would invite me along to join him on his chartered flight if his fiancée and bit on the side were there too. Even Tom Farley would know that was beyond inappropriate when he was trying to win me over. I'm better than that, I reminded myself. I'm not going to join a queue for anyone and I'm glad he has realized that.

I see him glance around and check his phone while crazed, screaming, lust-filled women corner him for selfies and autographs. He is wearing dark glasses and I can tell he is exhausted and dying to get away from it all. The rest of the band is attacked too by the fans but it's obvious there's only one main man, and that's the very rugged, very sexy and very charming Tom, of course. A burly security guard tries to call some order on the gathering crowd and I wonder when I should make my move. I don't even think he has seen me standing here, watching on like I'm looking in through a window on his crazy, wild life of women, music, travel and partying.

I fold my arms and keep watching. It's just gone eleven a.m. and I hear my tummy growl with hunger, even though

I'd managed to eat a small breakfast at the B&B. The flight will be leaving soon. I've no idea where in the airport a chartered flight might leave from but I imagine that where Tom and the guys are standing might be a clue.

'Did you get to see your Dublin girl?' I hear one of the fans shout in his direction. He doesn't answer but just shyly dips his head and keeps writing as he leans a piece of paper on a fan's back.

It's been a strange yet very awakening number of days since Jack left for Canada and I felt I was leaving much more than Howth behind when I drove off this morning. As I reversed out of the car park by the marina, I saw Peggy and Bouncer walking along the pier, taking their usual seat at the bench without anyone to disturb them. Routine and habit, comfort and familiarity – all the things we often take for granted, but oh how we'd miss them if they were gone from our lives.

I spent the journey to the airport reminding myself of who I am as a person and taking the very best of what I could from seeing Tom again. In such a short time, I've come to realize so much.

I'm a great teacher, I know that from how the children and parents used to heap praise on me when I'd change just one child's day with a comforting word or even a song.

I'm a risk-taker, a chancer, and sometimes those chances don't always go my way. I know that by the decision I made to go to Howth yesterday and how I told Miss Jean Brady exactly what I thought when I knew I wasn't being used for my full potential in her horrible school.

I'm a caring person, a person who knows what love is and who loves deeply. I know this because for the past three years, no matter what has been going on in my own life, my biggest desire, even bigger than finding closure with Tom, has been to see my brother walk again. To see him happy with Martin in Galway, to witness and feed off his grit and determination, and to hear his sweet voice sing even if he's only scraping the surface of his talent fills me up in a way that nothing else can.

I'm a funny and attentive friend. I know this because of how Sophie keeps reminding me how much she loves my company and how I make her laugh and allow her to be herself. I'm a sister who drops everything to hear Emily out when she's wrung out with grief and despair at not being able to conceive her much wanted baby.

I'm a daughter who accepts that my mother can see my flaws but who loves me all the same, maybe even more actually, for them. I'm an exceptionally proud woman, one who knows that I've struggled against the odds to get the qualifications and career opportunities that have come my way from my humble beginnings. I love how my father did his best for us all, even though he didn't have much to offer us financially. Thanks to him I grew up knowing the importance of family values and how, no matter what, when the going gets tough he's the one who will always be on my side.

I'm a music maker and a singer and I can find words that can move people, even if it's just a smile on a child's face when I remind them they've a lucky star and a lucky number. I know how to make a child feel special. Music is my passion, but teaching is my vocation and I can't wait to find a school that respects and appreciates all I have to offer, no matter where on the map that might be.

I feel better to have reminded myself of all of this. I stand up taller, prouder, and I know that coming here today to the airport is exactly where I'm meant to be. It's important to remind ourselves sometimes of what we were put on this planet for. We spend far too much time focusing on what we do wrong, beating ourselves up over mistakes and wrong decisions instead of learning from them. Every decision, every experience, every person we meet gets us to where we are meant to be in life. Being wrong, feeling confused, battling through the fog of life can only make us grow and shape us to become better people.

I'm flawed, I'm imperfect in so many ways but I'm still learning and I will continue to do so every day as I weave my way through whatever decisions life wants to throw at me next.

I shuffle my feet, I check the time and then when I look up I see him coming towards me. I inhale this moment; my eyes are bright and starry and I feel a rush of excitement race through my veins, running right to the tips of my fingers. I want to hold him tight and never want to let him go again. I want to cherish every single moment we have together from now on. I'm so grateful he has given me another chance to be the couple I've always believed deep down we could be.

He looks even better than I remembered, and when he puts his arms around me and pulls me into the warmth of his body, I can't help myself from nuzzling into his neck and letting the tears of relief and love flow. I inhale his familiar smell, and when he kisses me full on the lips in the midst of this busy airport, I don't care who sees us as I feel my knees weaken as they always do under his hungry embrace.

I look into his eyes to see that he has been crying too.

'Thank you for coming to meet me,' he says. 'I'd an awful, awful feeling you might change your mind.'

I shake my head.

'No way,' I tell him. 'I'm never going to make that mistake again. I promise you. I didn't even have to think twice about coming. I wouldn't have missed this moment for the world.'

The crowd of fans in the near distance disperses at last and the airport security team are able to get back to their day jobs, relieved to have some normality again, it seems. I take one last fleeting glance towards where they were all standing just minutes ago, and I watch Tom Farley walk away into the distance, feeling nothing – only closure at last. Then I look up at my darling husband and he pulls me towards him again.

'I was going to surprise you by coming home early, but I couldn't wait to see you so I had to just tell you when I'd be here. It's so good to be back.'

We walk away, arm in arm, out of the airport doors and into the morning sunshine.

'I can't wait to see Ardara again, just to kick off my shoes and lie up on the sofa with you, Charlotte. Being away made me realize just how much you mean to me. I love you so, so much and always will.'

He has no idea how glad I am to see him again too. I was so close to making the biggest mistake of my life while he was away.

'And I love you too, Jack,' I tell him, feeling my heart strain at the thought of ever losing him and all we have. 'I really, really do.'

We drive away from the airport and I can't help but notice a plane taking off in the distance, one I know carries Tom and his band back to London and to the life he craved and is now living. I hope he finds love one day, just like I have. I hope he learns to be happy and, like me, takes a chance to make sure it comes his way.

'I can't wait to get home,' I say to Jack, and then we put the windows down and turn the radio up loud. It's

Blind Generation on as usual, but I don't turn it over this time.

Instead we just laugh and sing along with Tom as he makes his own way home, back to London, across the sky.

Epilogue

I jump up like a child on Christmas Eve waiting for Santa when I hear the first car arrive to our home in Ardara. The living room is decorated, the tree is up and both Jack and I have been busy in the kitchen preparing food and drinks for our expected guests. A smell of mulled wine and cloves lingers in the air and the sound of Sinatra fills my ears with joy.

We're hosting a bumper festive season this year, and I can't wait to see everyone who has been invited, even if some of them have agreed to sleep on the floor in the makeshift beds we've put up for them all.

I peep out of the curtains to see who has got here first. Since I started my job at the local primary school here in Ardara where they put the most wonderful emphasis on outdoor life and alternative teaching, where they love my music and songs, I haven't been able to see my family as much as I used to, which makes this holiday season even more special.

'It's Emily!' I squeal, racing out through the hallway where I bear hug my sister, minding her growing bump, which I then kiss and stroke in total awe. 'How are you feeling? Boy, you've got so big! Not fat, pregnant, I mean!'

She laughs and pats her belly. Kevin's chest swells beside her.

'You're right, he sure is going to be one big boy,' she says, letting Jack and me know she has found out the gender of her much anticipated arrival.

I feel my own belly flutter.

'Ah! A nephew!' I coo. 'Oh, we're all going to love you so, so much, little boy!'

I hug her again, and then I maul Kevin who has big welling tears in his eyes at the mention of his unborn son while Jack gives me a look that pleads with me if it can be us next. He doesn't know yet, but I've some very exciting Christmas news for him that I'm saving for the day itself. I can't wait to see his face.

Also, I've some amazing updates from a lady called Dianna Thompson from Moville Records in London who wants to hear more of my songs after I sent her some samples, having found her details on the back of Tom Farley's note that day. Looks like Tom was right about one thing – maybe I will end up hearing my songs on the radio one day soon.

Sophie and Harry are next to arrive, with Harry carrying their new six-month-old puppy Rufus like he is made of gold, and I tilt my head to the side and open out my arms to welcome them. Harry hands me the pup on his way past, which is not what I was expecting, while Sophie comes behind him, struggling with their older two pets, Milo and Jess.

'Give me triplets any day,' jokes Harry as he marches down the hallway. 'I swear I'm ready for a beer and a chat with Jack about sport and women and anything but animals. I'm not sure I can clean up after any more dogs. I'm off duty, it's official.'

Sophie kisses me on the cheek and rolls her eyes as her husband disappears into the kitchen.

'My mother is absolutely fuming that we got another dog,' she giggles, her mischievous face reminding me why I love her so much. 'I'm not sorry, Char, I'm really not even one bit. I just can't make someone else happy when it's not what I want myself.'

She lets the dogs loose and they go bounding into the sitting room, much to Emily and Kevin's delight where they ruffle and play with them on the sofa. Mam and Dad are running late, but when they do arrive Dad confesses how they stopped in with Mary at the art gallery to pick up my Christmas present, which he's been saving up for months now. I don't have to ask what it is as I can tell from the size and shape, but my dad's excitement and the look of pride on his face that he managed to buy a real, original piece of art tells me I need to open it straight away.

We go into the kitchen and I lay the painting down on the table, and then carefully begin to unwrap the paper which Mary has securely taped to keep it safe on the short journey up the hill.

'Oh Dad, if this is what I think it is!'

'Open the card first!' he says, so for a change I do what my parents tell me. I take the Christmas card out of the envelope and I almost choke with emotion when I see my own daddy's handwriting. Dad never writes Christmas cards, or birthday cards or any type of cards for that matter. He always leaves it to Mam, which makes this moment even more special. He watches and waits with his hands in his pockets as I read his words.

To Charlotte,
Our youngest, our baby, and always our pride and joy. You have made me so proud since the very first day you were born, I hope you know that. Don't ever change, because as Oscar himself said (or did he?), you must be yourself as everyone else is already taken.
All my love,
Dad

I purse my lips and my eyes fill up, then I hug my darling daddy who has given me absolutely everything he could to get this far in life. For so long I feared I'd disappointed him along the way, but this gift and card have let me know that he loves me just the way I am.

'This is from me,' Mam says, not wanting to give Dad too much of the limelight. I swoon at her beautiful floral arrangement, which she reminds me three times she made all by herself at her new class, then she launches into stories of her fellow classmates, even though no one has a clue of who she is talking about.

'This painting will take pride of place in the sitting room,' says Jack, admiring the rather unusual portrait of the famous Irish poet. 'Maybe he might even inspire you to write some more, Char?'

I snuggle into my husband. I was thinking the exact same thing.

'You never know, I might even treat you all to a song after the turkey tomorrow,' I tell him. 'I've been practising lately and the words are starting to come my way again.'

Jack looks at me with great delight.

'Well, that would be the best Christmas present ever!' he tells me and kisses my forehead.

When everyone has drinks in their hand and the conversation is flowing about everything from puppy toilet training, to pregnant bumps, to my new job at the tiny rural school in Ardara (which I absolutely love and adore), to Jack's promotion and the opening of his new practice, to Dad's back trouble and Mam's new flower arranging class, we just have two more guests before our party is complete. And when I see the headlights come onto the driveway, I know my brother and his partner have finally arrived safely.

I go to the door to see them in, and Martin parks right at the porch as he always does so that Matthew doesn't have to manoeuvre far in his chair. It's raining lightly, so I open an umbrella and hold it outside to shelter them both on their way in. Martin normally races to the boot to get the wheelchair and bring it round to the passenger side to Matthew but as he opens the boot this time, he tells me to go inside and keep dry.

'I can manage, honestly,' he says to me. 'We've a present for you all and it's in the boot so I'd rather you waited inside. Don't want to ruin the surprise so gather everyone up, will you, Charlotte?'

'OK,' I tell him, my face puzzled. 'I'll leave the door open then and gather the others into the sitting room, shall I?'

'Perfect!' says Martin. I lean down quickly before I go in and give my brother a wave. He has dyed his hair a blinding shade of blue, taking me back to my student days when my father used to joke that Matthew had experimented with every colour of the rainbow.

'Martin doesn't want us to see our Christmas present,' I tell the rest of my family, 'so he's asked me to bring you all into the sitting room.'

Harry, Kevin and Jack grunt as they make their way in from the kitchen, unimpressed, I can tell, that I've interrupted some very important rugby chat, and Dad needs convincing that Martin doesn't need any help with getting Matthew into his chair.

Mam, Emily and I share glances of confusion. Normally our Christmas present from Matthew is something totally impractical and his effort at a joke, which sometimes can be irritating. Like the time he bought Emily a 'Grow a Boyfriend' kit when she was sixteen and heartbroken, or when he thought it would be funny to present me with a 'Hot Firemen' calendar which ended up in his own bedroom . . . With hindsight I can see now how that all makes sense.

I hear them shuffling into the hallway and almost have to sit on my hands to stop myself going to their aid, and Dad just can't control himself.

'Let me at least get your bags!' he calls out from his pew on the armchair by the fire.

'In a minute,' calls Martin. 'Just let us get in first. We're nearly there and don't want to ruin the surprise.'

Mam starts to chatter, as usual unable to be quiet for long, and then Matthew calls in at her to give it a rest for just five minutes.

'Well, that's me told off.'

'Ssh!'

Then, what seems like minutes later but is only probably seconds, Martin comes to the sitting room door by himself, flustered, soaked from the rain and slightly out of breath. A cool shiver runs up my arms and goose bumps spring up on the back of my neck as I realize he is waiting on Matthew now to follow him in, but he isn't looking down towards a chair. He seems to be watching Matthew at eye level. Could this really be happening?

Martin nods out into the hallway, spurring my brother on, and I feel a lump form in my throat and tears flow down my cheeks.

'Oh Matthew! Oh my God, Matthew!'

I clasp my face in disbelief and everyone in the room falls silent, except for my mother's gentle sobs as she watches her only son hold onto the doorframe and take small, shuffling steps in towards us. Emily gasps and I watch my dad wipe his eyes as he stands up to greet his boy.

'I'd forgotten . . . I'd forgotten just how tall and fine a man you are, Matthew,' he says, hugging him tight, then Mam, Emily and I join them in the middle of the sitting room floor in a group huddle.

'More to the point, do you like my hair?' asks Matthew amongst the sniffling and sobbing around him. 'I thought a change would do me good.'

Mam ruffles his damp, bright blue hair and holds him into her again, and then Jack puts his arm around me, knowing I need his arms to stop me falling as I witness a moment I've been waiting on for so long.

'I knew he'd do it,' he whispers into my hair. 'I knew it would just take some time, faith and lots of love.'

'Thank you for everything, Jack,' I say to my husband.

'Thank you for believing in him and for believing in me all along this bumpy road. This has got to be the happiest day of my life. I'm so, so happy.'

I watch as Matthew gets all the praise he deserves for his determination and dedication to get back on his feet again, I watch as Martin looks on at every move he makes with beaming pride, I watch my sister and her husband who are both glowing with their impending parenthood, I watch Harry and Sophie argue over whose turn it is to take their dogs outside then agree to go together, and I watch my mam and dad whose love and guidance got us this far in life, no matter how many tears and struggles we've all felt along the way.

I remember Peggy on the pier in Howth that day last year when she reminded me that everything we experience is sent to us as a lesson, and that no one or nothing will leave our lives until it has taught us what it was meant to. Matthew's accident has taught us so much about love, patience and gratitude and it also led me to Jack, the man I love and who I was always meant to be with.

I think of Tom Farley, who never did marry Ana in the end, and who has probably scrawled another few names on his tattooed arms since. I continue to wish him well in my heart, but my thoughts of him are different now and from a distance, just where they belong and where they'll always be for as long as I live.

I think of the love I have, right here in this room, and I

vow that I will never take anything for granted again. I will make mistakes, I know I will, but I also know that I will continue to learn and grow with whatever life throws my way, as we all will.

I've learned so much in my thirty-one years so far, but most of all I've learned that, although we can try and control our destiny as we take twists and turns in life, turning right, left and even taking the odd wrong turn – no matter how we try and shape it, fate will always make sure we end up exactly where we are meant to be.

I've learned that there is no other me out there, and there never really was, of course. I'm exactly where I'm meant to be right now and I want to cherish every single moment.

I want to live in the present. I want to sing again, to teach many more smiling children. I want to love and appreciate my life as I learn and grow.

This is my life. This is where I'm meant to be. This is me.

Acknowledgements

I've always had this inkling that in another version of my life I'd have travelled the world and ended up somewhere like Nashville as a songwriter (seriously!). But of course, here I am working in an equally dream career as a novelist with the very best publishers and I have my gorgeous children to enjoy the journey with me, so I wouldn't change it for the world.

The whole concept of this got me thinking though – how many of us have an alternative path we may have gone down had destiny and fate not led us a certain way? I do believe we meet people and find ourselves in places for a reason, and that's how the idea of *Rewrite the Stars* was born.

This is the beginning of a new writing chapter for me as I've stepped across to join the team at HarperFiction, so I'd like to firstly thank three absolutely wonderful women for making this happen:

— To Charlotte Ledger, my publisher at HarperFiction, thank you from the bottom of my heart for your belief in me since our paths first crossed just over five years ago. I hope we have many new adventures ahead.
— To my agent Sarah Hornsley of The Bent Agency – I'm beyond excited and so grateful for all you have done for my career so far and for what will come next. I'm so privileged to have you on my side.
— And to my editor Emily Ruston who continues to bring out the best of me as a writer. Thank you for 'getting me' and all I aspire to be, especially for the very inspiring GIF of Bradley Cooper when I was having an off day on the writing front!

A huge, huge thanks to all the bookshops (Sheehy's in Cookstown especially) for flying my flag; to all the hard-working book bloggers in the UK, USA, Ireland and Germany for their encouraging reviews; to the various media near and far who give me column inches and airtime when I need to get the word out (Pamela Ballantine, Gail Walker, Martin Breen, Annamay McNally, Ian Greer, Jenny Lee, Steven Rainey, John Toal to name a few) and to the book clubs who have read my work and taken the time to send me photos of their bookish adventures everywhere from the beaches of Boston to the snowy mountains of Keystone, Colorado!

Thank you so, so much to all my loyal readers for your

continued support and messages on social media – please do keep them coming! I love hearing how you relate to the themes of my stories and how you connect with the characters – there simply is no bigger compliment. Massive thanks to Mona Carson Simpson who, as a reader, goes that extra mile to spread the word about my books. Thanks, Mona, for giving me a laugh when I needed it badly with 'Betty the book' and for being such a source of enthusiasm and support. I owe you a lunch in Café No 47 next time you're home in Donaghmore!

I wrote this book around what was possibly the most challenging times in our family and for that I dedicate it to my children – Jordyn, Jade, Adam, Dualta and Sonny – for being so brave and strong as we tackle this new way of life. Jim and I love you all very much and you will always be our number one priority.

Thanks to Jim as always for everything, especially your support and comfort over the past few months while we both worked intensively to meet our own deadlines amongst the heartache and pain. I'm so proud of you and all your achievements in art and music, but most of all for how you have minded me in such difficult times.

I want to also give a special mention to my sisters, my brother and my dad who have also shown immense strength and courage lately. We are so lucky to have each other and will celebrate many good times ahead.

Huge, huge thanks to singer/songwriter Gareth Dunlop

and Dianna Maher (Moraine Music Group, Nashville) for the amazing song, 'You'. I can't express how exciting it is to have an actual song attached to this story – it really is the pièce de résistance!

Finally, the biggest lesson I learned while writing Charlotte Taylor's story was that we aren't here for very long, tomorrow is never guaranteed and so there's nothing like the power of 'now'. We should never be afraid to take risks and make the changes we need to, to be the person we want to be.

I hope you agree.

Lots of love,

Emma x